T 9689

D0000669

Spells & Sleeping Bags

WITHDRAWN

Hastings Memorial Library
505 Central Avenue
Grant, NE 69140

Spells & Sleeping Bags

sarah mlynowski

delacorte press

Published by Delacorte Press
an imprint of Random House Children's Books
a division of Random House, Inc.
New York

This is a work of fiction. Names, characters, places, and incidents either
are the product of the author's imagination or are used fictitiously.
Any resemblance to actual persons, living or dead, events,
or locales is entirely coincidental.

Copyright © 2007 by Sarah Mlynowski

All rights reserved.

Delacorte Press and colophon are registered trademarks of
Random House, Inc.

Visit us on the Web! www.randomhouse.com/teens

Educators and librarians, for a variety of teaching tools,
visit us at www.randomhouse.com/teachers

The Library of Congress has cataloged the hardcover edition of this
work as follows:
Mlynowski, Sarah.
Spells & sleeping bags / Sarah Mlynowski. — 1st ed.
p. cm.
Summary: Rachel and her younger sister, both witches,
spend the summer at Camp Wood Lake, where Rachel tries to
have a normal camp experience while surreptitiously honing her
newly discovered talents.
ISBN: 978-0-385-73387-8 (hardcover)
ISBN: 978-0-385-90401-8 (glb edition)
[1. Witches—Fiction. 2. Camps—Fiction. 3. Sisters—Fiction.
4. Adirondack Mountains (N.Y.)—Fiction. 5. Humorous stories.]
I. Title. II. Title: Spells and sleeping bags.
PZ7.M7135Sp 2007
[Fic]—dc22
2006017018

ISBN: 978-0-385-73388-5 (tr. pbk.)

Printed in the United States of America

10 9 8 7 6 5 4 3 2 1

First Trade Paperback Edition

Random House Children's Books supports the
First Amendment and celebrates the right to read.

For the girls of Bunk 9

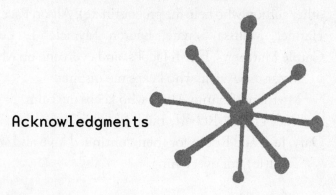

Acknowledgments

Thanks to the power of a zillion to:

Wendy Loggia, my amazingly brilliant editor. Laura Dail, the best agent a girl could have. Beverly Horowitz, Pam Bobowicz, Melanie Chang, Chip Gibson, Isabel Warren-Lynch, Tamar Schwartz, Rachel Feld, Linda Leonard, Kenny Holcomb, Timothy Terhune, Adrienne Waintraub, Jennifer Black, and the rest of the incredible Random House Children's Books team for all their hard work. Gail Brussel, the best publicist in town. Über-talented artist Robin Zingone. Lisa Callamaro and everyone at Storefront Pictures.

Pripstein's camp, the magical and much-loved sleepaway camp where I spent my summers—thank you, world's best camp director Ronnie Braverman. Special thanks to Melanie Fefergrad, as well as Sohmer, Christine, Samara, Elissa, Brian, Spike, Ronit, and Sam & Jess for helping me remember all the fun we had.

My mom, Elissa Ambrose, who must read everything first. Lynda Curnyn and Jess Braun for their always superb advice. My number-one fan, Avery Carmichael.

The people I hang out with at the watercooler (aka the

other authors who help me procrastinate): Alison Pace, Kristin Harmel, Melissa Senate, Lauren Myracle, E. Lockhart, Carole Matthews, Farrin Jacobs, and everyone on MySpace.

My sister, Aviva, who keeps me inspired.

My friend Bonnie Altro, who keeps me calm.

Dad, Louisa, Robert, Bubby, Vickie, John, Jen, Darren, Gary, Jess, and Robin for their continued love and support.

Todd(ie), for everything.

Spells & Sleeping Bags

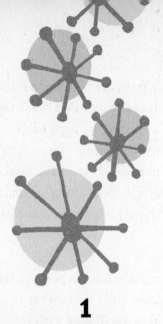

1
ALL ABOARD!

I'm pretty sure my camp knapsack is not supposed to be levitating off the sidewalk of Fifth Avenue. Whoopsies. I make a (somewhat) discreet lunge for one of its red straps and plant it back next to my feet.

Tee hee.

My mother, who is fortunately too busy eyeing the parked camp buses lining the street to notice my infraction, asks, "Do you know where you're going?"

"Yes, Mom," my sister says, rolling her eyes. "We know how to read. We're both on the same bus. The sign says 'Girls grades seven thru nine,' and since that's both of us, that's where we're going. Unfortunately."

Miri is not happy about being shipped off to Camp Wood Lake in the Adirondacks for seven weeks. She'd much rather stay in the city, free to spend the summer as she pleases, helping the homeless. That's her cause du jour.

Unfortunately for her, she can't help the homeless when she is being sent to a summer camp filled with spoiled rich kids. Those are her words, not mine. I'm perfectly happy to spend the summer with spoiled rich kids. No, wait. That didn't come out right. What I mean is I'm perfectly happy to be going to camp, because I'm perfectly happy doing *anything* these days. Deliriously happy. Jumping-on-couches-like-they're-trampolines happy.

Why? Because I'm finally a witch!

No, not *witch* as in mean or cranky. I don't pull my sister's hair or rip off her Barbies' heads. (Not that either of us still has Barbies. Okay, fine. Not that I still play with them. Sure, they're in a bag at the back of my closet, and I sometimes take them out just to see how they're doing, but that's it, I swear.) I have powers, like Hermione and Sabrina. Like my sister. And my mother.

We found out in February that my sister is a witch. My mom, who chose to live her adult life as a nonpracticing witch, had never mentioned anything about this particular family trait because she was hoping her powers would somehow skip over her kids. And for a while it looked like they had with me. But oh no, they didn't. Both of us are witches. Finger-snapping, broom-riding, spell-canting witches. Yes! And since I am a witch, nothing that could possibly happen this summer can burst my bubble of glorious happiness. I mean, hello? I finally have magical powers! I can zap up anything I want. More handbags? Presto. Tastier food? Kazam. Friends? Zap! Nah, I probably won't cast spells on any possible friends, since enchanting individuals is so morally wrong. But I could if I wanted to.

Why? Because I'm a witch!

But even if *nobody* in my bunk wants to be my friend this summer—and I don't see why they wouldn't, since none of them goes to my school, and therefore they don't know anything about my previous social mishaps (we were a bit wild and carefree with Miri's powers in the early days)—I won't care.

Why? Because I'm a witch!

Even if Raf doesn't fall in love with me this summer—yes, Raf Kosravi, the hottest guy in my class and, I should mention, the love of my life, is going to be at Wood Lake too—so what? It will be his loss.

Why? Because I'm a witch!

Okay, that's a lie. Not the witch part (yay!) but the part about Raf. I'd care a lot if he didn't fall in love with me. But you get my point.

My ego has gained about seven hundred pounds since I discovered my magic at prom last month. My mom and sister were thrilled for me, of course. Thrilled that I was happy—and thrilled that they would no longer have to listen to me complain about not having powers.

For the first week after prom, I could not resist zapping everything in sight. Lights. The television. Miri's stuff. "I'm doing it, I'm doing it!" I cheered while gleefully lifting her pillow.

Which is when my mom walked in and told me that I'd better relax with my magic. "If you want to go to camp, you have to promise to control yourself."

"Of course," I said. "But check it out! I've finally got game!"

Since my mom scores frighteningly low on the hip-ometer, I had to explain. "Technique. Ability. Style."

3

"Got it," she said, and left. And that was when the pillow exploded. Feathers and Miri's pink pillowcase shot across her room like confetti. "Sorry," I squealed.

"Game over!" Miri screamed, cowering against the wall.

"Tiny accident," I said sheepishly. "Don't tell Mom." I didn't want our mother to have any excuse to keep me home and away from Raf.

Where is he, anyway? I step up on my tiptoes and peer first into the busy street, then into Central Park. The six waiting buses are supposed to be picking up all the campers from Manhattan, but unfortunately, Raf doesn't seem to be one of them. I know he's going to be a camper at Wood Lake this summer. He told me he signed up. And he's been going for years. So where is he?

There are certainly lots of other cute boys, though. Not that I'm looking. Oh, no, my heart belongs to Raf.

Honk! Honk! Honk!

It's so loud in this city. And the noon sun is scorching and everyone looks uncomfortable and sweaty. Unlike Miri, I'm seriously looking forward to getting off the disgustingly smoggy island of Manhattan. Good-bye school, subways, and skyscrapers. Hello summer, suntan lotion, and sleeping bags!

My mom grabs me in a hug. "You two are going to sit together, right?"

"Yes, Mom, we'll sit together," I say from under her left armpit. She'd better not mess up my flawlessly applied mascara or perfectly straightened hair. It took me half an hour to get my ocean of a head to look flat, and this is probably the only time all summer my hair will be de-rippled. I bought myself one of those megapopular hair straighteners, and let me tell you, it makes my hair look flatter than the sidewalk we're standing on. But no matter how much I begged (I'm talking down-on-two-knees plead-ing), my annoying mother was convinced I'd burn down not only my cabin but the entire camp and forbade me to bring my flatiron with me. She's spent the past month *mucho* para-noid that I was going to burn down our apartment, and every time I emerged from my room minus my usual fuzzy crown, she ran straight inside to make sure I'd unplugged the iron.

I don't know what her problem is. I've only left it plugged in once.

Okay, twice, but still, I never started a fire.

Wait a sec. What am I even worried about? If my hair gets curly, I can just zap it straight. Hah! Straightening irons are for mere mortals. I am a witch. An über-powerful, glori-ous witch.

Crap. My stupid knapsack is rising again. Why is it doing that? I pull away from my mom to grab it, but this time I swing it over my left shoulder to keep it in place. I furtively look around the crowded street to make sure nobody saw my uplifting experience.

Nope. People do not appear to be scratching their heads in confusion or gasping in shock. Whew.

Lex, my mom's new boyfriend, returns from finding a parking space and takes hold of her hand. They've been in-separable since they started dating. Whenever I see them, they're holding hands, gazing lovingly into each other's eyes, or they're—

"Ugh," Miri says. "Can you please stop smooching in public? It's going to make me carsick."

"Bus sick," I say, and cringe. Now, that would make a great first impression. Still, I don't blame my sister one bit. All that smooching is, well, nauseating. And yes, my mom and Lex are kissing. Right here. On the street.

They're always kissing. They kiss in the kitchen when they don't realize we're watching. At restaurants when they forget we're sitting across from them. On Fifth Avenue between Eighty-fourth and Eighty-fifth when we're leaving for camp. Not gross, open-mouth kisses, but constant little love pecks that are highly embarrassing. I mean, really. I can't help noticing that random kids and tourists keep glancing over at the pair and grimacing. This is one of the reasons I begged my dad and my stepmom not to come see us off today. If it freaks me out, imagine how it would weird out my dad. The other reason is that my mom would have had to talk to Jennifer, and my dad would have had to meet Lex, and honestly, the idea of the four of them being on the same continent, never mind the same street, makes me want to hide under my covers. Divorce issues, anyone?

My mom giggles. Ever since she hooked up with Lex (or Old Man Lex, as Miri and I call him secretly, since he's like a hundred—okay, fine, probably only fifty—and since his bushy eyebrows and the eight strands of hair left on his head are gray), she's been doing a lot of giggling. "Miri," she says

6

now, still clutching Lex's hand, "you'll keep an eye on your sister this summer, right?"

"Hey!" Is it normal that my mother is asking Miri, two years my junior, to look out for me? I think not.

"I want her to make sure you're careful with your"—she lowers her voice—"Glinda."

Is Glinda a doll? A Barbie that I'm insisting on taking to camp despite the risk of other campers mocking me for my infantile attachment?

Nope.

Glinda is my mom's new code word for magic. And yes, she named it after the good witch in *The Wizard of Oz*.

"I promise, Mom," I say. "I'll be careful with my Glinda."

Lex looks at my mom and then at me. He obviously has no idea who this Glinda is or why I have to take such good care of her. As close as they've become, Mom still hasn't told him her deep, dark secret. But since she never told my dad, I wouldn't hold my breath waiting for her to spill the beanies to the new man in her life.

She runs the bitten fingernails of her free hand through her short tinted blond hair. "Please don't use it, unless you absolutely have to."

Whatev.

"Have fun, girls," Lex says, squeezing both of us on the shoulder. Even though he spends every day with Mom, he hasn't quite reached the potential-stepfather, hug-the-daughters level yet. As nice as he is, we're not just going to start hugging some old man.

Fine, he's not *that* old. But he's pretty old.

7

"Take care of our mom, Lex," I say while tugging on Miri's wrist. "Let's go."

"Will do," he says. "Have fun, and remember to write home."

"We will!" I sing as I inch closer to the bus. Time to get this party on the road!

My mom makes a hangdog face. "Bye, girls. Love you."

"Love you!" Miri and I say simultaneously as we lean into yet another group (minus Lex) hug.

"I'll miss you," my mom says, her voice catching.

Aw. Oh, no. Itchy eyes! Itchy eyes! No, don't, don't . . .

"We'll miss you too," Miri says, and bursts into tears.

Sob. My tears are so going to mess up my mascara, run down my cheeks and my neck, and make my hair frizz.

"Name?" asks the pen-chewing girl standing in front of my gateway to happiness, aka the bus door. Her short blond ponytail is peeking out of her Mets baseball cap, and she's chomping on the end of the pen like it's a pretzel.

"Rachel Weinstein."

Chomp, chomp. "What grade did you just finish?"

"Ninth," I say proudly. I'm going into tenth grade. That is so old. I've practically graduated. I'm practically in college! I'm *practically* an adult. Next thing you know, I'll be driving my own car, having kids, sending them to camp. Omigod, that is so cute! My kids going to the same camp that I went to! The same camp that I'm going to, if this pen-chewer ever lets me onto the bus.

"You're an oldest Lion, then."

Roar? "Alrighty."

She takes another bite of the pen and it explodes into a navy blue mess on her lips.

"Um, you got some ink on you," I tell her.

She touches her face, then stares at the sticky blue on her fingers. "I hate when that happens," she says with a sigh. She ticks off my name and sighs again. "I'm Janice, your unit head."

I have no idea what a unit head is, but apparently it's stressful. "Hello, Unit Head Janice," I reply.

She studies her clipboard and sighs yet again. "You're going to be in bunk fourteen. And who are you?" she asks Miri.

As Miri introduces herself, I skip up the three steps into the excruciatingly hot bus. The backseats are filled with sweating and chattering teenage girls, all of whom abruptly stop talking the second they see me. They collectively look me up and down—I have no idea why, since we're all wearing the same assigned pale brown Camp Wood Lake cotton T-shirts and matching shorts—and resume their conversations.

9

Of course, at first I balked at wearing any kind of uniform, but these aren't too bad. A little boring, but not awful. The shirt says Camp Wood Lake in bubbly white and orange letters, and underneath there's a cute drawing of a girl and a boy in a white canoe. The shorts just say Camp Wood Lake across the butt. The glossy *Welcome to Camp* brochure explained that we'd have to wear it only today and during any out-of-camp trips. The brochure came with a funky DVD that flashed images of all the camp amenities (tennis courts, lakefront, arts and crafts, indoor swimming pool) while playing set-the-mood camp songs, like Green Day's "Time of Your Life" and Frankie Valli's "Stay," in the background.

Some of the seats in the middle are empty. I look for a place where Miri and I can sit together. Thank goodness she's on this bus. Imagine if I were all by my lonesome and had to sit by myself! I'd be known all summer as the girl who sat alone because no one wanted to talk to her. Just as I'm about to scoot into an empty seat, a tall brunette sitting three rows back stops talking to the two girls behind her, turns her head, and waves at me.

Huh? I look behind me to see if she's motioning to someone else. Nope, just me. Unless she's a nutcase who waves arbitrarily. Or maybe she's just done her nails and is air-drying?

"Hi, there," says the girl, looking into my eyes. "You can sit with me, if you want."

I am dumbfounded. The girl is smiley and not at all loserish-looking. Her layered curly dark hair is tied into a low ponytail, bangs clipped back, showing off clear skin, bright eyes, and a big smile. And she's friendly. "Sure," I say, plopping myself down next to her on the sticky leather seat, my knapsack at my feet. Perfect! Miri can sit in the empty row across the aisle. It will be just like we're sitting together . . . except not.

"I'm Alison," the girl says.

"Rachel," I tell her.

"Trishelle and Kristin," she says, motioning to the two girls in the row behind her.

"Hi," I say, not believing my luck. I've been on the bus for only thirty seconds and I've already met three people! Trishelle has long highlighted hair and is wearing a lot of makeup. I'm talking foundation, bright pink blush, heavy lip liner, and a thick ring of eyeliner. I hope it won't melt right off her face. Next to her is Kristin, whose cropped blond hair, tiny features, and pearl earrings (which my mother would never in a million years have let me bring to camp) remind me of a Connecticut housewife. "What bunk are you guys in?" I ask.

"Fifteen," Trishelle and Kristin say simultaneously. "You?"

"Fourteen."

"Me too," Alison says with a big smile.

Wahoo! This nice girl who invited me to sit with her for no reason is in my bunk!

11

"Rachel!" my sister calls. "I got us a place up here."

I turn to see Miri claiming the front row. "Mir, I'm sitting back here. Come join us," I say, pointing to the empty row next to me.

Instead of skipping over to me—come on, Miri, get with the program!—my sister glares my way. "I'd rather stay in front in case I get nauseous. It's less bumpy."

There is no way I'm budging from this spot. "All right, but I'm right back here if you need me. My little sister," I explain to my new friends. New best friends? Soon-to-be best friends?

"So," I begin, "is this your first—"

I'm interrupted by the blue-lipped Janice, who has motioned to the bus driver to close the door and is now looking nervously around the bus. "You're all here, right?" Janice then points at each of us while silently counting. "All right, you all seem to be here. Everyone ready?"

"We're ready," announces Trishelle.

Janice's blue lips stretch into a half smile. "Ready to start the summer?"

The girls around me all holler and applaud.

"Then let's get this bus rolling!"

As the driver pulls onto the street, the girls cheer. I feel like cheering a bit too, but I don't want to look weird. Ah, what the heck. "Yay!" I pipe in.

I lift my knees into the fetal position and place the soles of my pink sneakers against the back of the seat in front of me. "Is this your first year too?" I ask my new BFF.

"No way," Alison says. "My ninth."

"Wow."

"I know. I started going when I was seven. My older brother had been going to Wood Lake for years, and I begged my parents to let me come as soon as I was old enough."

"Were you in the starter program? My stepsister is doing it next month."

"Nah, that's new." She gives me a big smile. "So how did you hear about Wood Lake?"

When I was dating Will Kosravi (don't blame me for going out with the older brother of the love of my life; blame a love spell gone wrong à la Miri), he happened to mention that he was going to Wood Lake for the summer, and I happened to mention it to my stepmom, who was trying to get some alone time with my dad and decided it would be ideal for Miri, Prissy (my stepsister), and me to go off to camp. "Through someone at school," I answer, not quite ready to spill my heart. She might be my new BFF, but I've known her for only ten minutes. "Is your brother still at camp?"

She shakes her head. "Not anymore. He's twenty-three and in med school."

"That's a big age difference."

"Half brother," she explains. "His dad got remarried to my mom."

A divorce in the family! We have something in common besides being in the same bunk!

"It sucks that he's not here, actually. He was head staff. Hey, your sister is motioning to you," Alison tells me.

I look up, and indeed, Miri is frantically waving. "What's wrong?" I call to her.

Come here, she mouths.

Five minutes, I mouth, holding up five fingers, then turn back to Alison. "Sorry."

"Well, it was great when he was here. Our bunk never got in trouble for anything. Last year we were raiding the kitchen, and Abby, the head of Koalas, caught us, but my brother begged her not to rat us out."

"Lucky. What was your brother head of?"

"Waterfront. Swimming and boating."

Although I'm intrigued by the idea of boating, I'm not really looking forward to the swimming part of the summer. I mean, I know how to swim, sort of, if you count cooling off in my dad's pool after suntanning. And I can hold my head underwater for at least six seconds. That has to count for something, right? At least I have two cool new bathing suits,

13

a funky black and white one-piece and a sexy orange bikini. I also brought an old stretchy one-piece that belonged to my mom, which I am only planning on wearing when I have no other options, because that's like sharing a used tissue.

Anyway.

"Your sister is trying to get your attention again," Alison says. "Is she okay?"

She's certainly giving me a cramp. A cramp in my style. "I'll be right back," I tell Alison, then carefully maneuver my way down the center of the bus and into the seat next to Miri.

She is an alarming shade of green. "I don't feel well. I think I might—"

And that's when she throws up all over herself, the seat, and me.

Suddenly, the entire bus is silent. And then choruses of "Gross!" and "Nasty!" echo through the vehicle, turning my sister tomato red.

"You okay?" I ask, mortified for the two of us.

Her lips are trembling like she's about to cry. "Would it be too obvious if I disappeared?" she whispers.

"Yes," I whisper back.

"Oh, no." Janice has jumped up to inspect the atrocity. "We have a puker. Stop the bus!" she orders the driver. The driver turns off the highway and pulls into a gas station. My cheeks are burning up, but it's not because of the heat. This is *excruciatingly* embarrassing. I can't believe Miri did that.

We mope our way into the gas station's scummy, egg-scented bathroom. Once we lock the door, Miri takes off her shirt and carries it over to the sink.

"Is it coming out?" I ask, stripping off my own shirt and

wiping it under the faucet. Meanwhile, I study my reflection in the mirror. "Do you think my boobs are growing?"

She looks up from her rinsing. "Your left boob looks bigger."

"Bigger than what?"

She peers closely. "Than your right one."

I adjust my shoulders and then take another look. Omigod, she's right. My boobs are finally growing! Yay! The left boob is definitely bigger than it was the last time I measured. (Not that I measure often. Only every day or two.) I've been wishing for bigger boobs for forever. I mean, is it fair that I'm an A-cup and my little sister is a B? I think not. Wahoo! But how did I not notice this when I was in the shower? Wait a sec. "Why isn't the right one growing too?"

Miri shrugs. "That's what I was wondering."

Oh God. Oh, no. Panic washes over me like acid rain. Not that I know exactly what acid rain is, but I know it's bad. "How can one boob grow faster than the other? They're supposed to grow at the same rate! One arm doesn't grow longer than the other! One leg doesn't grow longer than the other! One foot doesn't—"

"Actually, lots of people have different-sized feet." Miri wiggles her own sneaker-clad foot as if to prove her point.

"No, no, no. Isn't there a spell we can use to even them out?"

"You know what Mom said about using boob spells before you've finished puberty. You could really mess up your body. Your hormones are already whacked out enough. I'm sure the other one will grow eventually."

"But what if it doesn't?"

"Then you'll have two different-sized boobs."

I think I might cry. "It's not fair!"

"It's not *that* much bigger than the other one."

"Yes, it is." My life is officially over. I mean, come on! Camp is all about bathing suits. People are going to *see* my deformity.

"Yeah, it's huge. So big it's practically another person. Let's call her Melinda."

How can she joke during a crisis like this? Hmm. "Why Melinda?"

"I don't know. It rhymes with Glinda?"

"Too confusing, I'll get them mixed up. Let's call her Bobby."

"Bobby is a boy's name."

"Get with it, Mir. Boys' names are very trendy for girls these days."

"Great. I'll change my name to Murray." She continues scraping at her shirt and then sighs. "It's not coming out. I should try a clean spell from A^2."

Miri is referring to *The Authorized and Absolute Reference Handbook to Astonishing Spells, Astounding Potions, and History of Witchcraft Since the Beginning of Time*, which we renamed *Authorized and Absolute* (hence the A^2). I do not yet possess my own copy.

"Really? Let me try it." Now's my chance to practice a real spell, a *published* spell, and not some limerick I made up on the spur of the moment.

"Now? People are waiting for us, and your magic hasn't been that dependable. . . ."

What is she talking about? "My magic is just fine, thank you very much."

She raises an eyebrow. "So you were purposely levitating your knapsack out there?"

"Oh, shut up. Come on, just tell me the spell."

"You're so difficult," she grumbles. "Just touch the stain with a drop of soap. Then pour some salt into your left hand. Turn the hot water on with your other hand and let it wash over the salt while you repeat three times 'Mark upon these robes be gone.' "

"Miri, I don't have any salt on me."

She reaches into her knapsack and pulls out one of those skinny-minny restaurant salt packets. "A witch always carries around salt. It's, like, the miracle ingredient."

Yay! Problem solved. Almost. I can't believe it; I'm about to do my first real spell! Of course, I've been using my raw will all over the place, but since my mother hasn't given me my much-deserved copy of A^2, I haven't yet tested an existing spell. She wouldn't let me begin my training earlier because she wanted me to focus on studying for my finals, and since I can't train from camp, she insists I wait until fall, when she will zap me up my very own copy of the book. So you can understand how excited I am about performing this spell. It's my very special rite of passage. Kind of like a bat mitzvah. A bat mitzvah in a gas station bathroom.

Hands trembling, I dab the soap on our shirts and then on the shorts we're still wearing. Then, after I rip open the packet and dump the salt in my left hand, I turn the water back on and say:

"Mark upon these robes be gone,
Mark upon these robes be gone,
Mark upon these robes be gone!"

17

The power boils from somewhere deep inside me, through my arms and into my fingertips. The room gets really cold. And then, suddenly . . . our clothes are spotless! Yes! Yes, yes, yes! They're clean and they're . . . tie-dyed? Huh? The three colors in our outfits have somehow merged and turned into swirls on our clothes. Oh, man, is my magic cool!

"Oh, no," Miri whines. "I knew I should have done it myself."

"Give me a break, we're going to look awesome." The uniforms are far less boring now. People will think that we just happened to have extra camp outfits in our knapsacks and that we're über-creative.

"We are not. We'll look like we're wearing psychedelic pajamas. Yikes! Look what your butt says!"

"What?" I turn around and try to stare at my behind in the mirror. Instead of saying Camp Wood Lake, my shorts now say Oodle Wamp Ack. As does my shirt. As does Miri's. Oops. "Can you fix it?"

We hear a honk.

"There's no time," she says anxiously. "I don't know how, and A^2 is in my duffel bag. At least people will be so busy trying to read your T-shirt, they won't notice your misshapen breasts."

Gee, thanks.

When we return to the bus, Janice has already wiped up the mess and now looks more nervous than ever. She's also chewing a brand-new black pen. If this one explodes, she's going to look like a bruise.

Head down, Miri squirms into her new seat in the second row. "Please stay up front with me?"

Aw. First it was panic, then it was hot water and salt. Now guilt washes over me. How can I abandon my sister on her first day of camp? Though in all fairness to myself, camp hasn't officially started, since we're not there yet. Nevertheless, I take the seat next to her. And then I look back—forlornly—at my new friends in the middle.

And we're off again. Off to a not-so-magical start.

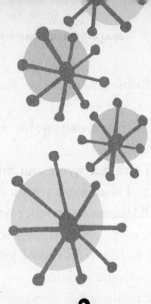

2
BAD TIGGER

Miri stares longingly out the window. "I wish I could poof myself off the bus."

Unfortunately for her, she can't. The one and only spell Mom has cast in the past month is a location charm that keeps Miri and me shackled to camp. It's essentially an invisible anklet made of distilled vinegar and cactus essence that works like a high-powered magnet. All we know is that we can't take it off without Mom's permission. Mom wants to keep us from zapping ourselves to Africa (Miri) or the Caribbean (me) when she's not around to monitor our comings and goings.

"No broom flying or transporting for you," I say.

Miri looks back at all the girls and her shoulders tense. "I should have refused when Dad said he was sending us to camp."

"Too late now," I say.

"It's so unfair that Prissy gets to come for only two weeks, and we have to stay all summer. Why can't they have a starter session for older kids too?"

My poor, socially inept sister. "Unlike Prissy, you're not six. Anyway, Mom is going to be in Thailand with Lex for most of August and it's not like she'd let us stay home alone." It's weird that my mom is suddenly so serious about Lex. I'm happy for her, of course. But what if I need to get in touch with her while she's away? Shouldn't she be at my beck and call 24/7?

She'd better bring me back some exotic clothes, or some hair chopsticks or something.

Miri kicks the railing. "It's like I'm in prison." Her eyes start to tear up. She has pretty much the same eyes as mine, big and brown, but her eyeballs are really white and sometimes they glow in the dark. Not in a creepy way. More like the moon.

21

I tickle my sister's arm. "You're going to love camp. I promise."

Eventually, Miri curls into a ball and falls asleep with her head on my knee. Through the window I watch the passing of mountains and lush green trees, counting the seconds until we get to camp. I can't believe I'm going to be away from home for seven weeks and one day.

Fifty days without chores! Fifty days without having to watch my mom make out with Lex! Fifty days without my stepmother calling me every five seconds to discuss her plans to get pregnant! Fifty days without having to bounce back and forth between my mom and my dad!

Fifty days *with* Raf. Single, unattached Raf.

"Did you hear?" my best friend, Tammy Wise, asked me ten days ago when we sat down at two empty desks for our math exam.

"About what?"

"About Raf and Melissa."

My heart leaped straight out of my chest, hit the ceiling, then bounced back in. Okay, not really, but it felt like it. Melissa Davis, my redheaded nemesis, had started dating Raf after Raf and I broke up back in April. Not that we'd really been going out, more like quasi going out. You know, him looking at me that way, me looking at him that way—there was a whole lot of *looking* going on. And one almost kiss (code for closed lips with no tongue action). "No, what?"

"They broke up!"

Yes! Yes! Yessssssssssssssssssssssssssssssssssssss! "When?"

"Saturday night!"

"What happened?"

"He broke up with her, and she's none too pleased."

My heart was hammering; my fingers were dancing; my legs were spasming. It was like I was on an upside-down roller coaster, only I wasn't moving. "I need details, Tammy. Details!"

"Apparently he told her that it's because he likes someone else." Her eyebrows went into overdrive.

The moderator flicked the lights off and on. "Please turn over your test booklets." And that was when I felt the tingling. The raw will. The rush of cold. More specifically, the back window flew wide open.

"What the . . . ," said the moderator as he rushed to the back of the room. "Who did that?"

I did. Did I?

The lights started flickering; the teacher's desk flipped smack over; the window slammed shut. It was as if a poltergeist had taken over the classroom. And I had the twitchy yet sure feeling that I was responsible, or more precisely, my fantabulous powers were.

I did some yoga-like breathing exercises to calm myself and tried to focus on the formulas in front of me. Thank goodness this was math, a subject I knew like the back of my hand.

Unfortunately, from that moment on, I noticed that whenever I got overstimulated, my magic tended to get a bit . . . unruly.

For example, while chomping Mom's cheese-and-tofu ravioli, I began picturing moonlit walks with Raf, canoeing with Raf, kissing Raf . . . and my heart started beating faster, and suddenly a ravioli square went soaring off my plate, bounced off the ceiling, and landed in my mother's carrot juice.

My mom dropped her fork in midchew. "What was that?"

If my mom knew I'd done that, I'd be eating tofu ravioli for the entire summer. Quick! I needed an excuse. A scapegoat. "Bad Tigger! Bad, bad Tigger."

Our cat, who was curled up in his favorite corner nook of the kitchen, licking his paws, narrowed his little yellow eyes as if to say *Are you kidding me?*

My mom jumped up to clean the mess. "Bad Tigger," she said, and I exhaled in relief.

I'm sad to admit that during the past week, I've started blaming Tigger for pretty much everything. Chair knocked

23

over? Tigger. Lights flickering? Tigger. Toilet paper roll unraveled all over the apartment? Tigger.

Okay, that last one *was* him, but it was because he was so pissed off at me.

I must have fallen asleep, because the next thing I hear is Janice's nervous voice.

"We're here, girls. Everyone ready?"

My eyes shoot open. Our bus has pulled onto the side of a dirt road, behind a row of already-parked buses. A few feet away is a wooden bridge crossing a murky pond. Beyond the bridge is a winding road that leads into thick trees.

We're really here. Watch out, world! Miri, my socially inept sister, and I, a newly minted witch, both of us in swirly tie-dyed Oodle Wamp Ack psychedelic pajamas, have arrived!

And let's not forget Glinda and Bobby.

Kids are already streaming out of the buses, and I peer ahead, looking for Raf. Still no sign of him. I take a few slow breaths to calm myself. After all, I wouldn't want the buses to rise into the sky and fly off to another planet, E.T.-style.

That's something I couldn't possibly blame on Tigger.

"All right, girls," Janice says. "Since you all sent your duffel bags earlier in the week, they've already been brought to your cabins." A Camp Wood Lake van picked up the bags at our apartment, which was a lot easier than carrying them ourselves. There must be a lot of campers from Manhattan. But I only care about one.

"In bunk two," Janice continues, "we have Jenny Boland, Heather Jacobs, Jessica Curnyn—"

I zone out for a few names before I hear "and Miri Weinstein."

Miri squeezes my hand.

"Hey, look, there's Natalie!" Trishelle announces. "The Canada bus must be here already."

"Cana-bus?" Miri whispers to me. "What kind of place is this?"

"Canada bus, you dork," I whisper-enunciate back.

Janice continues listing. "And in bunk fourteen," she says five minutes later, "we have Morgan Sweeney, Jan Winters, Carly Engels, Rachel Weinstein, and Alison Blaichman."

Yes! Alison *is* in my bunk! I turn back to her and wave.

After listing the names of the girls in bunk fifteen, Janice says, "If you have your sun hats or baseball caps with you, please put them on before leaving the bus."

I hate hats. I don't mind them on other people, but they always make me feel like I'm wearing a cardboard box. My baseball hats are all stiff. I'll just pretend my mother didn't force one into my backpack.

Miri pulls hers out and slaps it on. "Aren't you going to put your sun hat on?" she says rather loudly.

"Shhh! Come on, let's go." Since we're at the front of the bus, we're the first ones off, and since we have no idea where we're going, we huddle together to wait for

25

instructions. Janice said she would show us the way, but she is deep in conversation with some of the counselors. Great. Now what? Wander around until the summer ends and we're buried in snow?

"Bunk two sounds awfully far away from bunk fourteen," Miri says, her voice all shaky.

"Come on, it can't be that far."

"Hi again," says a voice behind me. Hurrah, it's Alison, my new BFF.

"Hi," I say with relief.

"Lost?"

"Just a little."

"Follow me." Alison is much taller than I am and therefore takes bigger steps.

"Did you meet my sister, Miri?" I ask while practically running to keep up.

"You guys look alike," Alison says as we follow the trail over the bridge and onto a narrow gravel road lined with tall green pine trees.

"Is that a bunk?" Miri asks, pointing to a small white building peeking out on our left.

"No, it's the camp office. Colton! Hey!" she squeals, waving at a guy up the road.

"Howdy, Al-ison!" he hollers back in a thick Southern drawl. "How was your year?"

"Not bad!" she yells, and then says to me, "Colton's our age, too."

"He's cute." He has dimples and a buzz cut. "Where's he from?"

"Houston, I think."

Funny, I feel like I'm in Texas. The sky above us is still overwhelmingly bright and blue even though by now it must be at least four. I take a deep breath. It smells dewy and clean. Kind of like the air freshener in our bathroom back home. But, um, real.

As we continue along the road, the trees clear and we pass through a shopping center–sized massive field, behind which are postcard-perfect lush green mountains. Grass! Trees! Hills! Sky! I have never seen so much nature in one place.

There'd better not be bears here. Or any wild animals, for that matter. After six hours of online searching (fine, procrastinating studying for finals), I learned all about how bats, raccoons, and foxes carry scary diseases like rabies, Lyme disease, and plague. I didn't know plague still existed, but apparently lots of rodents up here are teeming with it.

27

And let's not forget mosquitoes. Those little monsters are bursting with West Nile virus. But they're not getting me. No way, no how. I packed about ten gallons of mosquito repellant.

"This is Upper Field," Alison says. "There're the baseball field, the kitchen staff housing, the soccer field, the Upper Field showers, and back there are bunks sixteen and seventeen, where Colton and some of the other Lion guys live."

"What does *Lion* mean exactly?"

"The oldest unit at camp. People finishing grades seven, eight, and nine. Koalas are the youngest and Monkeys are in the middle."

Ah. I scan Upper Field, wondering if that's where Raf

sleeps. My heart makes like a deer and gallops. (Deer do gallop, right? Hopefully, I will never have the occasion to meet one to find out.)

"Here we are," Alison announces, pointing with a flourish to a large green and white cabin on our right. "Bunks fourteen and fifteen are in this cabin."

Phewf. At least it's a cabin. A tiny part of me was concerned that I would be spending the summer in a tent. That would be way too much nature for City Rachel.

Two girls, a blonde and a redhead, are standing on the long porch, and when they spot us, they begin waving madly.

"Poodles! Morgan!" Alison shrieks. "You're here!" She scurries up the hill and the cabin's steps and throws her arms around the girls.

Poodles? People bring their dogs to camp?

"Check it out, Alison," the redhead squeals. "Poodles got a butterfly tattoo on her ankle and I finally got tits!"

Did she just say the T word? I hate that word. It's so vulgar.

"You're blocking the way," someone says. I turn around to see a thin, glossy girl glaring at me. She looks me up and down and flips her black hair. Then, without a word, she pushes past me, nearly knocking me over. Her hair storms behind her, and without so much as an "excuse me," she heads up the hill to the cabin.

How rude. I hope she's in bunk fifteen. But I know better than to whine about someone on my first day at camp. I wouldn't want to end up the picked-on girl. There's always one in every crowd, the girl nobody likes. It's terrible the way some kids gang up like that on one specific person, but I have to admit, I'm terrified of becoming that person myself.

I find my balance and say to Miri, "Do you want me to walk with you to your cabin?"

She looks nervously up the road and then back at me. "Nah, go ahead. I'll find it."

"Rachel, come meet everyone!" Alison calls from the porch. "Miri, just walk down the road to Lower Field, then take the path up the hill between bunks one and three, and your bunk will be on the right."

"You sure you can make it on your own?" I ask my pale-looking sister.

She gives me a brave smile. "I'll be fine. How lost can I get?"

I decide not to remind her about the time she got lost in the basement of our apartment building. Anyway, if she gets lost, she can always zap herself back to her cabin, can't she? "Good luck," I say, and squeeze her arm. "See you at dinner." As I make my way up the hill, I feel butterflies (not tattooed ones) going haywire in my stomach.

There are already towels and a few pieces of clothing hanging over the porch railing, giving the place a homey feel. A few empty duffel bags are piled in the corner. Alison has resumed her group hug with the two other girls, and I can't help feeling left out. What if I'm always the outsider? What if they think I'm just the weird new girl?

I feel a tingling in my fingers. Then in my elbows, then in my head, then—

The towels and clothing that were carefully hung over the railing all go skyrocketing into the air like kites. But unlike kites, they have nothing anchoring them to the ground and continue to soar higher and higher and higher and . . .

Gone.

Hah! I totally did that! I didn't mean to, but still! I just made towels disappear! I am the queen of magic! I might have to make myself a tiara in arts and crafts.

I wonder where they went?

Oh, there they are, caught in the branches. Hope someone has a ladder.

Like me, the three girls are staring at the towel-covered trees. Unlike me, they have perplexed expressions on their faces.

I might have to try to control my magic just a teeny bit. If towels shoot up into the sky every time I get freaked out, people are bound to notice, and then they're going to start wondering about me, and the next thing I know, they'll be tying me to a three-legged stool and dropping me into the lake like they used to do to witches in the Middle Ages.

Or maybe I'll get my own talk show. One of those psychic shows where they make people talk to the dead!

Wow, can I really talk to the dead? "Hey, dead, are you there?" No response. "Granny Esther, can you hear me?"

"Rachel, who are you talking to?" Alison asks.

I feel my face redden. "Um, I thought I saw an old friend, Esther. We call her Granny because she's so old. At least seventeen."

Oh God. They think I'm a moron.

To my relief, Alison laughs. "You are *so* hilarious!" She

30

grabs my hand and leads me up the steps. "Come meet the girls."

"Hi," I say shyly.

"This is Morgan. She's been coming to camp as long as I have."

Morgan has short, curly red hair and a spatter of freckles across her nose. If I were a director, I would so cast her as Annie.

"Where are you from?" she asks as we check each other out. If only I weren't wearing the most ridiculous outfit in the world.

The redhead is adorable. She's already changed out of the camp clothing and is now wearing a tight black T-shirt, gold-heeled flip-flops, and a short jean skirt that exposes her pale, freckled legs. I bet she has to wear a lot of sunscreen.

"Manhattan," I answer. Maybe she'll think my tie-dye is some sort of New Yorker fashion statement. We are normally ahead of the curve, even when we do retro. "You?"

"I live right outside Chicago. What camp did you go to before?"

"I didn't," I reply. "I mean, I went to day camp, but never sleepaway."

"Hope you don't get homesick," she says.

Puh-lease. I've been counting the days until I could venture out on my own. I'm practically ready for college.

"She won't," Alison says. "She's going to love it. This place is the best camp."

"How would you know?" asks Morgan. "You've never been to another camp."

31

"Neither have you!"

The blond girl—the gorgeous blond girl, I should add—pats my arm. "I'm Poodles."

"She's our California chick," Alison says. "She's been coming here forever too."

"Poodles?" I can't help asking. Is that some sort of California name? I knew they were New Agey, but being named after an animal?

"My unit head nicknamed me on the first day of camp back when I was a Koala."

"She used to wear her hair all poufy," Morgan says, and fluffs up her friend's hair.

"Cool shirt," Poodles says to me. "Did you get it specially made?"

Yes! "Oh, definitely," I say, and turn around. "The shorts too."

Poodles smiles. "Funky."

"So what's your real name?" I ask, turning back.

"Jan, but nobody here calls me that. Even my friends in Cali call me Poodles."

Poodles definitely looks like she's from Cali. (Hmm, can I call it Cali if I'm not from Cali? Cali sounds so cool. I wish I were from Cali. Maybe I can move to Cali?) First of all, she's tall, towering over even Alison. Also, her hair is naturally blond (I think). And she has big blue eyes and perfectly tanned arms and legs, which her short pink shorts and white tank top show off. Surely her mother is a famous movie star.

"We saved you a bed," she says to Alison.

What if there's no bed left for me? No, that's stupid; they

must have one for everybody, right? And anyway, I can just zap myself up a new one. Of course, that might cause a little confusion.

There are two green wooden doors on the porch, one that says "14" and one that says "15." I follow the other girls through the one on the left, which says "14" in black paint, and immediately enter a smallish square room.

"Here we are," Alison says. "Bunk fourteen, home sweet home."

I look around my new (jury's-still-out-on-sweet) home. The walls of the bunk are paneled with beige faux wood that have names and years scribbled in black and red all over them. *Michael Solinger was here '95–06!, Farrah and Carrie BFF! Lynda D. loves Jon C.*

Sunlight streams through the large screened windows that overlook the porch, making the room feel superbright. The two lightbulbs hanging from the white ceiling aren't even on. Directly opposite the door we just came through is an opening to what looks like a huge closet, but my feet are too glued to the dark gray floor to explore.

Glued because I'm terrified.

On both sides of the entranceway to the closet are metal bunk beds, pressed against the back wall.

No one said anything about bunk beds. Bunk beds were not in the brochure. I cannot sleep on a top bunk. It's way too far off the ground.

Next to where I'm standing, sandwiched between the two windows overlooking the porch, is a lone single bed that (surprise, surprise) has already been claimed with a

33

pink comforter and ruffled pillows. A small silver fan is attached to the metal railing on the bed, blowing air onto the marked territory, so to speak.

"Carly, what are you doing?" Alison asks a dark-haired girl, who appears to be doing sit-ups on a beach towel in the middle of the room.

"Forty-one, forty-two . . . ," says the girl. "I'm doing my stomach crunches . . . forty-four . . . hold on, I'll be done when I get to fifty . . . forty-seven, forty-eight, forty-nine, fifty." She rolls back onto the towel. "Done. I have a new plan. If I do fifty sit-ups every day, my stomach will be flat by the end of the summer."

Alison squats down to hug Carly. "Still a nut job, I see."

"Am not," she says, and then stands. "I'm just fat."

"You are not fat! Nut job, meet Rachel. Rachel, Carly."

"Hi," I say. How am I going to remember all these new names? Maybe I need tricks. For example, Carly is lying on the floor doing sit-ups on the first day of camp. Alison thinks she's nuts, so I'll call her Crazy, which starts with the same letter as *Carly*, which is making me . . . Confused.

Think I'll skip that idea.

"Hey," Carly says, shaking out her towel. She hangs it over the railing of one of the top bunks. Then she heaves herself onto the bed and pushes aside at least ten teddy bears to find a clear spot.

"Rachel, looks like you're on the top bunk above me, since it's all that's left," Alison says, depositing her knapsack on the bottom bunk right where we're standing. "Unless you want my bottom bed?"

Of course I want her bottom bed. But I probably shouldn't ask for it. "No, I'm fine on top," I lie. Hurrah to sharing with Alison, boo to the top bunk. What are the chances I won't roll off in the middle of the night and break my head? Maybe I can zap up an invisible net.

Morgan has set up her bed under Carly's. She has a Betty Boop comforter, and a matching calendar on her wall. I wish I brought something more fun than a boring old gray blanket and drab white sheets.

The pink and frilly single seems to belong to Poodles. She is kneeling on her bed, taping photos of hot guys to her wall.

I look around for that rude black-haired girl who nearly knocked me over and am glad that she's not here. "Are there five girls in every bunk?" I ask. Five beds equals five girls, right?

"No, fifteen has six," Alison says. "They set up the beds and the bunks based on how many people are coming to camp. Last year all the girls in our age group were together in bunk four because we were eight, but this year we're eleven, so they divided us into bunks fourteen and fifteen, which are connected back there through the cubby room." She points to the opening between the bunk beds.

"We were supposed to be six," Poodles says. "I convinced my friend Wendy to come, but she got a small role in an NBC pilot and decided to stay in Cali and take it."

"Lucky," Carly says.

"As is Poodles," Morgan says, "since she now gets a single."

Alison sits down on said single and leans her back against the wall.

I'm not sure exactly what to do with myself, so I pick up the communal Lysol can that's sitting on one of the empty shelves, climb up the brown, not-so-sturdy ladder, spray and spray and spray some more, and then deposit my knapsack on the saggy, stained mattress. Okay. I've claimed a bed. I will not be sleeping on the floor (unless I fall out, that is). Now what? I sit down on the edge of the bed, try to ignore the loud creak, and let my legs dangle off the edge of my dirty-looking mattress.

This. Is. Terrifying.

I'm going to have to zap the bunk bed into two singles. Sure, it'll be tight in here, but if I can squeeze the extra bed into the corner, I can make it all fit. Of course, I'll have to wait until no one is here before I attempt any Sabrina-style interior decoration.

"Hello, missy," chimes a new girl from the room's back entrance.

Alison jumps off the bed. "Cece!"

The two girls throw their arms around each other.

"You got braces!" Alison screams.

Cece clamps her mouth shut and mutters, "I hate them."

"They look cute."

"How can braces look cute? A railroad is running across my face. I'm hideous. I don't want to talk about it. I'm not smiling all summer."

"Come on!"

"It's true," Cece says. "Anyway, I'm sad that I'm not in the same bunk as you this summer."

"We're practically in the same bunk. We're connected."

"Not the same and you know it. We're not going to be at the same mess hall table or have all our activities together."

36

"Cece!" screams a voice from the other side of the wall.

"See you later," she says, then disappears back through the opening, bumping into an older teen along the way.

"Hello, my chickadees," sings the older teen, sauntering into the room and clapping. "Welcome back! Ready to part-ay?"

My bunkmates hoot and holler. "Deb!" they scream.

"We missed you," says Poodles, jumping up to give the counselor a hug.

After saying hi to all the girls, Deb walks over to my bed. "Hiyee! Welcome to camp." Her hair is dirty blond and tied back with a red and black checkered bandana, do-rag-style. Up close I notice that she has big eyes, big white teeth, and a big smile. "You lucked out," she says. "This side of the cabin is way better than the other."

More hoots and hollers from the girls.

"I bet Penelope is saying the same thing to the new girls in bunk fifteen," Morgan says.

"I'll have you know that Anthony let me choose which side of the cabin I wanted, and I chose you guys."

"When we were all in one bunk last year, both Penelope and Deb were our counselors," Alison explains to me. "Frankly, Debs, I'm surprised you weren't sick of us. I thought you would have requested Koalas after last year."

"I could never get sick of you girls!"

Morgan snorts. "We got sick of you." She's sitting cross-legged on her bottom bunk, her flip-flops kicked to the floor.

Deb parks herself next to Morgan and starts poking her arm. "Let's see the C-cups you've been e-mailing me about."

Morgan sticks out her chest. "Nice tits, huh?"

Ew, she said it again!

"Not bad." Deb sticks out her own chest. "But not as big as mine."

"Debs, you're five years older. I should hope yours are bigger. Mine are going to look huge, though," Morgan continues. "You should see the bikinis I bought. They all have ridiculous padding. Will Kosravi will have no choice but to fall in lust with me."

I almost choke on my tongue. They're talking about my Will!

"Keep drooling, Morgan sweetie," Deb says. "First of all, he's staff, and staff are not allowed to date campers. And second of all, he told me in precamp that he has a serious girlfriend back home."

Morgan's freckled features crumple in disappointment. "No way! Who?"

Deb shrugs. "I don't remember her name."

"It's Kat," I pipe up.

Everyone looks at me.

Morgan puts her hands on her hips. "How do you know?"

"I, um, know the Kosravi boys pretty well."

"Do you go to school with them?" asks Poodles, not turning around from her postering.

Oh yes. "Uh-huh."

I must be bright red, because Morgan asks, "Did you date Will?" at the same time that Poodles asks, "Did you date Raf?"

Funny they should ask. "Well . . . kind of."

Alison looks up at me. "Which one?"

Here comes the weird part. "Both?"

All four of my new bunkmates' jaws drop. So does the counselor's.

"You dated Raf *and* Will Kosravi?" Carly squeals.

"Kind of."

Alison whistles. "You're like a legend."

Even Poodles is now paying full attention. "Who's a better kisser?"

"Girls, less gossiping and more unpacking," Deb says, now fully recovered. "Dinner's in one hour and I expect this place to be perfectly put together by then, got it? Off to the cubby room you go."

I step down from my bed, happy to avoid answering the question. Because unfortunately, I don't know the answer. Raf and I haven't *really* kissed.

Sorry, let me rephrase. Raf and I haven't really kissed *yet*.

When I realize that my bunkmates and my counselor are all vacating the bunk for the cubby room, I see my opportunity to fix my bunk bed situation. If I leave things the way they are, I will surely end up rolling off in the middle of the night and breaking my head.

I wait a few seconds for the room to clear out, and then I hurry to the far corner of the room, where no one can see me. Unfortunately, I don't have A^2. But at the prom, I made up my own spell, and that seemed to work, so . . .

I clear my throat, close my eyes, focus my raw will, and chant under my breath:

"Bunk bed, split in two.

Two single beds are what I need from you!"

The air gets sucked out of the room, and I jump up and down as the metal frame starts to quiver. It's working!

39

Now the bunk bed is swaying from side to side like a rocking chair.

Clank! Clank! Clank!

Uh-oh.

Suddenly, the frame cracks in two, sounding like a firework and causing the top bunk to crash into Alison's bed below it.

See, the thing is, I was kind of imagining two perfectly formed single beds, not one bunk bed sawed in half. I was planning on telling the other girls that the bunk bed had been desperately needed in one of the other bunks, and that I had reluctantly agreed to let them have it in return for two singles. . . .

Yeah, my plan was obviously not very well thought out.

"What was that?" Poodles asks, rushing back into the room with Deb and Carly.

"Omigod, my bed!" shrieks Alison from behind them. "Rachel, are you okay? You could have been killed!"

"If this had happened when you were asleep, you *both* could have been killed," Deb says, eyes wide.

"I'm fine, I'm fine," I tell them sheepishly.

"I'll call the office and tell them to get a new bunk bed pronto," Deb says. "Plus I'm making them check over every bed here to make sure they're secure. In all my years here, I have never seen that happen!"

What can I say? She's never had a witch for a camper.

Just one more thing I can't blame on Tigger.

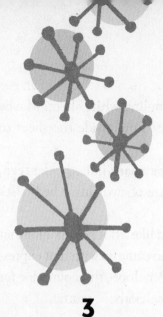

3
THE ART OF UNPACKING

Once everyone calms down, I explore the rest of the cabin. The cubby room is a large rectangular space filled with—you guessed it—wooden cubbies. Some of the cubbies are already stuffed with clothes, though most of them are empty. Duffel bags are piled in the center of the room.

Omigod. You've got to be kidding me. I'm expected to change right here and prance around naked in front of all these strangers? They're going to see my deformity!

From inside the cubby room, I can peek into bunk fifteen. Instead of two bunk beds and one single, it has three bunk beds.

The cubby room leads to the bathroom, which I realize I very badly have to use.

Yes, the bathroom! I can change in there, can't I?

I squeeze through the girls and the bags and step inside. There are three stalls on my left and four sinks on my right.

But where are the showers?

Beyond the bathroom is a dangling white sheet. Maybe the showers are on the other side? I pull aside the sheet to take a look.

"You can't come in here," snaps a dark-haired older teen, who appears to be napping on one of two single beds. "It's the counselors' room!"

The sheet drops out of my hand like a hot potato. Not that I would ever hold a hot potato. Who came up with that expression, anyway? The girl must be Penelope, the counselor for bunk fifteen. Good thing I got Deb. "Sorry," I mutter.

I vaguely remember Alison mentioning showers being on Upper Field. Does that mean there are no showers in the cabins?

I retreat into one of the stalls. One of the *tiny* stalls. There's no way I could ever change my clothes in here. I lock the door, cover the seat with flimsy one-ply toilet paper, bang my knees against the door, and pee.

I also read all the graffiti on the back of the door. Lynda D. seems to still really love Jon C.

Once done and out of the stall, I smile at myself in the mirror, pump some of the communal soap into my palms, wash my hands, then dry them on someone else's black towel and look around. I think I'm finally getting my bearings. The cabin is shaped like the letter *T*. First you have the two sleeping rooms, which both lead into the cubby room, which leads into the bathroom, which leads into the counselors' room.

No problemo. Now back to the cubby room . . .

Or shall I say, the disaster zone.

There are bags, clothes, and girls everywhere. I try to tune out the loud chattering ("My butt got so much wider over the year!" "You have to see my adorable running shoes." "Did you get your belly pierced?") while I locate my two bags. Of course, I find one of them under a pile of others and practically break my arm yanking it out.

I don't understand how I'm expected to keep this cubby organized. Honestly. How am I supposed to cram

8 T-shirts

3 pairs of shorts

2 pairs of jeans

2 pairs of sweatpants

1 pair of black pants (dry-clean only, so they'd better not get dirty)

2 long-sleeved shirts

2 sweatshirts

12 pairs of socks

12 pairs of underwear

8 bras

3 bathing suits

1 jean jacket

1 pair of sneakers

1 pair of flip-flops

1 pair of cute strappy black sandals

9 towels (3 hand, 4 beach, 2 shower)

1 alternate pillowcase

2 alternate twin-size sheets (1 flat & 1 fitted, both boring and white)

2 laundry bags

43

1 invisibility shield, aka enchanted umbrella (Let me tell you, it was no easy feat sneaking this past my mother's snooping eyes to pack. Though it's a good thing it becomes invisible only when cloaking someone. Otherwise, how would I ever find it?)

1 bathrobe

into a space the size of my school locker? What I need is some sort of organizing spell. While waiting for the room to clear, I brainstorm, trying to come up with rhymes. Not that spells have to rhyme, but all the coolest spells in A^2 are in verse, and I'm not about to take a chance with my wardrobe. Now, what should I try? I want to zap my clothes into being folded neatly. The way they look on a store shelf. What rhymes with zap?

Wrap? Tap? Map?

I got it! I open my bag and shove all my stuff into the cubby; then, when the room has pretty much emptied out, I stand right in front of my cubby (blocking any potential snoops), close my eyes, focus, ram my hands inside the cubby, wiggle my fingers, and say:

"*With this zap,*

Let my clothes look like they do at the Gap!"

Here comes the rush of cold air . . . and presto!

I step back and study my creation. Omigod! My clothes are folded into flawless squares and, oh yes, color-coordinated, too. From light to dark, like a rainbow.

Yes!

I unfold a flattened shirt. It's a pale green and white striped short-sleeved V-neck top. That doesn't belong to me. That doesn't have my *Rachel Weinstein* camp label. Instead, a price tag is dangling from its neck.

Um . . . did I poof up new clothes?

I look at my now empty duffel bag with longing. Where art thou, oh, favorite jeans? What am I going to do? Are they all gone forever? Even my cute new bikini?

Although . . . maybe these clothes are even better! Designer clothes! I shake out the shirt with excitement.

A glance at the label tells me that the shirt is a women's large. I hunt through the clothes, looking for a piece of clothing that might fit.

Oh good, here's something smaller. *Much* smaller. It's a size 1 girls' jean dress with a lace trim.

A toddler size 1.

I said Gap, not BabyGap, didn't I?

I frantically search through my cubby, looking for something—anything—I can wear. A linen maternity skirt? No. Boys' cargo pants? Also no. Men's black and white checkered boxer shorts?

Definitely not.

I wish I had my old stuff back. But since the world of magic tends to like exchanges, my real clothes are probably heaped in a big mess on a shelf at a suburban shopping mall.

I'm making my new bed (a brand-new top of a brand-new bunk bed—oh joy) when a voice comes from the sky. "Attenthion all camperth and counthlorth. Attenthion all camperth and counthlorth. Pleathe head to the meth hall for thupper."

"What was that?" I ask.

"It's Stef," Alison says.

"Or Thtef," Morgan says.

"Don't be mean," Alison says. "It's not her fault she has a lisp."

"You mean lithp?" Morgan says.

"Stef is the head counselor's sister," Alison explains. "She's been running the office and doing the announcements for years."

I look down at my new Gap jeans (with rolled-up cuffs, because they are two sizes too long) and my too-tight scooped-neck shirt. The girls are giving me weird looks, but there's nothing I can do until I can get Miri to swing by with a spell reversal—which she hopefully can . . . if she brought the enchanted crystal to camp. I was kind of wanting to look my most gorgeous for my first Raf sighting, but this is the best I can do.

Changing in front of all the other girls was completely humiliating. They all threw their clothes off like they were starring in some kind of camp porn movie. I kept my eyes on the dusty floor and changed quickly and furiously.

"Let's bust a move, girls!" Deb hollers while stomping and clomping through our bunk.

I follow my bunkmates onto the porch and down the tree-lined gravel road to the mess hall. Along the way, we pass a few green cabins on our right and the waterfront on our left. Even when it's calm, the lake scares me. As do the tied-up sailboats. At some point I'll probably have to mention my nautical inexperience to Deb. But one issue at a time. First I have to make my way to the mess hall.

The chaotic, earsplitting, overwhelming mess hall.

Our bunk's table is all the way in the rear, by the back window. The kitchen is near the entrance. "Why are we so far from the food?" I ask.

"All the Lions sit back here," Alison answers.

The wooden walls are decorated with hand-painted plaques that make me wish I had been coming to camp forever. *Army versus Navy, Color War 1975. Empire versus Rebels, Color War 1989. '50s versus '60s, 2001.* I've heard that color war is like mock Olympics, but I've never done one before. Fun!

Any minute, I realize, I'm going to see Raf. I take a deep breath and try not to obsess.

47

When I get to our table, which is right next to bunk fifteen's, I scoot onto the bench up against the window so that I can keep my eye out for He Who Should Not Be Obsessed Over. On the table are a pile of cutlery, a pile of paper plates, a stack of Styrofoam cups, two yellow pitchers filled with some sort of purple liquid, a basket of sliced French bread, and a basket of mini peanut butter and jelly packets.

"Want some bug juice?" Carly asks from across the table.

I assume that's the purple drink in the plastic pitcher and not some sort of disgusting smoothie. "Sure, thanks."

My stomach grumbles, so I nab a piece of bread. I'm wondering where the food is when I spot Deb in the long line of counselors going into the kitchen. When she finally returns, she places two large plastic bowls of food in the center of the table, one filled with steaming mac and cheese, the other filled with salad. Alison and Poodles leap up to make themselves a plate.

And that's when I see him. Raf. My breath gets lost somewhere between my lips and my lungs. I think I might have swallowed it. He's still dark and handsome and lean and handsome and did I say handsome? His dark hair seems so soft and touchable. He looks the same as he always does, but he's the summer version in a thin white T-shirt, which shows off his lean muscled arms, and khaki shorts and navy flip-flops, which show off his lean muscled legs.

He's standing in the doorframe, talking to a scruffy-looking blond guy near our age while looking around the room.

Is he looking for me? He might be looking for me. Please say he broke up with Melissa because he likes me. It must be me. It must. Please say he's looking for me. Maybe I should wave.

Nah, I don't want to be too obvious. But I want him to see me. But I don't want him to think I was looking for him. But I want him to think I'm glad to see him. But not too glad.

Don't obsess, don't obsess, don't obsess. . . .

Contact! Yes! Our eyes have made contact! He sees me! By George, he's smiling! He's walking over to me! I start to stand up.

"Freeze!" screams Deb.

Huh? I look around our table to discover that my four bunkmates are frozen in place. Yes, frozen. As though they're on a TV show and someone has just pressed Pause on my TiVo. Carly is in mid-peanut-butter-and-jelly bite. Alison is standing in mid-mac-and-cheese scoop.

I must look confused, because Deb orders, "Rachel, freeze!"

Am I under arrest? I freeze just in case. Since I was in the middle of standing up to greet Raf, this isn't easy. Raf, meanwhile, laughs when he sees me, and mouths, *I'll talk to you later.*

No, no, no. Talk to me now! I was so close!

"When a counselor calls 'freeze,' you have to freeze," Deb explains. "First person who moves has to stack."

I don't know what *stack* is, but since my four bunkmates are remaining in their frozen state, I'm assuming it's something I don't want to be doing. So I stay frozen.

Unfortunately, staying frozen is becoming increasingly painful. It feels like I'm in the middle of one of those squats they force us to do in gym.

Poodles was about to pour herself a glass of juice, and now her hand is shaking from holding up the pitcher. Carly is still in mid-peanut-butter-and-jelly bite. Deb stands up and balances a paper plate on Poodles' head.

My butt is majorly hurting. Need to sit down. Is this over yet? When is someone going to move?

Deb then opens one of the strawberry jellies, dips her finger inside, and dabs it on Morgan's nose.

Morgan cracks up.

49

"You stack!" Deb tells her, howling with laughter.

The girls resume their activity. I rest my butt back on the bench (ahhhhhhh) and ask, "What is stack, exactly?"

"Cleaning the table," Alison says, returning to her mac and cheese. "Counselors call 'freeze' at every meal. Whoever moves first, stacks. Or they call 'pig.' That's when they go like this"—she puts her index finger on the side of her nose—"and the last person to do it stacks."

It's like moving to a new country and having to learn all the customs.

After filling my plate with salad and mac and cheese, I look at Raf's table (three over from mine). Should I go say hi now? Probably not, since he's currently wolfing down his food. Now what? Do I wait for him to talk to me? Do I go over in front of everyone? I don't want to interrupt. What if he just stares at me like I'm crazy? What if he doesn't think we're going to be a couple? What if we spend the entire summer playing the camp equivalent of phone tag and I never talk to him again?

I try to control myself and not stare. I don't want all his bunkmates wondering who Crazy Stalking New Girl is.

Don't obsess, don't obsess, don't obsess. . . .

"Ketchup?" Alison asks me, interrupting my panic.

"No, thanks." Miri puts ketchup on her mac and cheese. I do not, as that is disgusting.

By the time I finish eating, Morgan is already halfway through clearing the paper plates and tossing them into the garbage. My sister the environmentalist is going to hate that.

Suddenly, there's a tap on my shoulder. Raf?

Miri. "Hi," she says. "Move over."

I push over so that she can squeeze in beside me. "Hey! Did you like dinner?"

She shakes her head. "I can't believe how much paper they waste."

"I thought that might annoy you."

"It should bother you, too," she says, taking a sip of my bug juice.

Perhaps, but my brain is too busy being bothered by the fact that Miri can get off her butt to say hello to me but Raf can't. I mean, I saw Miri this afternoon and Raf hasn't seen—

Raf is standing directly across the table, behind Carly.

"Hey," he says.

I can't breathe or speak. What is wrong with me? I've been waiting for this day for so long, planning the entire conversation. Really. I have it all scripted in my head. I'll casually flick my glimmering brown tresses over my shoulder and say hello as demurely as possible, and then I'll ask, "What's up?" ever so casually. He'll then declare his undying love for me and grab me in his arms and kiss me so passionately that—

"Rachel? You okay?"

Now is not the time for fantasizing, Rachel! Now is the time to speak up, Rachel! Now is not the time for referring to oneself in the third person, Rachel!

"Hi, Raf," I squeak.

"How are you liking your first day of camp?"

"Fun. Cool. Good." So what if I can manage only one-syllable words? At least I'm speaking. Unfortunately, my entire bunk is intently listening to the conversation.

"Did you like Oscar's mac and cheese?" he asks.

"Oscar?"

"The chef. He's been the chef for, like, twenty years."

"Oh yes. Very cheesy." Brilliant, Rachel.

Raf waves hello to the girls at the table. "Hi, ladies."

"So how long have you two known each other?" Alison asks, her mouth full.

"Rache and I go way back."

"We hear she knows your brother, too," Morgan says.

The edges of Raf's cheeks turn pink.

I might have to zap her into a bug. Or even better, bug juice. I can't believe she brought up Will. I can't believe I dated Will, even though it was accidental. I hope Raf won't let all that come between us. I know it would totally weird me out if Raf dated Miri.

Oh, right. Miri. "Raf, have you met my little sister, Miri?"

He gives her a smile. "Yup. Once. I forgot how much you guys look alike."

That's good, right? Miri's adorable. We blush simultaneously.

"I also saw you in the fashion show with Rachel," Miri says, which leads to an awkward silence, since I was, um, awful in the fashion show. Miri, obviously realizing her faux pas, mutters, "I'd better get back to my table. I promised my counselor I'd only be gone for a minute."

"Me too," Raf says.

"Hey, Raf, how come you weren't on the bus today?" Omigod, I can't believe I just asked that! A cool person wouldn't have asked that. A cool person wouldn't even have noticed he wasn't on the bus.

"I drove up with Will. The counselors had last night off after pre-camp, so he came into the city to see Kat. Anyway, I'll see you later, Rache."

I love that he's calling me *Rache*! "Cool. Later."

Later. I'm going to see Raf later.

I'm not even going to obsess over what he meant by *later*. I'm going to be cool.

La, la, la. La.

But did he mean later like in five minutes, later tomorrow, or later as in he'll stop by to say good-bye on the last day of camp?

53

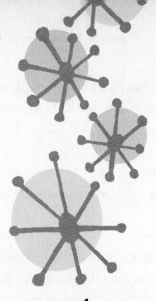

4
BREAK OUT THE MARSHMALLOWS

After dinner is free play. We return to the bunk to hang out and eat barbecue chips, brownies, and peanut M&M'S.

"Are there ever going to be activities?" I ask as my hand turns multicolored from the candied chocolate. I am lying on Alison's bed, my feet propped up against the ladder. "Or do we just get to hang out and eat all summer?"

"The first day is always a get-to-know-you day," Morgan explains. "And don't get too used to the food. They give us two days with the junk we brought from home and then they toss the rest."

"They don't toss it," Alison says. "They put it in a big garbage bag and take it to the counselors' lounge, where they snack on it all summer."

"That is so unfair," Poodles says with a sigh. "I can't wait until we're staff and can steal our kids' food. Alison, pass me another one of your mom's brownies."

"Sure. Want one, Carly?"

Carly is on the floor in sit-up position. "No, thanks." *Huff, huff.* "I'm on a diet."

"You can be on a diet once they've confiscated our food," Alison says. "Right now you should enjoy the brownies."

Carly ignores her.

"I'm not letting them take all my stuff," Morgan says. "No way. I'm finding a better hiding place this year."

If only I had stuff to hide. At least they share. I reach over and take another handful of Alison's M&M'S. "Can't you just stash the stuff in your laundry bag or something?"

Morgan snorts. "Please. That's the first place they look."

Alison nods. "Last year, Anderson—Rachel, have you met Anderson yet?"

"Nope."

"He's good friends with Raf. Anyway, he—"

"He uses way too much hair gel," Morgan says.

"*Anyway,* he hid his cell in an empty deodorant can. But his counselor heard it ringing, and it got confiscated."

"I agree with the cell phone rule," Poodles says. "They ruin the camp experience."

"Attenthion all camperth and counthlorth! Attenthion all camperth and counthlorth! It ith now the end of free play. Pleathe protheed to Upper Field for the annual firtht night'th campfire."

"Speaking of camp experiences," Alison says, "this is one of my faves."

Morgan smirks. "Just don't forget to bring a thweat-thirt."

"School is done.
It's time for summer fun.
Canoes and mosquitoes too.
Back to camp, where the friends are true."

Since I don't know any of the words, all I can do is bop my head and clap along with the 350 counselors and campers who are all singing (aka screaming) at the tops of their lungs around the massive campfire. Somehow our bunk has managed to score seats on the ground only a few rows back from the fire, so even though it's cool out, the flames are warming my face.

Anthony, the head counselor and an enormously tall and stunningly attractive olive-skinned man in his late twenties, is leading us along on his guitar.

"W-O-O-D!
A home away from home for me.
L-A-K-E!
There's nowhere we'd rather be!"

I spot Miri sitting diagonally from me with her bunk. Instead of pretending to sing along, she's writing in some book. Writing! At a campfire! How can she even see?

"Wood Lake counselors are the best.
If only our cabins weren't a mess!

Koalas, Monkeys, Lions, and C-I-Ts,
Oscar, can we have more cookies, please?

On days of rain or days of sun,
From the bridge to Lower Field's bunk one,
We're glad we're here,
But we wanna stay all year!

In the fall we go our separate ways,
Counting down the days,
With longing and heartache,
Until we're back at Camp Wood Lake!"

Alison and Poodles put their arms around my shoulders and sway, and I join in for the final chorus:

"W-O-O-D!
A home away from home for me.
L-A-K-E!
There's nowhere we'd rather be!"

57

Everyone erupts into cheers and applause. Anthony waves his guitar in the air and the hollering gets even louder. Even the Lion boys, including Raf, who are standing a few rows behind us, are cheering.

"Welcome back to camp, everyone!" Anthony says, his voice echoing through Upper Field. "It's going to be a killer summer."

More deafening cheers.

"Time to introduce you to this year's head staff. Welcome back Abby, the returning head of Koalas."

All the little kids cheer.

"Hi, everyone!" says the tiny twenty-something in an

unexpectedly booming voice. She stands next to Anthony near the fire. "Go, Koalas, go!"

The kids all wave their tiny hands in the air and cheer.

"How adorable?" Poodles says to me.

"So adorable," I say. Second session, when starter camp begins, Prissy will be sitting with them!

"Now say hello to Mitch," Anthony says, "head of Monkeys." The ten-, eleven-, and twelve-year-olds cheer. Mitch is Will and Raf's older brother, the only Kosravi brother I haven't dated. He looks like them too. All dark, brooding, and sexy.

"Monkeys are going to rock the house!" Mitch announces, punching the air.

"And we all know Janice," Anthony continues, "the head of the Lion unit."

All us Lions whoop and scream.

"Hello, everyone," she says, standing up and looking around anxiously, her lips still blue, the only unit head with her clipboard in hand.

"Give a cheer for Houser, the returning head of CITs."

The CITs all leap up, wave, and howl.

"And for Rose, the head of waterfront."

It's suddenly quiet around the fire. Seriously, I can hear the crickets. Apparently, no one likes Rose. Eventually, some of the lifeguards and the other head staff clap halfheartedly.

"She's awful," Alison whispers to me. "My brother had her job last year, and everyone *loved* him."

She's in her late teens; has clear porcelain skin, a tiny pink mouth, and glossy blond hair; and is wearing a whistle around her neck. She doesn't look *that* bad. But what do I know?

Rose glares at the campers.

"Um, thank you, Rose. Now please give a big round of applause for the lady you never want to see, Dr. Dina!"

A middle-aged woman with big brown hair joins the line, and there's more cheering.

"And finally, put your hands together for Oscar Han, our extraordinary camp chef!"

A grandfatherly Chinese man dressed in an all-white chef's outfit stands up and waves hello.

The crowd goes wild. "Oscar! Oscar! Oscar!"

"He makes the world's best lasagna," Alison tells me.

Bzzz, bzzz, bzzz. A mosquito attacks my ear, and I wave it away. Damn, I forgot to douse myself in bug repellant.

Anthony raises his hand to quiet us. "We are here to ensure that you have a terrific summer. For the last hundred and six years, this camp has been a summer home to campers of all ages."

Lots of cheers.

"But for us to keep you happy and safe, you have to follow the rules."

"Screw the rules!" one of the Lion boys hollers, and everyone laughs.

"Very funny, Blume," Anthony says. "I'm hoping you'll stay clear of the boats this year."

More laughter.

"Last year, Blume, Raf, Colton, and Anderson put all the canoes and kayaks in the pool," Alison explains. "My brother thought it was hysterical. But of course he had to zap them."

I have a feeling their zap isn't the same as my zap.

"What's zap?" I ask, turning to get a look at this Blume character. He's kind of scruffy in his ripped jeans, layered shirts, and backward hat. He's standing right next to Raf. I turn around quickly before Raf sees me and thinks I'm staring at him. Not cool.

"If you're zapped, you're grounded."

"So, as I was saying. Rules. Flagpole," Anthony continues. "Be on time. Rest hours are to be spent inside your bunks. If you are not at your scheduled activity, your counselor must know why. You're on your own for free play, but no woods, and no boys in girls' bunks or vice versa, *ever*."

"Boo!" scream the Lion boys.

Anthony flashes his blinding smile. "No pool or beach without staff supervision. And curfews are there for a reason and must be followed. Koalas, after evening activity, your counselors will take you to snack and then straight to bed."

"Boo!" shriek the Koalas.

"Monkeys, you have free time, known here at Wood Lake as lawn time, until quarter of ten. Lions, you have lawn time until ten-fifteen."

Excellent. Free time to make out with Raf!

"Why is it called lawn time?" I ask Alison.

"The Lions used to hang out on the lawn."

"What lawn?"

"They tore it up when they built the pool. But the name stuck."

"The final rule is absolutely no smoking anywhere on the camp grounds."

The crowd gets quiet.

"After last year, this rule has become even more important. As many of you know, one of our campers"—

"A Lion named Jordan Browne," Poodles whispers
to me.

—"snuck cigarettes into camp, tossed a lit one into his
cabin's garbage pail, and set it on fire. The entire porch was
burnt down and had to be rebuilt. Luckily, no one was hurt,
but this year we are implementing a no-tolerance cigarette
policy. Any camper caught with cigarettes will be sent home
immediately. No exceptions. Got it?"

We all nod.

"What happened to Jordan Browne?" I ask. Bzzz. Bzzz.
Bzzz. I slap the bug away again with the back of my hand.

"He wasn't asked back as a CIT," Alison whispers. "And
his parents had to pay for damages."

"If you have cigarettes here, you should give them to head
staff when we come to collect your food," Anthony says.

"So they can smoke them in the parking lot," Morgan
grumbles from the other side of Alison. "Annoying that
they can smoke and we can't."

"You shouldn't smoke as it is," Alison tells her, wrinkling
her nose. "It's disgusting."

"I don't!" Morgan cries. "But I should be allowed to if I
wanted to."

Anthony picks up his guitar again. "Now let's get back
to our singing! Does everyone know the words to 'One Tin
Soldier'?"

Everyone knows the words. Everyone except me.

I wonder if anyone would notice if I zapped myself up a
songbook so I could follow along.

61

"Listen, children, to a story that was written long ago . . ."

I look around the crowded campfire. Hmm, too many people watching. In light of my previous experience, namely zapping up my new wardrobe, I think I should probably practice a bit more in private before I attempt magic in front of the entire camp population.

Bzzz. Bzzz. Bzzz.

Oh, for goodness' sake. *Mosquito, be gone!*

I feel a rush of cold, then the little bugger disappears midbuzz in a puff of purple smoke.

"What was that?" Poodles asks, her head snapping back.

It worked! "I didn't see anything," I say quickly. I know I should feel bad for zapping him to Never Never Land, but I so don't.

"Weird," Poodles says, shaking her long hair.

"Wild," says Alison.

Wonderful, I think but don't say.

"Lights-out in ten minutes!" Deb announces from the front of the bunk. "If you need anything, I'll be in my room."

"Let's get washed," Alison says. She shimmies off my bed (where we were chatting) as I—a bit fearfully—climb down the ladder.

We grab our toothbrushes, toothpaste, hand towels, and facecloths from our shared blue shelf, stuff our socked feet into our flip-flops, hurry through the cubby room and into the bathroom, and then wait behind Cece, Trishelle, Poodles, and Carly for our turns at any of the four sinks.

"Yowza!" I shriek when I'm finally up. "Does the water ever warm up?"

"Nope."

I practically freeze my face off while washing it. I quickly brush my teeth, retreat into the cubby room to change into oversize flannel pj's (courtesy of the Gap), and climb into bed.

"So, Carly, what's the story with you and Blume this year?" Poodles asks.

Morgan starts making kissing noises.

"Shut up!" Carly orders.

"You going to dump him if he tries to french you again?" Morgan asks, laughing.

The girls crack up. It's weird being plopped down into a new group of friends with all this backstory.

"I dumped him because he always had a crust of spit around his mouth and the idea of kissing him made me want to vomit," Carly explains, sitting up in her bed. "But I'll have you know that I had a boyfriend this year, Michael Miller, who was a *very* good kisser."

"Ooh-la-la," says Poodles.

"Was there tongue in the kiss?" Morgan asks.

"You are so gross!" Carly shrieks.

Morgan laughs. "No tongue, then?"

"It's none of your business! Anyway, I'm not interested in Blume."

"You're going to break his heart," Alison says.

Poodles raises an eyebrow. "Why don't you go for him this summer, Alison?"

"Me?"

"Yeah, you. Do you like him?"

63

Morgan turns to Poodles. "Why are you always playing matchmaker?"

"Why not?"

"What about the spit?" Carly asks.

"He does *not* have spit issues," Poodles says. "I kissed him when we were Monkeys, remember? He's a sweetheart."

"Then why don't *you* hook up with him again?" Morgan asks.

Poodles smiles mysteriously. "I already have my eye on someone."

"Who?" they all ask.

"Harris," she says, lowering her voice.

Of course I have no idea who Harris is, but I don't want to be annoying and butt into their catch-up.

"You can't go out with Harris!" Alison tells her. "He's staff."

"So what?"

"It's against the rules," Alison says.

"Oh, whatever, he's only seventeen and people do it all the time. He was totally flirting with me at the campfire today."

"That is so not fair," Morgan complains. "If you're going to hook up with Harris, I'm going to hook up with Will."

"Slight difference there," Carly says. "Poodles has a chance with Harris, and you have no chance with Will."

"Alison, want me to talk to Blume for you?" Poodles asks.

Carly looks disturbed. "Wait a sec—"

"You just said you weren't interested!"

"I know, but still. This is all kind of sudden."

"I'm not interested in Blume," Alison says. "I like boys who are more studious."

Morgan snorts. "Nerdy, you mean?"

"Bookish."

Deb interrupts them by turning off the lights.

"Good night, everyone!" Carly says.

Poodles: "Good night, ladies."

Morgan: "Good night, horndogs."

Alison: "We're not horndogs."

Morgan: "I was talking about myself."

Everyone laughs.

"Teddy says good night," Carly pipes up in a squeaky voice.

Morgan groans. "You're not going to talk in that teddy bear voice every night again this summer?"

"Of course she is," Poodles says. "It's part of her charm. Did you see her new bear? He's wearing a tuxedo."

"He's not a bear," Carly says. "He's a penguin."

"You seriously need a life," Morgan tells her.

"Missed you guys," Carly says.

"Missed you, too," the other girls sing back, and then Alison adds, "And we're glad you're here, Rachel."

Moonlight streams through the blindless windows, casting a silver glow over the floorboards.

"I'm glad I'm here," I say.

The bunk is so quiet. Too quiet. I hope I'll be able to fall asleep without the sound of honking New York taxis.

Squeak! Scrape!

Every time any of the girls move, creaks echo through the room.

Ah, I think. That's better.

I turn onto my side, smiling to myself.

65

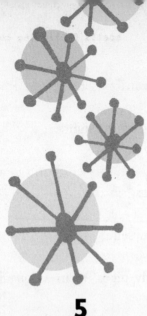

5
MORNING GLORY

"Time to get up! Let's go!"

Why is my mother screaming?

"Flagpole in thirty minutes!"

Oh, right. I'm at camp.

My eyes spring open, and I sit up and look around the cabin. The sun is streaming through the windows, but my bunkmates are all still fast asleep.

Itch. Ouch. My knee is on fire. A mosquito bite. Another one on my ankle. And another . . . on my nose. The nerve of that mosquito! Now I really don't feel guilty about banishing him to Never Never Land. I am so getting West Nile virus.

"Time to get up," Janice says, stomping through the bunk like she's wearing tap shoes. "Flagpole's in thirty minutes."

Yikes, it's freezing in here. My nose has morphed into an

ice cube. An itchy ice cube. I'm about to climb down the ladder, but nobody else is budging. Well, if they're not moving . . . I lie back down, pull my flimsy blanket over my face, and go back to sleep.

About twenty minutes later, I hear squeaks and peeps and remove my blanket to see Carly on the floor doing her stomach crunches. Morgan is on her feet and yawning.

It's so cold in here I can practically see my breath. I hope the Gap makes ski jackets.

Alison groans in the bed below me. "It's not morning already, is it?"

"It is," says Morgan.

"What time is it?" Alison whimpers.

"Ten past eight."

My bunk bed creaks as Alison pushes herself out. She grabs her glasses from our shared blue wooden shelf, pops a piece of gum into her mouth, throws her baseball hat over her messy brown hair, slips her socked feet into her Tevas, and says, "Ready."

Is she kidding me? "You're going in your pajamas?"

"Of course. It's breakfast."

"You're not even wearing a bra!"

She shrugs. "I'm pretty flat."

There is no way, nohow I'm wearing these oversize flannel pajamas to breakfast. They are so not for public viewing. "I think I'd rather put on clothes."

"Then you'd better hurry," Carly says, peeling herself off the floor. "We were supposed to leave, like, two minutes ago."

"Bunk fourteen better be on the porch in five seconds!" orders Deb.

67

I fly down my ladder and sprint to the cubby room, where I frantically search for a new pair of women's underwear. Nope. (Mental note: ask Miri for reversal spell!) I put on yesterday's jeans and a sweatshirt that looks like it might fit but doesn't. No time to change. I need to find my shoes. Where did I put them? After finding them in a heap under Alison's bed, I run to the bathroom to pee. I'm in midflush when Deb screams, "Move it, girls!"

I slam open the door and hurry to wash my hands. And that's when I spot my hair in the mirror. Omigod. It's a disaster. Where is my brush? I need to find my brush! Did I bring a brush?

Poodles struts out of the end stall as I'm staring at myself in despair. She's wearing silky pink pj bottoms and a tight white hoodie. Her long blond hair is pulled back into a high ponytail. No fair. Why does she look dining-room presentable even in pj's while I look like a lumberjack whose head got caught in a thunderstorm?

I need a hair spell, pronto. I close my eyes and wish.

Hair, I'm running late.

I really need you to get straight!

Cold air! Zap!

I open my eyes. The results stare back at me from the mirror.

Well, it worked. It's straight. It's standing straight up like porcupine quills, or like I stuck my finger in an electrical socket, but it *is* straight.

Now what?

I rummage through the stuff on my shelf for an elastic,

return to the bathroom mirror, and tie my hair into a high ponytail.

Not terrible. Kind of cheerleadery.

"Weinstein, on the porch!" Deb commands, coming to get me. I notice with a smidgen of anxiety that she's still in her pj's. Will I be the only one *not* wearing pj's?

The flagpole is beyond the mess hall, on Lower Field. Since this is my first time on Lower Field, I can't help feeling awed as I make my way down the road with the rest of my bunk. This camp is humongous! We pass a small park and then the infirmary, a place I hope never to visit. I mean, can you imagine getting sick at camp? Whenever I get sick, my face gets all puffy and my breath reeks like week-old un-cooked chicken.

After the infirmary, the road opens up into Lower Field, which is basically a flagpole, a baseball diamond with bleachers, and a basketball court, also with bleachers. Surrounding the field is a circle of green cabins that look like the tiny green houses on a Monopoly board. Kids are now streaming out of these bunks to line up at the flagpole. "Let's go, let's go!" counselors are shouting. We all line up by bunk, and I scan the circle for Raf.

It's not until I spot him (in his flannel pajama bottoms and a sweatshirt!) talking to one of the other guys that I re-alize I didn't brush my teeth.

Omigod.

How could I have forgotten that? I have never left my apartment without brushing my teeth. This is not good. Not good at all. I have horrendous morning breath. It's worse

69

than my sick breath. Honestly, when I first wake up, my mouth should be declared a nuclear wasteland.

I will not utter a single word until I return to my bunk.

Anthony begins tugging on a rope, pulling up the flag. "Can the Koala unit please lead us in the national anthem?"

The counselors of the youngest unit cue their campers to begin singing. "One. Two. Three! *Oh, say can you see . . .*"

Obviously, I cannot sing. Instead, I cower behind the other girls, keeping my lips zipped throughout the entire "Star-Spangled Banner," realizing that almost the entire camp (including Miri) is wearing pajamas, or at least pajama bottoms.

As the end of the song approaches, the campers start getting fidgety and moving toward the mess hall, even though their counselors are attempting to hold them back.

"Walk, don't run!" Anthony hollers as the younger kids ignore him and take off toward the mess hall.

On the walk to breakfast, I do my best to mime instead of talk. "How did you sleep?" Shrug. (I don't know the hand signal for lumpy mattress.) "Did you lose weight? Your clothes seem kind of big on you." Nod, nod. (Why not?) "How do you like camp so far?" Big smile. (Big closed-lipped smile.)

I hide when I spot Raf. I cannot let him see me this morning. With my porcupine hair and killer breath, forget it. I follow Alison up the stairs and then have a brainstorm. Hello? Why do I keep forgetting I'm a witch? I can just zap up something that will help. Once inside the mess hall, I sit down at the end of our table, shut my eyes, and wish.

My morning breath is quite obscene.

Please help me make it clean!

My body turns cold, so it must be working. I open my eyes, cover my mouth with my hand, exhale, then breathe in with my nose. Ew. Guess not.

And then I notice the basket of cutlery in the center of our table. Or what used to be a basket of cutlery. It is now a basket of multicolored toothbrushes.

Whoops.

I have to fix that before anyone notices. How do I fix that so no one notices?

Since my bunkmates are still shuffling into their seats, no one has spotted my most recent magic snafu just yet. I nonchalantly yank the basket toward me and dump it onto the floor. I hold my breath (both because I'm praying no one saw and because I'm afraid of scaring them all with its smell).

"Deb, they forgot to bring us cutlery," Carly complains.

"I'll get some when I get the food," Deb says.

Phewf. Problem solved. And luckily, no one seems to have noticed the random toothbrushes on the floor. I exhale with relief.

Ew to the power of two. Not totally solved.

I miraculously manage to avoid talking all through breakfast and all the way back to the bunk for cleanup. The first thing I'm cleaning is my mouth. I head straight for the sink. When I return to our side of the cabin, I discover that my bunk-mates are back in bed. "I thought it was cleanup," I say.

"That's code for extended sleep," Alison explains from beneath her duvet.

Fine by me. I kick off my sneakers, climb up my ladder, disappear under my covers, and fall right asleep. It must be the cold air that's making me so tired.

Deb bangs on the wall. "Girls, you've got to get up."

No one moves or responds.

"I'm serious! You know Janice is going to bust my butt if this place is a mess. I made you a work wheel"—

Alison and Morgan both groan. Slightly curious about what's causing all this groaning, I peek through my covers. Deb is sitting on Poodles' bed, holding up some sort of red and yellow wheel-thingy.

—"that tells you what your chores are. I have sweep, dustpan, bathroom, porch, and free. 'Kay? And Penelope made the same one for fifteen except it has cubbies instead of porch, and two frees."

Our work wheel looks like pizza pie with five slices. Our names have been written in block letters around the wheel. "Today, Poodles, you have sweep; Rachel has dustpan; Alison, bathroom; Morgan's on porch; and, Carly, you're free."

Carly cheers. "More sit-ups for me!"

No fair! Each of us gets excused from chores one out of every five days, but in fifteen, two of them are excused every six days, which means the girls in fifteen end up being free 33.3 percent of the time while we're only free 20 percent of the time! Humph. But I don't say anything. I wouldn't want the others to think I'm some kind of math geek.

"We'll get up in five minutes," Poodles says. "Hey, Debs,

why don't you go check the schedule to see what activities
we have today? Tell Janice that we want to have sailing."

"Definitely," Morgan says. "Harris is hot."

Poodles nods. "Since he's a leader for canoe trips, I'd like
to put in a request for an overnight."

"One day at a time," Deb says, heading toward the door.
"I'll go see what I can do, but you have to get out of bed."

Poodles plants her feet firmly on the floor. "No worries,
I'm up." As soon as Deb leaves the bunk, Poodles giggles and
gets back under her frilly covers.

We all go back to sleep for another ten minutes, then we
hear, "Guys! You promised you'd clean up! We have our
swim tests in ten minutes!"

Swim test? So soon after breakfast? Is that legal?
Anyway, people should be prohibited from using the
word *test* during the summer months. I wonder if I can wish
that up?

"Boooo!" says Poodles. "I told you I wanted sailing."

"Unfortunately, Janice makes the schedule, not you,
Poodles. If you want sailing so badly, choose it as one of your
electives."

"When do those start?" Alison asks.

"In the next few days. Today: swimming tests, then
drama, pottery, lunch washup, lunch, rest hour, soccer, tennis, snack, and then general swim, or 'GS.' So throw on your
bathing suit and sunscreen and grab a towel."

Poodles shakes her long blond hair. "I can't take my
swim test today anyway. I have my period."

Why didn't I think of that?

"Me too," says Carly.

73

"Me three?" I try.

Deb laughs. "You are such little liars," she says, standing up and stretching her arms above her.

"I swear, I do!" insists Poodles.

"What, you've never heard of tampons?" Deb asks.

Poodles pulls her covers tightly around her. "But I have cramps."

"Exercise is good for cramps," Deb says.

Poodles exaggerates an eyebrow raise. "I assume you'll be joining us in the lake?"

"Not on your life," Deb says, laughing.

"Way to lead by example," Poodles grumbles.

"Wait till you guys see my new bikini," Morgan says, slipping on her flip-flops. "I look like a Victoria's Secret model."

Carly snorts. "I think you have to be taller to be a Victoria's Secret model."

Morgan wags her finger. "Watch it, or your penguin teddy bear is going to accidentally fall into the lake."

"Let's clean up now, so we don't have to later," Alison says, getting out of bed.

"Attenthion all camperth and counthlorth! Attenthion all camperth and counthlorth! It ith now the end of cleanup. Pleathe protheed to firtht morning activity!"

Deb: "Move it, girls, move it!"

Morgan laughs. "Saved by the announthment."

Unfortunately, since I forgot to ask Miri to stop by my bunk and reverse my clothes, I don't know if I have a bathing suit. And I'm quite sure the camp frowns on skinny-dipping.

74

I search through my cubby. Here's one! A plain navy suit that looks about my size.

Perfect. Now all I have to do is change into it—which means I have to get *totally* naked in front of everyone. Hello, embarrassing.

My heart starts racing and I try to calm it.

I notice that Carly keeps her shirt on while she changes, and kind of sneaks her bra out. Interesting technique. I pull my suit on and try to do the same, but I somehow end up strangling myself, with my bra tangled around my neck, and then I feel hot and cold and hot and cold and—

Poof.

Ouch! Omigod! I look down at my bare stomach. Then I turn around and get a glimpse of my mostly exposed backside.

My one-piece bathing suit just morphed into a thong bikini.

Why did I do that? And now what am I going to do? I can't have my butt on show for the entire camp!

I grab a towel off the top of my cubby and cover my butt.

Breathe in, breathe out. I need to calm down, or who knows what will happen next?

What if the Lion boys are taking their swim tests too?

Poof!

Holy crap. My thong bikini just lost all its color. In fact, it's completely see-through.

No, no, no! I wrap the towel around me, shower-style. Did anyone see? I peek at the girls still changing, but they don't seem to have noticed.

75

I need to think of a swimsuit spell. . . .

"I'm counting to ten and whoever is not on the porch is stacking lunch!" screams Deb. "Ten. Nine. Eight—"

Ready, Alison heads for the front of the bunk.

"Seven. Six—"

I can't be creative under all this pressure!

"Five. Four. Three—"

I pull the checkered boxer shorts and a new T-shirt from my cubby and throw them over my practically invisible suit. I'll just have to swim in clothes.

"Two—"

With my towel in hand, I bolt for the door. Here goes nothing. At least I've covered up my see-through bathing suit. If I hadn't I'd have to say here goes, and shows, every-thing.

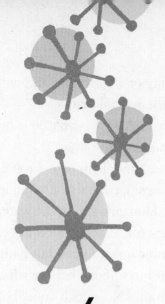

6
WHY I HATE DOLPHINS

Help! I'm drowning!

Okay, fine, I'm not really drowning—not yet, anyway—but I'm quite close. My arms and legs and even Bobby are numb with cold, and if I have to stay in the water for one more second, they might all fall off.

I touch the dock, then push off again for my eighth lap.

Campers are allowed to swim only in a designated area, which is marked by three docks that make a square with the beach. The swimming area is divided into three sections, from shallowest to deepest: turtle (up to my knees), dolphin (up to my chest), and whale (way over my head). This place is obsessed with naming things after animals. Anyway. I'm currently in whale, trying not to drown, taking my swim test.

I'm expected to swim twenty laps and tread water for ten minutes to get my whale bracelet. Those who don't get one won't be allowed to go windsurfing or waterskiing and will be able to go up only to dolphin for general swim.

But of course I'm going to get it. And if I can't do it on my own, I'll just whip up a swimming spell.

Almost there, almost there . . . Nine, I think as I touch the other dock and then push off again, careful not to bump into any of the other twenty or so Lion girls still in the water taking their tests. Not an easy feat for someone who never officially learned to swim. I do know how to float, but lying on my back doesn't seem to get me anywhere. I believe what I'm doing is called the doggie paddle. Not much style, but hey, so far it's working.

Eleven more. Groan. Cough. Swallow? I just swallowed a mouthful of water. I hope no one has peed in it. Why did I have to think of that? Now I have to go.

Ten!

This time I hold on to the dock a little longer than necessary. I think my wet shorts and T-shirt are weighing me down.

Eeep! Eeep! Eeep! Rose, the head of waterfront, is blowing repeatedly into her whistle and glaring at me from her perch on the dock beside the other swim staff (including two cute boy counselors, which no one but me seems to find *mucho* embarrassing). She spits the whistle out of her mouth and lets it dangle around her neck. "Holding! You have to do that last lap over again. Let go immediately." She is as evil as Alison said she was. She even looks like the devil in her one-piece red suit and matching red sun visor.

"Are you chewing gum?" she shrieked at Poodles when we first went down to the beach and sat in our bunk lines.

Poodles rolled her eyes. "No?"

"Don't lie to me. There is absolutely no food, no gum, no anything down on the beach. Do we understand each other?"

Poodles swallowed her gum.

I don't know why Rose acts like she's forty when she's only, like, twenty, tops. Anyway, I cannot believe she just gave me an extra lap. I think I'll switch over to my back. Maybe if I kick a little, I'll make some progress. Hey, it's working! I'm moving! I might be a little slow, but who cares? I get to look at the sky, which is like a big blue painting with a few clouds that look like marshmallows.

I wonder what's for lunch. I'm kind of hungry. And thirsty. I could use a glass of water.

Why am I thinking about water? (Um, maybe because I'm surrounded by it?) It's making me have to pee even more. I really have to go. Is it gross if I just let out a small drop? It's not like anyone would see—

Smack!

I would say ow, but I just swallowed another gallon of water. And the sky is spinning, since the smack was me knocking my head against someone else's head, bumper car–style, and the crash has sent me flying in another direction.

"Are you crazy?" asks the girl I smacked. "You have to stay in your lane. You were going diagonally."

Maybe swimming on my back and admiring the sky

79

wasn't my best idea. I struggle to tread water and catch my breath. I turn to the girl, recognizing her immediately. She's that rude black-haired girl from fifteen who practically knocked me over yesterday outside the cabin. "I'm so sorry," I say. "Are you okay?" I at least have manners. I at least apologize when I nearly take someone out.

She narrows her almond-colored eyes into slits, then shakes her head while continuing to glare at me. "Hardly."

"I'm just learning how to swim," I say by way of an explanation.

"Save your excuses for the fish," she snaps, then kicks off in the other direction. "The entire lake doesn't belong to you."

Well, excuse me. Annoyance bubbles inside me, and I take a deep breath to steady myself. Must not lose temper . . . must not lose temper . . . As rude as Miss Attitude was, I wouldn't want to accidentally turn her into a minnow.

With my luck, I'd probably turn her into a whale and then she'd swallow me.

Anyway, I shouldn't be wasting my magic on something as insignificant as her. I should be trying to come up with some sort of swimming spell. Something, I think as I swallow another mouthful of lake while still in my treading position, that will keep me above the water. How about:

"It's time to float,
Just like a boat!"

Burst of cold, and . . . my legs are expanding.

More specifically, my knees are blowing up like they're balloons being pumped with helium. My legs look like two snakes that have swallowed television sets. Now my knees are rising out of the water! Sit, legs, sit!

My rising knees are pushing me on my stomach and forcing my head below water. If this spell makes me drown, I'm going to be really pissed off.

"Stop!" I gurgle at my knees. "Get back down!"

Carly, who's now swimming beside me, looks over with concern. "Are you okay? You look like you're having trouble."

I turn onto my back in an attempt to keep from drowning. "Fine, thanks." I need my sister. "Miri!" I gasp, arms flailing. "Come here!" She's on the beach, reading. Miri and her bunkmates were the first ones to take the test, and Miri, a super swimmer (she used my dad's pool for something other than cooling off), was the first out of the water.

"Can you focus, please?" Rose snaps from the dock.

"Miri!" I try again. My sister finally spots me, drops her book, and hurries into the water. "What?" she asks, swimming up beside me.

"Please tell me you brought the spell-reversal charm to camp."

She nods.

"Thank God. Okay. Go get it. I'm having a prob—"

Before I can finish the sentence, my personal floatation devices flip me headfirst upside down and underwater, into a quasi headstand.

Cough! Sputter!

Miri yanks my head out of the water. "Rachel, what did you do?" she asks in amazement.

"Tiny"—cough—"mistake."

81

Eeep! Eeep! Eeep! "Did I give you permission to enter the water?" Rose yells at Miri. "Did I?"

Miri drags me to the side and secures my feet under the dock so that they won't fly up. "I'll go get the reversal crystal from my bunk. And watch how cool this is—I discovered a new transport spell that will work in the lake!" With a dive under the water, she vanishes.

I dip my head under the surface to watch, but it's too murky to see anything.

Eeep! Rose is anxiously searching the waterfront. "Where did she go?"

"Um . . . who?"

Rose waves her hands over her head. "The girl you were talking to!"

"What girl?"

Eeep! Eeep! Eeep! Eeep! Rose's whistle sounds like an overeager teakettle. "Campers out of the water!" she screams. "Search and rescue! Human chain, human chain!"

You've got to be kidding.

All the remaining girls, except me of course, because I'm too afraid to move, rush to the shore. Rose whips off her sun visor and dives off the dock, into the lake. Meanwhile, the swim staff all grab hands at the front of the beach and begin combing through the water.

Miri suddenly bobs up beside me with a splash. "Got it," she says, holding the spell-reversal necklace over her head. She looks around at the chaos. "What's going on?"

"Search and rescue," I say.

"For who?"

"You." I grab Miri's hand and wave it in the air. "She's right here!" I yell. "Stop the search!"

A flabbergasted Rose front-crawls over to us. "Where were you?"

"Around?" Miri says. She swims backward, circling me, as the spell reversal requires.

"But I . . . I'm going to be watching you two," Rose spits. "Search and rescue canceled!" she screams to the rest of the staff, climbing up the ladder, dripping with water.

As Miri finishes the reversal, my knees shrink to their nonengorged size. Ah. "Thanks."

"No problem." She starts swimming toward the shore.

"Wait, Mir, can I borrow the crystal?"

"Why?"

"Wardrobe malfunction," I say sheepishly.

She floats on her back. "I think you should stop using your Glinda until you can control it better."

83

"My Glinda is just fine, thank you very much." The nerve of her. As if my magic isn't on a par with hers. Honestly, my magic isn't that bad. A little rough around the edges, maybe. If you fall off your bike, you don't just sell it on eBay, do you? No, you get back on and practice. I doggie-paddle over to her, grab the crystal necklace from her hand, and place it around my neck. "If you'll excuse me," I say huffily, "I have some laps to swim."

Too bad the spell reversals didn't work on my outfit—my wet boxers and T-shirt are not exactly giving me extra speed.

I am unable to finish my laps.

It is beyond embarrassing.

I try one more swimming spell, but it somehow manages to make my legs and arms weigh six thousand pounds, so I can barely move and I end up sinking to the lake's sandy bottom, where I'm forced to reverse my spell.

Since I am now way too exhausted to complete ten laps, I get my dolphin, which means that, unlike all the other Lion girls, I get a chain bracelet with a blue bead. They also get a chain bracelet, but their beads are yellow.

"Could have been worse," Alison says, back on the beach. "You could have gotten your turtle."

"Not funny," I say, fingering my bracelet of shame.

"I'm just teasing. Honestly, it doesn't matter. We still like you."

The five of us are sprawled on our towels, soaking up the sun. The five of us and Miri, that is. As soon as I dragged myself out of the water, she joined us on the beach. Actually, only three of my bunkmates are sprawling. Carly is doing her stomach crunches. She's the only girl in the bunk (besides me) who went swimming in a pair of shorts, then covered herself with her shirt as soon as she got out of the lake.

"Guys, check out the pair of tits on the new girl!" Morgan says.

There's that word again. I can't stand it! It's like finger-nails against a—

"Can you not use the word *tits*?" Poodles asks.

"Tits, tits, tits," Morgan chants.

"Unlike you, we don't stare at people's chests," Alison says.

"I'm not staring! But she was walking around the cabin topless. Mine are nearly as gorgeous, but you don't see me parading around like that, showing them off."

"Cece told me she *was* being super-braggy," Alison says. "Showing off, talking about all the places she's lived."

"Where did she live?" Poodles asks.

"Apparently, she goes to boarding school in Switzerland," Alison says.

"Trishelle told me that she told the whole bunk she shops in Milan, London, and Paris," Carly says.

"I don't believe it for a second," Morgan grumbles.

"Well, I believe it," says Carly, midcrunch. "Did you see that bathing suit?"

"It must have cost a fortune," Poodles says. "Morgan, you'd better get out of the sun. You're burning already."

Morgan brushes off the warning. "I need to get some color."

"You always burn on the second day," Alison tells her. She turns to me and adds, "She always burns on the second day. She never listens."

"I don't think they're all that great," Carly says.

"What's not so great?" Alison asks.

"Her tits," Morgan answers for Carly.

Cringe.

"Which one is she?" I ask, searching the shaded area of the beach where the group from fifteen are clustered.

Alison props herself up on her elbows and points at Miss

85

Attitude, who pushed me yesterday and yelled at me in the water today. "The girl in the black bikini."

Miss Attitude is now animatedly talking to her bunkmates, her dark wet hair hanging down to her waist.

"Didn't you meet her?" Poodles asks. "Her name is Liana."

"I wonder how they decided to put me in your bunk and Liana in theirs," I say. "You'd think they would have put the two new girls together."

"There are two new girls in fifteen, actually," Alison says. She points to a pale blond girl sitting by herself at the edge of the circle. "Her name is Molly."

"Where's she from?" Poodles asks.

"Greenwich, maybe?" Alison says.

I study the girls from bunk fifteen. I recognize the awful Liana; the other new girl, Molly; Cece, who's friends with Alison; and Trishelle and Kristin from the bus. "Who's the girl with the glasses?" I ask, motioning to the only one I haven't met.

"Natalie," Alison says. "You'd like her; she's supersmart."

Morgan adjusts her bikini. "What a know-it-all. I'm glad I don't have to share a bunk with her anymore."

"You're not still mad at her for going to the camp social with Brandon Young last year, are you?" Poodles asks.

"Noooo." She considers her answer. "Fine, maybe a little. But I don't care about him anymore. He's such a child. Did you see him sticking Cheerios up his nose at breakfast? Puh-lease. I'm onto bigger and better things. Like Will."

"Didn't you hear?" Alison says. "Rachel says he has a girlfriend."

"Whatever. She's not here, is she?"

"Attenthion all camperth and counthlorth," says the voice in the sky. "Attenthion all camperth and counthlorth. Pleathe protheed to thecond morning activity."

"Let's go, girls," Deb says, clapping. "We need to change superfast and then motor over to the rec hall for drama."

I follow the lead of my bunkmates and wrap my towel tightly around me. That is, all my bunkmates except Morgan, who ties her towel around her waist.

"You okay?" I ask Miri as we head up the beach. She was pretty quiet on the sand. I was happy to have her with me, but I kind of wish she felt comfortable hanging out with her own bunk.

"Uh-huh."

We pause at the top of the beach, under the sign listing the rules, which include things like no gum, no horseplay, and always swim with a buddy.

Miri's going to have to find herself a buddy.

"Where's your bunk?" I ask.

"That way," she says, pointing away from where I'm going. "Bunk two is in Lower Field, but it's behind all the other bunks, near the Lower Field showers." She makes a face. "I have to hike all the way up a hill to get to my bunk."

"So do I."

"My hill is bigger than yours, trust me. Come see?" she asks hopefully.

"This second?"

"Yeah."

My bunkmates are already disappearing down the road. "Mir, I have to get ready for drama. Maybe later. Did you get a bottom bunk?"

She sighs. "No. Top. You?"

"Me too."

"But you hate top bunks!"

I shrug. "I'm sure it'll be fine. I gotta go. See you at lunch!" I say. I turn around to hurry after the girls. When I reach them, I can't help feeling good. I'm at camp. *At camp!* Who would have thought? I like camp! It's sunny! The girls are nice. If only I can seal the deal with Raf . . .

Omigod, there's Raf, right in front of me!

No, not Raf, it's Will. The two of them have the same sexy dark hair, dark eyes, and lean athletic body. Will is taller than Raf, though, and his hair is shorter. Raf has a wider smile. And a curl to his hair that Will doesn't have. Oh, no, what am I going to say to Will? We haven't spoken since his prom. I've been in minor denial about having to run into him someday, and here he is, coming down the road, laughing, looking as cute as ever. He's wearing shorts, a T-shirt, and sneakers without socks, none of which I've ever seen him in. His dark brown hair is messy, and his normally serious expression is relaxed and all smiley. Little boys are following him in a line like he's the Pied Piper.

Okay, I swear I don't have any romantic feelings left for Will, but how adorable is he?

About a second after I spot him, he spots me and turns a deep shade of watermelon. The inside of a watermelon, not the outside, since he's flushed, not nauseous.

I hope. I mean, no girl wants the sight of her to make a guy sick.

"Hi, ladies," he says to my entire bunk while looking at me.

Okay, the key to having an awkwardless summer is making sure Will knows that I am cool with him.

"Will, hi!" crows Morgan, heaving out her chest as far as she can without toppling over.

"Hey, Will," say the other girls.

"Hi, Will!" I sing extra-sweetly, and stop directly in his path. "How's Kat?"

He smiles. Of course he smiles. He's crazy about her. "She's great," he says with a wistful expression on his face. Aw. How sweet! He misses her.

"Is this your girlfriend?" one of the little boys sings.

"No," Will says a little too loudly, then gives me a wide smile. "But you might want to ask my brother if she's his."

Did he just say what I think he said? Really? Does that mean Raf talked about me? It must. And Will is cool with it! Wahoo! I try to remain calm.

"So, Will," says Morgan, practically wiggling her boobs right in his face, "did you have a good year?"

"Not bad. How was yours?"

"Oh, I really grew," she says, wiggling some more. "You know. Emotionally."

"All right, let's go," I say to Morgan.

"Congrats on graduating," she continues, fully ignoring me. "Where are you going next year? Somewhere near me?"

"Columbia."

89

"On scholarship," I add, sounding like a proud sibling—which is what I'll be when Raf and I get married.

One of Will's campers paws his hand. "Daddy, what do we have now?"

Will picks up the kid and puts him on his shoulders. "Mitchell, remember, I'm your counselor, not your dad. And we have baseball."

Another one of his campers tugs his pants. "And what's for lunch?"

"Grilled cheese," he says.

Really? "Yum," I say. "That's my favorite."

"They always serve comfort food for the first few days," Will says. "Comfort food for the homesick."

Homesick? What's that?

We change into fresh outfits (I use the spell reversal on my cubby and have my regular clothes back, finally), hang our wet clothes and towels over the porch railing to dry in the sun, and then head to drama (where we play improv games), then pottery (where we make bowls), then lunch washup (where we wash), then lunch (where we eat).

Rest hour is after lunch. Poodles and Carly are playing gin rummy on Poodles' bed; Alison is immersed in a cross-word puzzle; and I'm writing a letter to Tammy, telling her how much fun camp is.

We hear Liana yapping a mile a minute on the other side of our wall. She doesn't quite get the meaning of *rest* hour.

"All the girls at Miss Rally's Hall for Girls—that's the *exclusive* boarding school I go to in Switzerland—are wearing this perfume. It's the hot new scent."

"I got that on Paddington," she's saying now. "It's the most fashionable street in Sydney. . . ."

Poodles picks up a card, frowns, and slams down the queen of spades.

"Where did I get that old thing? I think it was last summer in Croatia. It's the new Paris. So not touristy. . . ."

Croatia? The new Paris? I've never even been to the old Paris. I try to focus on my letter, but Liana's nasal voice won't let me.

"Trust me," coos Liana, "you haven't lived until you've fallen in love with an Italian."

"Get her away from me," whispers Cece, coming into our bunk and sitting on Alison's bed. "We all want to kill her."

"She is awful," Carly says.

"Let's just ignore her," I say. I put down my pen and look at the girls. "I've always wanted to learn how to play gin."

Poodles waves her hand at me. "Come down; I'll teach you."

"I should probably teach her," says Carly, "if she ever wants to win."

Poodles rolls her eyes. "Ha-ha."

"Attenthion all camperth and counthlorth! Attenthion all camperth and counthlorth! It ith now the end of reth hour. Pleathe protheed to your firtht afternoon activity."

Already?

"No worries," Poodles says. "We'll teach you at free play."

"Soccer time," Deb hollers from the hallway. "Against fifteen, Upper Field. Let's go!"

We change into appropriate outfits in the cubby room.

I can't help noticing that now that my cubby is no longer magically organized, everyone else's cubbies appear to be in better shape than mine.

But most of the other girls have been coming to camp for years and have therefore had lots of living-out-of-a-cubby experience. Yes, that explains it. No, I am not a natural-born slob.

One cubby looks particularly neat. Crazy neat. Neater than mine did with the spell. This one is a level above the Gap. It's Banana Republic. Actually, it's more like an expensive boutique. It's so sparse.

Oh, no.

I am annoyed to discover that this cubby belongs to Liana. She reaches into it and pulls out a fancy-looking polo shirt without even causing a ripple. What is she, a Jenga champion?

She catches me staring. And smirks.

Ignore, ignore, ignore.

Or maybe mess it up when she's not looking.

Unfortunately, I suck at soccer. Luckily, I'm not the only one. Morgan and Poodles can't even kick the ball. Carly and

Alison are pretty good, so Carly plays goalie while Alison scores all the goals, and the rest of us run after the ball while laughing hysterically.

The girls from fifteen are equally clueless, and they're laughing even more loudly than we are. Since we're only five and they're six, Liana has volunteered to sit out, so instead of playing, she watches from the sideline, taking the sun in her glamorous-looking polo shirt, velvet shorts, and big sunglasses. Occasionally, she passes the girls in her bunk a water bottle, telling them they look dehydrated.

I thought soccer was oh so European. You'd think she'd be trying to show off how continental she is.

We tie four to four and enjoy every second.

"Quick, let's run to the showers before they get too crowded," Alison tells us.

I seriously need to bathe. I don't think I've ever been this filthy. It didn't help that it started drizzling right after soccer. At least GS was canceled. I had been slightly nervous about my dolphin status.

So we all put on our bathrobes (except for Morgan, who wraps herself in a flimsy towel), pick up our shower pails (stuffed with shampoo, conditioner, facial soap, a comb, body soap, and a loofah—yes! I somehow knew to bring the right things!), and bravely head out onto the porch. At least it has stopped raining for now.

"Which showers should we go to?" Poodles asks.

We huddle together to decide.

"Lower Field," says Carly, wrapping her bathrobe tightly around her. "I hate the Upper Field showers."

Morgan shakes her head. "Too grimy. And too far. What if it starts raining again?"

"Yeah, our legs will be all dirty from the walk back," Poodles says. "Let's just go to Upper Field."

Morgan winks at me. "Hope you're not shy, Rachel."

Huh?

We begin the trek to Upper Field.

"This is where the kitchen staff sleeps," Alison says as we pass some blue cabins. "But they're all in the mess hall now, preparing for dinner. These are the boys' showers, and then around the bend are the girls'."

Blume is lounging on the steps. "What up?" he asks.

"Hey, Alison, it's your new boyfriend," Morgan whispers.

Alison turns bright red.

"If Blume's here maybe Raf is too," Poodles says. "Rachel, wanna sneak in?"

Morgan makes kissing noises.

"Shut up," I say, but smile at the same time.

"What's the story with you two?" Carly asks.

"Good question." Sigh. "What about you guys? Any romances I should know about?"

"I still think Alison should go out with Blume," Morgan says.

"Not interested," she responds as she pushes open the door to the shower room.

"Crap, someone's using them," Poodles says.

The waiting room for the showers is pretty bare. Gray walls, hooks, and lots and lots of steam.

"It's bunk fifteen," Alison says, putting her pail down on a bench. "I hear Cece."

"How many of them are in there?" Poodles asks, and then peeks into the steamy room. "Hi, girls. Almost done?"

"We just got here," Cece says, more snarkily than necessary. "We'll probably be a while."

"What's her problem?" Carly asks.

Alison shrugs, bewildered.

"You'll have to wait," someone else says in an extra-nasal voice.

Liana.

Poodles rolls her eyes. "It's too hot in here. Let's wait outside."

I don't really want any boys to see me in my bathrobe. But standing in the steamy room is clearly not an option, so the five of us pile back outside, pails in hand. Ah, that's better. Except now we're pretty much facing the Upper Field baseball diamond, where some of the Lion boys are congregating. Not playing but hanging out. While we're in our bathrobes. Our not-so-sexy grandmotherly bathrobes.

"This place is making me miss my nice, simple shower at home," I say.

"The pool showers are the best," Alison says wistfully. "Last year my brother let us use them all the time."

"Showers are the one bad part of camp," Poodles says. "But I swear, you get used to it."

"By the second month," Morgan grumbles.

"Do you miss home yet, Rachel?" Alison asks.

I take in a nice, deep breath of fresh air. "Not really."

95

Morgan leans against the railing. "Remember how homesick I was when we were Koalas? I used to cry all night."

"You weren't the only one," Alison says. "Anderson used to cry through every meal."

"Has anyone else wondered what's up with his hair? It's like he's just discovered gel. He uses a bottle a day." Morgan glances down at her watch. "What the heck is taking them so long? They've been in there forever."

"I think he's cute," Carly says.

"Who? Anderson?" Poodles asks.

"Yeah. Did you see how built he got over the year?" She waggles her eyebrows suggestively. "He's been doing his sit-ups. And his chin-ups."

"You going to go for him this summer?" Morgan asks.

96

"Maybe."

Morgan laughs. "Remember, no kissing."

"Oh, shut up. If you're going to say dumb things, I'm so going to yank your towel," Carly threatens.

"Go ahead," Morgan says. "Then maybe the guys will see what I've got going on."

"You're such a perv," Carly says.

"Yeah, and you're a prude," Morgan says. "Do you know who else is looking kind of cute this year? Colton."

"It's the accent," Poodles says. "Who doesn't find cowboys sexy?"

"I don't," Alison says.

"We know, we know, you like nerds," Morgan says, shaking her head.

"Maybe we should fix him up with Cece," Poodles says. "Speaking of Cece, what is taking them so long?" She opens the door and screams, "Can you guys get a move on?"

We hear laughing inside the shower.

"They are so annoying." Carly sighs. "They'd better not use up all the hot water."

Hot water, huh? Maybe I can hurry them along . . . by concentrating. Hard.

And then: "Ahhhhhhhhhhhhhh!"

And then: "It's freezing!"

And then: "What the hell?"

Wahoo! It worked! I did it! You see, Miri? My magic worked exactly the way I wanted it to. I am full of control. I am like control-top panty hose. I am a witch-superstar. Go, me. Ten seconds later, all six girls pour out of the shower, cursing. "There's no hot water left," Natalie says, her glasses still foggy.

"You guys are screwed," Molly says.

"Try getting here faster next time," Cece says, running her tongue over her braces.

Alison blinks in surprise.

"Better luck next time," Trishelle, the last one out, says. And I don't know how this is possible, but she already has eyeliner on. Maybe it's a tattoo?

"Now what are we going to do?" Morgan cries.

Hmm. I didn't really think that far ahead.

"Let's go in," Poodles says. "Come on, we've done it before."

The shower room is a small white space with six

showerheads but no dividers. So we're all going to shower together. Terrific. How do I do this without staring? Look at the floor. Look at the floor!

I know I said I was comfortable at camp . . . but not this comfortable.

Each of the four girls chooses a shower. I take the one in the corner and try to turn it on. And try again. And again.

"That one has been broken for years," Alison says.

I try another one. Nope.

"That one too," she says. "You can share with me. Oh God, it's cold. I can't believe how obnoxious the bunk fifteeners were! What is up with them? Plus I can't believe they used all the hot water."

Morgan flips her head over so that the water gets her hair but not her body. "How rude."

Alison runs into and out of the water in two and a half seconds. "So cold! Ah! Your turn, Rachel."

I step under the stream of water and scream, "It's freezing!" Come on, raw will, you can do it! Make it warm again! But no go. What is wrong with my magic? Why is it so unpredictable?

"Hey, Rachel, did you know that one of your tits is bigger than the other?" Morgan asks.

I think I want to die.

"Morgan!" Alison shrieks. "You're ruder than bunk fifteen!"

Morgan clamps her hand over her mouth. "I just noticed! I couldn't help it!"

"What are you staring at her boobs for?" Carly asks.

I step out of the cold water and cross my arms in front of

my chest. "You're right, my boobs are developing at weird speeds." Just like my powers. "It's embarrassing."

"At least you have one boob," Alison says. She puts her arms up in the air. "I don't have any!"

"My boobs are different sizes too," Carly says. "My left one's a B, and my right one's a C. But Michael never complained."

Morgan laughs. "Oh, you're such a big talker. You think we're really going to believe you're not a prude anymore?"

"I was never a prude!" Carly insists, rinsing the shampoo out of her hair. "Blume has spit crust!"

"Sure, sure. And you're really a sex goddess in disguise," Morgan says. "Look, I'm sorry for staring, Rachel. But I was trying to understand what Will saw in you that he doesn't see in me. Maybe he likes uneven boobs. Do you think I should stuff *one* of my cups?"

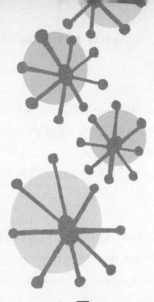

7
DANCING QUEEN

On my second camp morning, not only do I remember to brush my teeth, I wear my pajama bottoms to flagpole.

But my day gets worse soon after that.

First, at cleanup I have bathroom, which is majorly vile. Wearing plastic gloves, I rinse the toothpaste blobs and strands of hair down the sinks and dump the individual stall garbages into the main one on the porch. Then I have to re-stock the toilet paper and soap.

After that, Deb tells us we have dance for our first activity.

That's when I know the end is near.

I look like I'm being electrocuted when I dance. Instant anxiety sets in.

I follow my bunkmates to the rec hall with a heavy heart. After the dance specialist leads us in a warm-up, she puts on some R & B music and tells us to "dance" an activity or chore.

I have no idea what she means.

"I'll start," says Poodles. She snaps to the beat and then says, "The Sweep!" Suddenly, she's grooving to the music, miming the chore of sweeping, somehow making it look like a hot new dance move.

Everyone claps. I panic even more.

"Look at me, look at me!" Morgan sings, waving her hands from side to side while shaking her butt. "My new move is . . . the Window Washer."

"Go, Morgie!" Poodles hollers while the rest of the girls cheer in approval.

Wait a second. Her arms are stiff and she looks ridiculous. Could it be? Is it possible that Morgan has no rhythm? Yet they're all cheering her on anyway?

"My turn!" Carly lifts her knees in slow motion to the beat. "I call it the Climbing Man."

101

She can't dance either—yet there's more cheering and hollering.

Alison joins in, performing a series of kicks that would make the A-list fashion-show girls at my school cringe in horror. "The Soccer Player!"

Now even I'm cheering. Then, before I can chicken out, I say, "The Doggie Paddle!" and proceed to shake my butt and pretend I'm swimming. And they're still cheering! They are! I beam and throw myself into the moves wholeheart-edly.

I quickly deduce that out of the five of us, only Poodles can actually dance, while the rest of us look absolutely ridiculous. But as during yesterday's soccer game, we don't care. Instead, we make a game out of how bad we are.

And this is a game I can win!

"Rachel, you're hilarious," Alison howls as I try my hand at the Making the Bed and then the Brushing Your Teeth.

"Hey," Carly says over the music. "Speaking of tooth-brushing, does anyone know why there were fifty tooth-brushes under our table yesterday?"

La, la, la. I distract her with the Garbage Dumper.

I'm in such a good mood from dance that I don't even mind when Rose later puts me in the lowest swimming group, which is essentially remedial swimming. We learn how to flutter kick, which is basically holding on to the dock and kicking.

Gee, thanks.

Then we have newcomb ball against bunk fifteen. I had never heard of newcomb ball, but apparently it's a camp sport that's a lot like volleyball except easier, because you can catch the ball before lobbing it to the other side.

"Damn!" Poodles says as the ball slips through her fingers for the second time. Bunk fifteen keeps whipping the ball over the net.

We've been playing for only three minutes and we're already losing five to zero.

"What is up with you guys?" Alison asks the other side. "I've never seen you so competitive."

"There's nothing wrong with wanting to kick your butts," barks Kristin, her hands on her hips. She's somehow managed not to lose her pearl earrings. If they were mine, they would be at the bottom of the lake by now.

It's Natalie's serve and she hurls it straight at me.

"I got it! I got it! I got it!" I say as I hug the ball into my chest. Yes! I did it!

"Way to go, Rachel!" my team cheers.

Now all I have to do is throw it back over the net. The incredibly high-looking net.

It's time for a little magic.

It's time to fly!

Newcomb ball, reach for the sky!

And then I throw.

And the ball goes up. And up. Way up.

Over the trees, over the mountains, and then a distant splash.

"I think it landed in the lake," Trishelle says, rubbing her eye and smearing black eyeliner down her cheek.

"Nice going, Rachel," Cece says. "Now what?"

My face feels hot and my neck feels hot and now my arms . . .

Zap! Rush of cold!

"Careful!" Alison shouts as the newcomb ball net tips over and crashes down on the bunk fifteen girls, trapping them beneath the mesh.

Whoopsies.

Deb and Penelope declare the game over.

"We were raided!" Morgan shrieks.

We wake up the next morning to find our beds and bodies tangled in toilet paper. My pillowcase is covered in

103

shaving cream. Should I be concerned that I dreamed about eating ice cream?

"This is so gross," Poodles says, trying to comb the mess out of her hair. "How could anyone be so immature?"

Our bunk has been totally trashed. Our shelves have been emptied, and our stuff is lying on the floor, covered in toilet paper and sticky orange and pink string. It looks like Times Square on January 1.

"Do you think it was the boys?" Carly asks.

The boys? In our bunk? At night! How adorable!

"No, I bet it was *them*." Morgan juts her chin out at the wall separating us from bunk fifteen.

Less adorable.

"They wouldn't do this to us!" Alison exclaims. "They're our friends."

"They haven't been acting like our friends," Poodles grumbles.

Suddenly, we all realize how quiet the other side of the cabin is. And then we hear muffled laughter.

Oh yeah, it was them.

Of course they deny it. Naive Deb doesn't believe they would do that to us, and since we can't prove anything, we get stuck cleaning for most of the morning.

"We have to get them back," Morgan says, stuffing her foamy sheets into her laundry bag.

"We will," Poodles says. "But not tonight. We'll do it when they least expect it."

"This is so lame," Morgan says the next day as she opens the rec hall door for evening activity. The rec hall is an old wooden room with rafters on the ceiling and the names of campers graffitied all over the walls. "It's a sing-down, I know it."

I, on the other hand, do not think it's lame. I don't think it's lame because Raf is on the other side of the room. Evening activity is the best, because it's either the whole camp or the entire Lion unit.

"Rachel!" I look up to see Miri beckoning me to her.

In a minute, I mouth, then follow my bunk to a bench in the corner. As soon as I sit down, Janice, green pen in mouth (that can't be good), flicks the lights on and off. "Settle down, everyone," she says. "Sit with your bunks! It's time for a sing-down."

"Told you," Morgan mutters, taking a seat.

"Here's how it works. Every bunk gets a—"

"We know how it works!" interrupts Blume, looking extra-scruffy in a sweatshirt with its sleeves ripped off. His bunkmates laugh.

Janice starts pacing up and down the room. "Not everyone knows, Blume. Now be quiet, please. As I was saying, every bunk gets a pad of paper. I'm going to say a word or an expression or a theme, and together as a bunk, you write down as many songs that contain it as you can. Then each bunk will have a chance to sing one of the songs. Remember, if you repeat a song someone else has sung, you're automatically disqualified. Last bunk standing wins."

"What do we win?" Blume asks.

"Glory," says his counselor. "And for being a pain in the ass, you get to be secretary."

His bunk laughs again.

All of the Lion unit is here. I spot Miri sitting with the rest of bunk two, but she's slightly behind them. Aw, Mir. Why isn't she making friends? I'll have to give her a pep talk. She has to be friendly and outgoing, and she can't be afraid to put herself out there.

"All right, get ready," Janice says. "The songs have to have a color in them. Got it? You have two minutes, starting now."

No time to worry about Miri; must think of songs. I huddle with my bunkmates. Deb plays secretary.

" 'Brown Eyed Girl,' " Carly whispers.

Poodles: " 'Blue Suede Shoes.' "

Alison: " 'Yellow Submarine.' "

Me: " 'Follow the Yellow Brick Road?' "

Deb scribbles it down. Yes! I got one!

We throw out a ton of songs before Janice announces that our time is up and that bunk five will go first. The boys' counselors gather them and count, "One, two, three!"

"*Brown-eyed girl. You, my brown-eyed girl!*" they shriek in disastrous voices.

"Damn!" Deb crosses out our number-one song.

We're going clockwise, so next up is bunk fifteen. "Ready, girls?" Penelope asks.

"*It was an itsy bitsy, teenie weenie yellow polka-dot bikini,*" they sing. Kristin shakes her butt. Liana tosses her hair.

"Bunch of jerk-offs," Morgan mutters.

"Bunk two, you're up," Janice announces.

The girls from Miri's bunk lean in together. Well, all except Miri. *"Baby beluga in the deep blue sea!"* they sing.

"Bunk eleven!"

"Tie a yellow ribbon round the old oak tree!"

"Seventeen!"

That's Raf's bunk. The group counts to three and then sings, *"Red, red wine, you make me feel so fine."*

"Seven!" says Janice.

"Blue moon," the youngest Lion boys croon, *"you saw me standing alone. Without a dream in my heart. Blue moon!"* And that's when they all spin around, pull down their pants, and moon us.

"Ew!" we scream. All the girls, anyway. The boys just laugh.

Janice bites her pen like she's a rabbit with a carrot. "You're eliminated for lewdness!"

The boys are bent over with laughter. I doubt they care. Poor counselors. They're definitely going to have their hands full with this cheeky group. Pun intended.

"Fourteen, you're up!"

Poodles pretends she's a conductor. "One, two, three . . ."

"We all live in a yellow submarine," we sing, and then cheer. Wahoo! Fun!

We go around the circle again, and we have to cross out some of our songs. Then Miri's bunk sings "Brown Eyed Girl" again, which makes no sense. I mean, how hard is it

107

to put an X beside one of your entries once someone else sings it?

"You're out!" Janice shouts.

We go round and round and round, and bunks get eliminated, either for duplication or for not being able to come up with something new, until it's just us, fifteen, and Raf's bunk.

And then Raf's bunk sings "Yellow Submarine," which we already sang, and they're out.

Now it's between us and fifteen.

This is no longer a game. After the way they've been treating us, it's war.

"We're out of songs," Deb whispers. "Someone think of one, quick!"

Come on, magic! I need a remember-a-song spell! What can I do? I need to think of something!

And that's when I look up at Janice and see her green pen, which makes me think of the green song.

Me: "Kermit's song. You know? Green. How does it go?"

" 'It's Not Easy Being Green,' " Poodles says, high-fiving me.

"Brilliant!" Deb says, scribbling it down.

Liana whispers something into Natalie's ear, then motions to the rest of the bunk. Two seconds later, they belt out, *"It's not easy being green!"*

Aaah!

My whole bunk groans. "She was so eavesdropping," Morgan says. "I hate her."

She totally *was* eavesdropping! How dare she steal my green!

"Fourteen, you're up."

"Hold on!" Poodles says, and motions us in. "Anyone got anything?"

"Count with me, everyone," Janice instructs. "Ten! Nine!"

"Anyone have anything?" Alison begs. "Carly?"

"Seven! Six!" The whole unit is cheering now.

"Poodles? Morgan? Rachel?"

Liana is a thief. She sucks. I wonder how she'd feel if she were *really* green, as in poof, you're now Kermit's sister.

"Three! Two! One!" Janice makes a loud buzzer sound, and her pen explodes all over her mouth and chin, giving her a green beard. "Fifteen wins! Nice game, everyone. Off to snack. Be back at your bunk for curfew at ten-fifteen. No excuses!"

Thief, thief, thief.

"Hey," says someone behind me.

I look up to see Raf. Yay! "Hi."

"You going to snack?"

I'm going anywhere you want me to go, mister. I shrug oh so casually. "Maybe. You?"

"Sure. Come with me. Do you know my boys? Blume, Colton, and Anderson?"

Come with me, he says! Finally. I can't believe it's taken me over four days to get some quasi-alone time with him.

The scraggly guy, the cute Texan, and the guy who really *does* wear too much hair gel say hello.

109

The five of us skip down the stairs of the rec hall. It was light when evening activity started, but now it's pitch-black. I look up to see a sky layered with shining stars. Wow. This is amazing. I fill my lungs with night air. "It's so nice here," I say.

"It is, huh? Are you cold?"

I am a bit chilly. My arms are covered in goose bumps. "Maybe I should stop back at my bunk and get a sweater."

Raf pulls his black sweatshirt over his head. "Take mine."

Omigod. I am wearing Raf's sweatshirt. Raf's deliciously yummy-smelling sweatshirt. Does this mean he likes me? Or is he just being polite?

We talk all the way down the hill to the back of the dining hall and then meet up with some of the others. Raf, Colton, Anderson, Blume, Morgan, Carly, Alison, Poodles, and I get our cookies and then debate what to do next.

"Let's go hang out on our porch," Morgan says.

Poodles steers Carly toward Anderson. Carly turns pink but goes up to him anyway. Guess she does have her eye on him after all.

Raf and I follow the rest of the crowd back to our bunk. I can't believe how much walking we're doing. I must have walked like a hundred miles since I've been here. Lower Field, Upper Field, Lower Field, dining hall. It's better than a treadmill.

"So how'd you do on your exams?" Raf asks me.

"Not bad. You?"

"Good, I think. But math was a killer. Bet you didn't think so," he says, teasing.

Raf knows that math is my best subject. I grin. "It was okay."

"What did you get?"

"My final grade?"

"Yes, your final grade."

"Ninety-nine."

He laughs. "What happened to the last two percent?"

"Very funny," I say with a happy smile. I love when he teases me. I look up at the endless sky. "Hey, there's the Big Dipper!"

He nods. "And here you are," he says softly.

"Here I am."

"I'm glad."

"You are?"

"Very."

And that's when he lifts his arm and puts it around me. Omigod. Raf's arm is around me. Around *me*.

You don't put your arm around just a friend.

111

"He likes you," Alison says to me. She's wearing her pj's and sitting at the foot of my bed.

"Yeah?"

"Oh yeah," says Poodles, who's standing in the center of the room, flossing her teeth. "Definitely. He was, like, giving you moon eyes the entire sing-down. He has it bad."

Yes!

"I saw it too," Carly adds. She's back on the floor, doing her stomach crunches, her feet anchored under her bed.

"You're lucky," Morgan says. "He's one of the best guys here."

Puh-lease. He's one of the best guys anywhere.

"Before lights-out, we need to do your electives," Deb says, sitting on Poodles' bed. "They start on Thursday after lunch, so tell me what you want to take for both elective A and elective B."

"What are the choices?" I ask.

"You have to pick two: A&C—that's arts and crafts, Rachel—pottery, sailing, windsurfing, canoeing, tennis, archery, drama, waterskiing, baseball, and basketball."

"Basketball!" Morgan says. "All the guys take basketball."

Brilliant! I'm going to take basketball too!

"Taking what *they* take is obvious," Poodles says, shaking her head.

That is so true.

"I'll take basketball with you," Carly says. "I have a killer shot."

"That's A for Morgan and Carly. What do you want as your B elective?"

"Drama," Carly says.

"Oh, me too," says Morgan. "We'll be in the play!"

"All right," Deb says. "Poodles? What do you want to take?"

"Sailing and sailing," she says.

Deb shakes her head. "You have to chose two different ones."

"Sailing and windsurfing, then. At least I'll get to stay at the beach."

"Done," Deb says, scribbling on her notepad. "Alison?"

"Same with me. Sailing and windsurfing."

"Rachel?"

"I'll take sailing and . . ." Windsurfing sounds a lot scarier than sailing. I mean, you have to do windsurfing alone, right? Just stand up there and hope the wind pushes you? I am so not into standing up there solo in my bathing suit for the world to see. Hmm, come to think of it, I'm not even allowed to go windsurfing because of my dolphin status. Crap. Now what? I've never canoed, played tennis, or arched (that can't be the right verb), and although hanging out with Raf at baseball and/or basketball sounds fun, how do I know which one he chose, if either?

"Um, A&C?"

"You know what?" Alison says. "I think I want to change my windsurfing to A&C too."

113

"Me too," says Poodles. "Can't be too obvious, right?"

After we're done, I head to the bathroom to get washed. As always, I practically freeze my face off while washing it. I quickly brush my teeth and then retreat into the cubby room to change into my pajamas. I gingerly remove Raf's sweatshirt. Instead of folding it and putting it away, I take it to bed with me.

Snuggling with Raf's clothing will be like snuggling with him. Well, not quite, but it will have to do.

Deb turns off the lights.

Hello, yummy sweatshirt. Of course, I can't help remembering that the best love spell involves a piece of the victim's (er, I mean, *guy's*) clothing. Not that I'm putting a love spell on Raf. This time I won't need one (hopefully). And this time I want the real thing.

"Rachel, wake up!"

I am being poked in the head. "Yes?" I ask, opening one eye. Poodles is motioning me to follow her. "It's time."

"For what?" I whisper.

"To get them back," Morgan tells me. She is dressed all in black.

The clock says 3:00 a.m. I throw off my covers and hurry to join them. "What's the plan?"

"We're painting their faces," Morgan says. "Poodles borrowed paint from A&C."

Trying not to giggle, the five of us get into position. Poodles is painting the girls on the top bunks while Morgan does the bottom ones. Carly and I hold the paint and act as artistic directors. Alison's duty is standing by in the bathroom in case Deb or Penelope wakes up.

Natalie gets red glasses painted on her, Trishelle becomes a Dalmatian, and Kristin gets the measles.

"What do you think?" Poodles whispers while painting green whiskers. "It's Molly the mouse."

I swallow my laughter.

Molly wrinkles her nose in her sleep but doesn't wake up. Next we visit Liana.

"Turn her into a cat!" I whisper.

"Actually, I have another idea." Poodles dips the

paintbrush into my jar of black paint and paints a goatee on Liana's chin and a mustache on her upper lip.

"That is so mean!" I murmur. Mean but funny.

Until Liana's eyes start to flutter.

Poodles jumps back.

Uh-oh.

"False alarm," Poodles tells me. "She's still asleep."

After Morgan puts the finishing touches on Cece (I'm not sure what she's supposed to be; she just has stripes and Xs across her face. A ticktacktoe board?), we sneak back to our side of the cabin.

"Won't they know it was us?" Carly asks.

"Probably," Poodles says, laughing.

"Maybe we should paint ourselves, too, to fool them," Carly says.

Morgan rolls her eyes. "Then we'd be painted."

115

"Let's just get rid of the evidence," Poodles says, tiptoe-ing toward the door. "Morgie, come with me. We'll leave the supplies in front of the A&C."

The remaining three of us get back into our beds. "You know," says Carly, "I'm going to hide the mirror so they don't know what they look like."

"But they'll still see each other," I try to explain, but Carly is already in the bathroom, removing the mirror from the wall.

Alison and I fall asleep, giggling to ourselves.

"Bunk fourteen, time to get up!" Janice says, stomping across our floor. Then she disappears into the cubby room and into bunk fifteen. "Bunk fifteen, it's time to get—" Audible gasp. "What happened to you?"

We all jolt up in bed, smiles on our faces.

"There's something on my face!" Trishelle shrieks.

Kristin: "Mine too! What is it, what is it?"

Cece: "It's red!"

Liana: "Well, it's all over my three-hundred-thread-count pillowcases."

"Now we're even," Poodles says.

They try to scrub the paint off, but without a proper shower, they are forced to go to flagpole with multicolored faces.

116

"They look like Teletubbies," Morgan snorts at breakfast over her stack of pancakes.

"Girls," Deb admonishes, "I hope you didn't have anything to do with this."

"Us?" Poodles innocently bats her eyelashes. "Why would we do such a thing? Pass the maple syrup."

Of course, bunk fifteen knows that it was us—not that they can prove it. They keep glaring at us from their table.

"We got them good," Morgan says.

Alison bites her lower lip. "And now we'd better watch our backs."

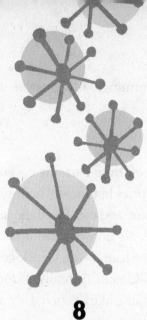

8
CHOPPY WATERS

It's Thursday, a few days later, and Alison and I are lying across the bow of a sailboat, legs stretched out as the wind whips through our hair and the sun kisses our skin. I can't believe I've been missing out on sailing my entire life! What else have my parents deprived me of?

After handing us life jackets, Harris, who is as über-hot as my bunkmates have described and in fact has a cleft in his chin that reminds me of a superhero in a comic book, divided up the Lions who had chosen sailing and then sent us out in boats.

Luckily for Poodles, Harris has chosen to come with us, sending the others (who include gelled-out Anderson; immature, nose-stuffing Brandon; and a few younger Lion girls I recognize from Miri's bunk—but no Miri) out with some of the CITs.

And now our boat is up and running, sailing across the glorious lake.

But the best part of sailing?

Raf's elective is windsurfing.

I literally cannot take my eyes off him. Partially because he's wearing bright yellow swim trunks but mostly because I watched him take off his shirt and expose his dark and smooth six-pack of a stomach. Fine, it's more like a four-pack, since he's only fifteen, but still. It's a lean, mean Greek-god-machine four-pack. Not that he's Greek. Actually, I don't know what his ancestry is. With a name like Kosravi, I always kind of assumed Russian.

"Coming about!" Harris calls as the boom swerves to the other side of the sailboat, turning us around. Alison and I cling to our seats, trying not to slide off.

Since we're now heading straight for the windsurfing section, toward my Russian-Greek four-pack, I suck in my stomach and strike my most enticing pose.

He's waving at me! Sure, his upper torso is now covered by his life jacket, but I think I just saw his arm muscles ripple.

A gust of wind emerges from nowhere (a gust of wind, my beating heart, whatever) and tilts the sailboat danger-ously onto its side. We all shriek as the cool water splashes our arms and legs. A growl echoes over the lake and I check out Colton, who has just fallen face-first off his board into the water, thanks to my little magical burst.

"I'm okay, y'all!" he hollers.

"Ouch," I say. "That looked like it hurt."

"Have you ever tried windsurfing?" Alison asks me.

We lean down as the boom swings around again. "Nope." Sounds scary. It's a good thing dolphins are restricted from doing it. Then again, how much more dangerous can it be than flying around on a broomstick?

"Canoeing?"

"Nope. I'm not so boaty."

"No worries," Poodles says from the other side of the boat. "You'll learn."

The sight of Raf maneuvering his sailboard distracts me. He seems genuinely in control of his sail, like it's a part of him. He's working the sail like it's a dancing partner and he's taken the lead.

I wish he'd look at me. Why isn't he looking at me? Look at me, Raf, look at me!

Look! At! Me!

And that's when another gust of wind, this one resembling a baby hurricane, sends him flying off his board, sideways, into the water.

"Did you see that?" Alison asks. "Poor Raf."

See it? I caused it!

Raf splashes around and then pulls himself onto the dock. This time he looks right at me—and gives me a sheepish smile.

Aw, he's embarrassed! How cute!

That must mean he likes me.

While Alison takes the sun for the rest of the period, Poodles and Harris flirt ("You're sooo funny, Harris." "You're so cute, Poodles."), and I ogle Raf. Of course, I ogle him discreetly. Very unobviously.

119

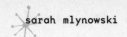

"You've got it bad," Alison says.

"Very bad," I admit.

"Attenthion all camperth and counthlorth! Attenthion all camperth and counthlorth! It ith now the end of thecond afternoon activity. Pleathe protheed to the back of the kitchen for thnack."

It's the next day, and Poodles, Alison, and I leave the A&C and head to Lower Field.

I spot Miri waiting in line for her snack and frowning. She's not going to make friends if she looks so miserable all the time.

"Try to pretend you're having fun," I tell her.

"Why? I'm not."

"What's wrong?"

"I don't want to talk about it."

I put my arm around her tiny shoulders. "What happened?"

"Do you care or do you just want to butt into line?"

"Both?" I tickle her side. "Oh, come on, Miri, lighten up. Aren't you having a little fun?"

She shrugs. "It's okay."

We take a few steps forward as the line moves. "Where's the rest of your bunk?"

She shrugs. "Who cares?"

"Come on, Mir. Don't you like any of them?"

"They're kind of cliquey."

"Miri, you have to try harder. I'm sure they'll love you if you give them a chance."

She sighs. "I'll try. Will you come swimming with me at GS? I'm dying to go in but I have no one to swim with."

"Um, Mir, you know I hate swimming." So far I've spent all GSs avoiding the water and working on my tan.

Her forehead crinkles into little folds. "Oh, come on, it's so hot out. And I need a buddy to go in the water."

"Ask someone from your bunk."

She sticks her thumbnail into her mouth and starts to nibble. "Maybe."

I push her hand away. "Don't! Your fingers are all grimy!"

"Hey, do you want to come check out my bunk at free play? You still haven't seen it."

"I can't. It's Morgan's birthday, and Deb made us cup-cakes. Tomorrow, maybe?"

"You're busy at free play, too? Aren't you going to spend any time with me at all?"

Oh, poor Miri. "You can come to the birthday party."

We step up to the counter.

"Enjoy!" Oscar pours us two glasses of milk and hands over two chocolate chip cookies each. I only take one.

"Thank you!" we say in unison.

"They won't mind?" Miri asks me.

"I don't think so. Alison," I say as I pass her in the line, "can we invite other people to Morgan's party?"

"Of course," she says. "I already invited Will."

I'm sure Morgan'll love that. "There you go," I say to my sister, accidentally dropping my cookie into my milk and then digging it out with my fingers.

"Oh sure, my fingers are grimy, but yours are perfectly clean?"

Good point. I sadly let the cookie sink back to the bottom of the cup. "So you'll come to my bunk?"

"Yes. And I'm taking back my crystal."

I was hoping to hold on to that for a while. Just in case. "Thanks for lending that to me, by the way."

"No problem. That's what sisters are for."

"Helping?"

She hands me one of her cookies. "Sharing."

I'm on my way back to my bunk when I run smack into Raf. He's in navy swim trunks; a red beach towel is casually thrown over the shoulder of a thin white T-shirt.

"Hi," he says. "Coming to GS?"

"Of course."

He tugs on his towel. "Wanna be my buddy?"

Coming from his lips, the word *buddy* sounds like *girlfriend*, not just *swimming partner*. (A girl can dream, can't she?) "Sure!"

"Great," he says while walking backward down the hill. "I'm just stopping for snack. See you on the beach in five."

My mother's bathing suit, which I'm wearing under my clothes (because my better one-piece was damp from that morning), will just not do. I sprint back to my bunk, the milk and cookies jiggling in my stomach like change in a pocket, take off my clothes, and put on my sexy orange bikini, Bobby be damned! Maybe the sexiness will distract from the abnormalness? I pull shorts and a shirt over my suit, grab a towel, and run back down to the beach.

Yes! I'm going swimming with Raf!

"Bunk lines, everyone, bunk lines!" Rose screams through her megaphone as she does at the beginning of every GS.

"Okay, everyone, remember the rules of the beach. You must check in with a buddy and we'll give each couple a number."

Ooh. *Couple*. I like the sound of that!

Sexy, shirtless Raf strolls over to me. "Ready?"

I strip off my shorts and shirt and cross my arms over my chest. No reason for him to get a view of Bobby if he doesn't have to. Hopefully, once we're in the water, he won't see anything.

123

We head to the check-in. "Do you both have your whale?" Rose asks, obviously forgetting our whole search-and-rescue experience.

"Yup," says Raf.

Uh-oh. My blue bead burns into my skin like a scarlet letter. I cannot admit that I have my dolphin. I absolutely can't. I need to use my magic to turn the bead yellow. I stare at my wrist with all my might and think:

Turn yellow this second, you stupid bead!

Nothing happens. Maybe it would help if it rhymed. One more time.

Turn yellow so I can get into whale

And go swimming with this gorgeous—

"Your bead looks blue to me," Rose says. "I'm checking you into dolphin."

Raf's eyes widen in surprise.

She exposed my secret before I had a chance to finish my spell! Which was going to end with the word *male*, in case you were wondering. I'm a rhyming machine.

Maybe I should become a rapper?

I'm too embarrassed to look Raf in the eye now that he knows my humiliating secret, so I walk ahead and dip my toe into the water.

"So, dolphin, huh?"

I turn back to see him smiling. "What's so funny?" I ask.

"Nothing." He's still smiling.

"Then why are you smiling?"

He laughs. "I think it's cute that you can't swim."

"It might be cute, but it's not funny."

He laughs again. "It's cute *and* funny. I can teach you."

"You're an expert?"

"No . . . well, a little. I'm up for my lifeguard badge this year." He steps into the water. When I don't follow, he takes my hand. "Come on," he says. "It's not that cold."

Takes my hand. Takes. My. Hand. Takes! My! Hand!

Yowza! Electricity smolders through our fingertips. Not real electricity, obviously, since we're in a lake, and if it was, we'd be fried.

Oh, I'm plenty warm now. Holding hands, we wade into the water. He uses his non-holding hand to lift the rope that blocks off the dolphin section. "Ready? Let's dunk."

He lets go of my hand (sigh!) and dives under the water. When he surfaces, he smiles devilishly and then sends a tsunami of a splash over my body.

"Oh, now you're in trouble." I spray him right back.

We continue splashing each other until Rose blows her whistle and yells, "Quiet on the beach! Buddy call!"

Behind us, a couple of girls from the Monkey unit scream, "One!"

Kids holler *two* through *ten*, and then Raf winks at me. "Eleven!" we scream in unison.

We're a couple! Can it get any better than this?

We swim and laugh and splash through two more buddy calls, then they order all the swimmers out of the lake and force us back into bunk lines.

"See you later," Raf says.

"See you later," I echo happily.

As I sit solo in my line on the sand, I scan the beach contentedly, a dreamy smile plastered on my face.

"Thanks a lot," I hear.

I look up to see Miri standing above me, glaring. "What?" I ask.

"I asked you to be my buddy, and you said no. But you went swimming with Raf."

Oh, crap. "Mir, I'm sorry. Really. But he asked me and—"

"I asked you too."

"You didn't technically; you just said—"

"Whatever, Rachel," she interrupts. "I had no one to go swimming with. I'm mad at you."

I stand up, my towel wrapped around me, and hug her. "I'm sorry. Really. But it was Raf," I whisper. "Try to understand."

"Humph." She does not hug me back.

"You can't stay mad at me."

"Bunk lines, everyone, bunk lines!" Rose orders.

"I'll see you at free play," I say. "There's going to be cupcakes. You can't come if you're still mad at me."

No response.

"Did I mention that they're chocolate?"

"All right, but only because of the cupcakes," she says, then returns to her own bunk line.

I stifle a yawn. All this excitement has made me exhausted. Maybe I'll take a nap instead of showering. The lake water is probably pretty clean.

"I peed in the lake again!" I hear one of the Koala boys yell.

Or not.

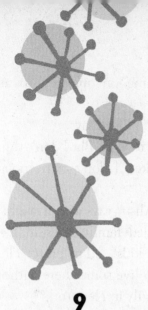

9

PASS THE POPCORN

After two weeks at camp, I feel like I've been here a year.

The junk food is long gone, my bed no longer feels strange (although it does still feel a little bit lumpy), I'm getting used to going to morning flagpole in my pajamas and washing my face in cold water, and I've somehow managed to find time to write my mom, my dad, and Tammy at least three letters each.

Every sunny, beautiful day is pretty much the same.

Now Poodles, Alison, and I are at A&C, sitting at a table, making lanyard bracelets. I'm just getting the hang of butterfly, the easiest stitch, which requires only three strands of the multicolored plastic lanyard, while Poodles and Alison are whipping through the more advanced techniques, like square and circle, which require four.

"The West Coast just has a relaxed vibe," Poodles says,

explaining why she's not planning on applying to any schools on the East Coast.

"But Manhattan is super-cool," Alison says.

"I know," Poodles says. "I love to visit. But I don't think I could ever be a real New Yorker. I don't own enough black."

"You have enough attitude," Alison says with a laugh.

"True. But my entire extended family lives in L.A. too. My aunts and uncles, their kids . . . I'm pretty close to them. I don't think I'd want to live somewhere without any roots. Do you have a lot of family in New York?"

"Not so much," I say. We don't see any of my mom's family. Her parents passed away a long time ago, and her relationship with her sister, Sasha, is a bit of a mystery. They got into a major fight years and years ago, when I was still a baby, and they haven't spoken since. It's the big family secret—which my mom refuses to share.

"I have a lot of family in New York, but we barely see them," Alison says. "Everyone's too busy."

"Would either of you ever consider moving out to California?"

"Maybe for college," I say, screwing up my stitch yet again and undoing it. "I do hate winters."

"What do you want to study?" Alison asks me.

"Well . . ." Here's where I sound really geeky. "I kind of like math."

"Really? That is so cool," Poodles says. "Do you want to be an engineer?"

"I haven't decided," I say. Am I dumb if I don't really

know what an engineer does? "Maybe I'll be a mathematician. Math professor? I'm good with numbers."

"What's twenty-two times thirty-three?" Poodles asks.

I close my eyes to calculate. "Seven hundred twenty-six," I say, opening them.

Poodles puts down her lanyard, impressed. "Twenty-seven times eighty-seven?"

"Two thousand three hundred forty-nine."

"Holy crap," Poodles says, laughing. "Fifty-two times—"

"She's not a monkey," Alison says.

Now I laugh. "What do you guys want to be?"

"I want to be a producer," Poodles says. "Like everyone else in L.A."

"I thought everyone in L.A. wanted to act," I say.

"They do. At first. Then they want to produce."

"You, Alison?" I ask.

"Physician," she says.

"Perfect!" I squeal. "I could use a new doctor. Mine still makes happy faces on my arm before he gives me my shots. When can you start?"

"In like fifteen years?"

"Damn," Poodles says, shaking her head. "I just screwed up a stitch. This has to be perfect." She leans over to us so that only we can hear what she says next. "I'm making it for Harris."

Natalie and Kristin have signed up for A&C too, and they're only a table away.

"You're making Harris a bracelet?" I ask. "Isn't that girly?"

129

Poodles bites one of her strands to tighten it. "It's the thought that counts. And I'm using black lanyard to make it macho."

"Do you think I should make Raf a bracelet?"

Poodles glances at my disembodied attempt at butterfly and grimaces. "Why don't you hold off a week or so? Until you've had more practice. It's not always the thought that counts."

"But I think I might have to make it more obvious that I like him," I say. Raf and I sat next to each other at last night's evening activity, which was "The Price Is Right." Then we hung out until curfew. We talked, we laughed, we joked. Basically we did everything couples do.

Except kiss.

"If you were any more obvious, you'd be wearing a sign," Alison jokes.

"Ha-ha. Maybe he just doesn't like me?"

Poodles shakes her head. "I've known Raf a long time, and I've never seen him spend so much time with one girl."

I blush happily.

"It'll happen," Poodles continues. "Maybe he's just waiting for the right moment. Or atmosphere."

Or century.

The atmosphere can't get any more right than this.

It's a few days later, and after a full afternoon of ponchos and rain boots and indoor activities like pottery, drama, and dodgeball and SI (aka swimming instruction) in the indoor

130

pool (which wasn't too bad, because the water was like a bath), it's movie night—the latest *Harry Potter*—in the CL (aka counselors' lounge). The CL is the only place at camp with a TV.

Janice is chewing a pink pen and flicking the lights on and off. "Find a spot. Let's go, let's go."

Raf and I have already settled into a space at the back of the CL, along the rear wall. Since I brought a blanket with me ("Set the stage!" Poodles instructed), I offer to share. Wink, wink.

I was kind of hoping for a romantic comedy and not the story of my life. But maybe Raf will cuddle me during the scary parts?

Janice turns off the lights, presses Play, and sinks into the oversize saggy seen-better-days brown couch in the center of the room.

131

Twenty minutes into the movie, I feel Raf's arm around me. Yes, yes, yes! My entire body tingles. The lights are off and everyone is absorbed in the movie. We're going to kiss tonight. It's going to happen. I just know it's going to happen. His face is only a few inches away from mine. All he has to do is turn a bit to the right. He laughs at something on the screen—as if watching the movie is possible at a time like this!—and now his cheek is only about two inches from mine. All I have to do is turn my face. *Turn!*

His laughing stops and I can hear his breathing. I can hear my own breathing too, and it's getting faster with every passing second, since my heart is beating a trillion times a minute.

I turn about a half inch. He turns about a half inch. I

turn a quarter inch. He turns a quarter inch. Omigod, we're so close I can barely stand it. If we both stuck out our tongues, they would touch—which is kind of the point. Tongue-touching. I wonder what his tongue is going to feel like. I've touched only one tongue in my life and it was his brother's. Probably best not to think about other boys' tongues when I'm about to kiss someone.

My mouth is drier than a cactus. I hope it doesn't taste like a cactus. Not that I know what a cactus tastes like, but I'm willing to bet it's not tasty. Never mind prickly.

Now our lips are only about an inch apart! And now a half inch and here it comes; it's really going to happen—

Suddenly, there's a rush of cold, and the lights pop on.

"Aaaah!" everyone screams.

I snap my head back. Eyes blinded. Can't see.

Janice leaps off the couch. "Who did that?"

Raf pulls away like a scared cat.

We all turn to look at the light switch. "Did someone turn on the light?" Janice asks again. No one answers. Janice tries to switch the lights back off, but they won't budge.

Did I do that? Was I somehow so nervous about kissing Raf that I turned the lights on so it wouldn't happen? What is wrong with me?

"Maybe it was Harry Potter," Blume says.

Everyone laughs. Everyone except me.

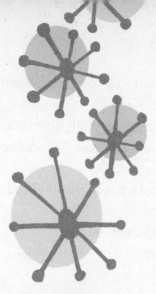

10
RAISING DVDs
IN THE CL

Crunch. The hairs on my arms stand at attention.

Just a twig, I tell myself. Nothing to be afraid of.

Crunch.

I run a little bit faster, just in case. I'm not sure why I thought it was a good idea to sneak through camp in the middle of the night. Oh, right, it's because I desperately and immediately need Miri's help.

I've finally found the path that leads between bunks one and three and am now trying to make my way to bunk two without a wild bear eating me first.

Ha-ha. There aren't really any bears at camp. Right?

Here it is. Bunk two. I creep up the wooden steps and close the invisibility shield—aka the enchanted umbrella. I gingerly open the door. Now all I have to do is figure out which bed is Miri's. I tiptoe around the cabin, peering into the top bunks at the faces of Miri's sleeping bunkmates.

In the moonlight, I recognize my sister's pale green comforter at the back, near the bathroom. "Miri," I whisper. "Miri, wake up."

When she doesn't respond, I poke her in the forehead.

My sister opens one eye. "What are you doing?"

"I need your help. Come outside with me."

"What time is it?" she murmurs.

"Three a.m."

"Are you crazy?"

"No, just desperate. You were right. My powers are out of control. I need your help. I need some training."

"Now?" she asks.

"You can't exactly train me in broad daylight, can you?"

"We're not allowed out of the bunks in the middle of the night! We're going to get into trouble."

"We won't if nobody sees us."

"What if someone's up?"

"Don't worry, I took care of that." I wave our invisibility shield over her bed.

"You brought that to camp?"

"Of course I brought it!"

"You didn't tell me you were bringing it!"

What, is she crazy? "Did you think I was going to leave a great toy like this at home?" I think not. "Come on!"

She climbs over the edge of the bed. "Am I allowed to get dressed?" She's wearing her blue Cookie Monster pajamas, which I can't believe I let her pack. At least she doesn't wear those to breakfast.

"Nah, let's just go."

She grumbles and stuffs her feet into her flip-flops. Before we leave, she snags a gray pencil case from the shelf.

"You're not going to have time to write," I snort.

"It's A^2. Camouflaged."

"No way!" I stifle a laugh as we hurry out the door. Why would she choose a pencil case? She's such a geek. I open the umbrella. Presto invisible.

"You didn't happen to pack our night-vision helmets, did you?" she asks.

Darn. I forgot about those. "No, unfortunately. But I brought something just as helpful." I wave a flashlight in the air.

"Where are you taking me, anyway?" Miri asks.

"How about the CL? It seems private."

And the counselors' lounge is carpeted, so I'm less likely to get hurt if training involves my crashing to the floor.

When we finally get there, we open the creaky door and then sit cross-legged on the saggy couch. Miri places the pencil case on the ground, sticks her hand into her pocket, and takes out a bag of white flour. Flour?

"What is that?"

"Baby powder. Quiet for a sec?" She clears her throat and says:

"From a caterpillar, a butterfly you became.
Now let this powder absorb your change!"

As she sprinkles the powder on the pencil case, it stretches and morphs into A^2. You know when you scrunch the paper wrapper off a straw and then drop water on it to watch it unravel? That's what it looks like. "Very cool."

135

She heaves the insanely heavy book onto her lap. From the outside, it looks the size of a regular hardcover novel, but it's actually two feet deep. And it smells sour, like month-old milk. "Okay, where do you want to start?"

"Good question."

"Well, what's the problem?"

"I don't know! I can't seem to control my powers. Like tonight. Raf was about to kiss me during the movie—"

"Thanks a lot for saving me a seat."

"Miri, you shouldn't be sitting with your sister. You should be sitting with your friends."

She shrugs. "I don't have any."

My heart sinks like a pound of lead. Even though she wasn't exactly Miss Popularity at home, I had kind of been hoping that things would be different here. "But why?"

She shrugs. "I told you. They've all been friends since they were seven."

"But so has my bunk!"

"Maybe," she squeaks, "but the girls in mine aren't interested in meeting new people."

The high-pitched tone of her voice makes the back of my neck stiffen. "Are they being mean?"

Her face flushes. "A little. Whatever. I don't care. It's not like I have so many friends at home."

"Not having friends is not the same as people being mean to you."

Her eyes cloud over. "I don't want to talk about it."

"You have to. I'm your sister."

She starts picking at her nails, and this time I don't stop her. "Well, yesterday I woke up and they were dipping my fingers in hot water to try to make me wet my bed or some-thing. And today someone put shampoo in my running shoes. But maybe that was an accident—"

"Are you kidding me? How does shampoo accidentally end up in someone's sneakers?" My cheeks burn, and I slam my fist into a couch pillow.

Ow. I don't have much of a right hook.

"Whatever," Miri says dismissively. "It doesn't matter. Honestly, I don't care. I don't want to waste time worrying about it. I want to be able to focus on helping the homeless when I get back, so I need to spend my free time researching."

"But, Miri, they're only ostracizing you because you don't make an effort to talk to them!"

She rolls her eyes. "But I don't even like them. Why would I make an effort?"

"Maybe if you talk to your counselors—"

"That would only make things worse." She juts out her chin. "I didn't come all the way here in the middle of the night to discuss my problems. Can we get back to yours?"

Although I'd rather keep talking about her, I don't want to upset her. "My powers are out of whack," I tell her, chang-ing the subject. "When I use my raw will, what I want to happen doesn't always end up happening."

"That's what A^2 is for."

"I know, I know. But it's not just that. When I get emo-tional, my magic goes nuts. For instance, I was so nervous about kissing Raf that I zapped on the lights."

"You were the one who turned them on?"

"Yes! It must have been me. My heart was beating like crazy and—" Pause. I wasn't the only person with magical

137

powers in here tonight. Is it possible that Miri was trying to sabotage my first kiss with Raf? Maybe she's worried that my relationship with Raf will make her feel even lonelier. Nah, she wouldn't do that to me. "Well, since *you* didn't do it"— I give her a meaningful look in case there's anything she wants to admit—"it must have been me. So I need to learn to control my powers. Did you ever have this problem?"

"Never. I guess I'm a more mature witch."

Like it's not annoying enough to have to ask my little sister for help—she has to rub it in. "Can you check the book to see if there's some sort of control technique I can use?"

She spreads open the book and flips through the wisp-thin pages. "Like an exercise?"

"Exactly."

"You need to be magic trained. Like toilet trained."

"Let's not get graphic."

"Maybe I should find you a magic diaper."

"Miri, I'd cut down on the toilet-training jokes if I were you. Don't forget that I am two years older and therefore have a very detailed memory of the time you ripped off your diaper and peed all over the living room fl—"

"I found something."

"Already?"

"I'm super-quick. Give me two seconds to read it."

I tap my sneakered foot for two seconds. "Finished?"

She ignores me.

"Hello?"

"Shush!" She continues reading and then looks up. "Okay, it'll work."

"Terrif. What is it?"

"It's called a megel."

"A what?"

"A megel exercise. You have to practice stopping the flow of your raw will. It'll make your magic muscles stronger."

"How do you do that?"

She points to the umbrella, which I left by the door. "See if you can mind-lift it."

"Um, I'm willing to play along here, but since the umbrella is my favorite toy, can I use something else as my guinea pig?"

She stands up. "Try the couch. It looks like it's already been through several megels."

"Too heavy."

She spins around, eyeing megel-able items. "The TV."

"What if I drop it?"

She skips over to the DVD player and picks up the *Harry Potter* DVD case. "Light enough for you?" She tosses it onto the carpet. "Go ahead."

Hello, pressure. I focus on the case. I try to summon all the energy I can feel inside me, and suddenly my arms are covered with tiny goose bumps. I try to direct all this energy at the case—fly, Harry, fly!—and the plastic starts to quiver. It's working! It lifts just an inch off the ground—

"Freeze!" Miri orders. "Keep it right there. Can you do that?"

I try to do that, but the case is trembling like crazy, my arms and legs are shaking, and the next thing I know, the case pops open, soars to the ceiling, then crashes back to the ground.

139

"Whoops," I say. "Sorry, Master Yoda. I have failed you."

She giggles. "You need practice."

No kidding. "But can't I practice using real A^2 spells? They're easier to control, right? The words and ingredients do most of the work, so how much can I screw up?"

"True, they're easier to control, but they're also much stronger. And since your raw will is so out of whack, it could be dangerous. Who knows what you could wish up? Or down," she adds, glancing at the broken DVD case on the floor.

Suddenly, we hear a loud creak outside the door.

"Someone's coming," Miri whispers in a rush.

"What do we do?" I ask, panicked.

She's waving her hand toward the door. "I'm trying to"—she huffs and puffs—"keep it closed."

"The door's stuck," a guy outside says.

"Push harder," says a second voice. A female voice.

"The invisibility shield!" Miri whispers, still struggling with the door.

Unfortunately, the umbrella is on the other side of the room. "It's too far away!" I try to use my raw will to float it over, but of course, *now* it won't work. "Can you zap it over?"

"Too tough"—huff—"to do"—puff—"two spells"—huff and puff—"at once! Use your feet!"

Oh, right. I forgot about those. I run over, pick up the umbrella, and ram it open just as Miri loses her battle. The door flies open as Miri dives next to me behind the umbrella.

"Good job," says the female voice.

I can't see who it is, since the umbrella is blocking our view. But I recognize the voice. It's Deb's.

I hear the door close. Terrific. We're trapped. My counselor is about to make out with some guy, and I'm going to be stuck here until they're done.

I think I'd rather watch my mom and Lex than listen to this.

"Now give me a kiss," I hear the guy say. He sounds like Anthony.

At least Deb has good taste.

Two hours later, Miri and I are finally free. Free, tired, and cranky.

"Next time we'll have to find somewhere with a little bit less traffic," I say as we cross Upper Field. "Hey, look, the sun is rising over the mountains. Wanna go down to the lake and watch?"

"Sure, why not?"

We scurry down to the waterfront. The lake is as still as a mirror but brimming with streaks of yellow and orange and blue. We leave our shoes on the sand, sit on the dock, and dangle our feet in the cool water.

I poke my sister's foot with my big toe, sending ripples through the lake. "Nice, huh?"

"Yeah," she says, almost wistfully. "Tonight was fun."

"Don't worry, Mir. Camp will get better. You'll see."

141

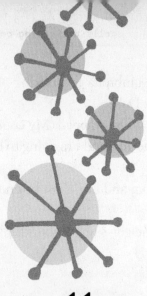

11
BEE MY SWEETIE

Whenever I get a moment alone, I practice my megels. I consider finding a secluded place in the woods, but I decide I'm still too afraid of running into a bear. Or a deer. Or a raccoon. Or any type of animal that isn't housebroken.

So I choose Plan B. Unfortunately, Plan B is using one of the bathroom stalls in our cabin. What can I say? Sure, it's slightly smelly, but it's conveniently close by, and it's the only place in camp where you can ever be truly alone. I practice my exercises on the extra roll of toilet paper sitting in the corner of the stall. Luckily, the stall doors go to the floor, so no one thinks I'm peeing like a boy.

It's rest hour, and I've been practicing in here for about ten minutes. I'm getting a bit better at it. Higher. Stop. Higher. Stop. . . .

Bam, bam, bam. "You've been in there *forever*. It's not your personal bathroom."

Whoops. I flush, even though I haven't done anything that requires flushing, and crack open the door. "Sorry, I—" I stop in midsentence. It's Liana. Why am I always apologizing to this girl?

"You can't hog the bathroom," she snaps.

Someone has some major hostility issues. "I said I was sorry."

She flips her hair and then slams past me into a stall—but not the stall I vacated. And that's when I realize something weird: the other two stalls were free. Huh. Why would Liana kick me out of my stall when two were empty? Does that make any sense?

Since there is still fifteen minutes of rest hour left, I walk through the cubby room to our bunk, pull down my pillow, and make myself comfy on Alison's bed, my feet flat against the ladder.

143

Poodles and Carly are playing gin rummy. "Wanna play, winner?" Carly asks me. "Kick our butts?"

It seems I have a knack for gin rummy. Who knew? "Sure, if there's time."

"I've got mail!" says Deb, arms full of e-mail printouts, letters, and packages. She reads the names as she hands out the e-mails first. "Alison, Poodles, Rachel, Carly, Poodles, Alison, Morgan, Morgan, Rachel."

Fun! I get an e-mail from Tammy (who's still dating Bosh and loving her summer babysitting job in the city) as well as an e-mail from my dad.

My dad's e-mails are adorable. And a wee bit illiterate, since they're sent from his BlackBerry. Take today's:

Enjoying very pleasant weather Going to conference tomorrow and will be home monday

Played golf yesterday. Jennifer sewing on P's camp labels. She excited to see you to.

Send e mail re your goings on and how enjoying camp. Love you girls lots.
Dad

_____

Sent from my BlackBerry Wireless Handheld

I've written him that we have no computer access (Deb prints out all the bunk's e-mails once a day), but the concept is obviously too foreign for him to grasp.

She tosses a thick pink package onto Poodles' bed. "For you, princess."

"I hope it's the new issue of *EW*," Poodles says, tearing the envelope open. "Oh good. *People,* too."

"Package for you, too, Rachel," Deb says, handing me a small padded envelope.

For me? A package? I am beyond excited.

"Who's it from?" Alison asks.

I flip the envelope over to read the return address. Jennifer Weinstein. "My stepmom," I say. That is so sweet of her! I wonder what she got me. A book? A CD?

I rip open the package and find . . . a bottle of Nair. *Hair removal for the upper lip.*

Huh? A folded handwritten note says, *Enjoy! Love, Jennifer.*

She did not just send me this.

"You have a mustache?" Morgan asks.

"No!" I say quickly, hiding the box behind me. I can't believe she would send me this. Is she trying to tell me something? "I don't think I do. Do I?" I wiggle my upper lip.

Alison examines my face. "I don't see one."

"Be honest."

"I swear! What a weird gift."

No kidding.

"Rachel, here's another letter for you," Deb says.

"Thanks."

I open it up and see that it's from my mom. It's your basic "I'm doing well, how are you, I miss you" letter. At least I have one normal parent.

Besides the whole witchcraft part.

"Don't you think Harris looks like a movie star?" Poodles asks while studying her new magazine.

"He's not that good-looking," says Morgan, tweezing her eyebrows in a handheld mirror. "Will, on the other hand . . . now there's a piece of eye candy."

"What's going on with Harris?" I ask Poodles.

Poodles keeps her eyes on her magazine. "Stuff."

"What?" we all scream.

Poodles smiles and shushes us with her finger to her lips. "I don't want"—she motions to fifteen—"them to hear."

Morgan tosses her hand mirror and tweezers onto her bed. "You'd better spill this second!"

Poodles twirls a lock of her blond hair around her long index finger. "Yesterday during sailing . . ."

We lean in eagerly.

". . . we tipped the boat, and when we were in the water, he kissed me."

"Oh! My! God!" we shriek.

"Alison and I were sailing and we didn't even notice!" I say in disbelief.

"That's why Harris sent you out with Anderson and Brandon," Poodles says.

"Ah," Alison says. "I didn't totally buy the 'they're training to be sailing instructors' part, since they tipped us twice."

"I think the tipping part was on purpose," I say. They thought it was hysterical every time we got dumped into the freezing water. Carly was so jealous when we told her.

"Can we get back to Harris, please?" Morgan whines.

"If any of you breathe a word of this to anyone," Poodles continues, "I will personally strangle you."

"You'd better be careful," Alison warns. "You could get into serious trouble."

"He could get fired," Carly adds.

Poodles looks meaningfully around the room. "That's why you all had better keep your mouths shut. Let's change the subject."

"What about you, Rachel?" Morgan asks, already back to her tweezing. "Any tongue action with Raf?"

"No," I say. "And now I feel even worse that it's taking so long."

"It's not the same," Alison says. "Harris lives in Boston. It's not like they're going to turn into a serious item." She looks at Poodles. "You're not serious about him, are you?"

"Me, serious? Get serious. My longest relationship was like a week."

"All they have is the summer," Alison continues, "so they have to get a move on. On the other hand, you and Raf—this is not just a summer fling. This has consequences! You guys go to school together. If it doesn't work out, you'll have to avoid each other not only for the next four weeks but for the next three years. Raf just wants to make sure."

Makes sense. I guess.

"And you know, you did date his brother," Carly adds.

"Lucky girl," grumbles Morgan.

There's always that. I sigh. "I suppose so."

But if Raf does make a move, what if my screwed-up magic messes it up again and makes me pop on the lights?

"Maybe the problem is that we're always around," Poodles says. "You need to go somewhere private. He's not going to make a move when the entire world is sitting on our porch."

147

"Now we're talking," I say. Maybe it'll work. After all, I've been doing my megels.

When we finish evening activity, I ask Raf if he wants to go for a walk.

His eyes widen in surprise (because of my brazen hussiness?) and then he quickly says, "Sure."

That was easy enough.

"Which way should we go?" he asks.

"Upper Field?" It has fewer bunks and therefore more privacy. We talk as we walk through the darkness. The night air is warm and dry.

"Let's go sit on the bleachers," he says, and we cross second base.

He steps up to the first level and takes my hand to help me along. Zing! Hello, electricity. We climb to the top and stretch our legs onto the row below.

"You can see the Big Dipper," Raf says, tilting his head back.

I forgot how cute his earlobe is. I have to stop myself from tugging on it. Instead I follow his lead and look at the sky. I'd make a wish, but there are too many stars to know which one I saw first. And it's not like I need stars to make wishes. "I wish we could stay at camp forever," I say anyway. "It's so pretty here."

"I know what you mean. A sky like this makes you wonder why you'd ever live in the city."

"Um, because our parents force us to?"

He laughs. "Right, there's that. But I'd like to go somewhere cool for college."

"Like where?"

The moonlight glows on his skin. "I don't know. Somewhere like this, in the middle of nowhere. University of . . . Iowa."

"Why Iowa?"

He tilts his head down and studies his hands. "They have a great writing program."

"Is that what you want to be? A writer?"

"I think so. What about you? What are your plans?"

My only real plan at the moment is to get him to kiss me. "I think I want to major in math."

"Cool. Do you think you'll stay in New York?"

"Lately I've been dreaming about California. Maybe I'll go to school out there." He hums the Mamas and the Papas' "California Dreamin'" and I join in.

We both laugh.

"Wouldn't you miss New York?" I ask.

"If I can make it there," he sings.

My turn: *"I'll make it—boom, boom—anywhere!"*

Together now: *"It's up to you, New York, New York!"*

"I love that song," he says.

Me too! Omigod, Raf and I have a song! "Admit it, Raf, you'll never leave Manhattan."

"I would miss it too much. And I'd miss my family. Wouldn't you?"

"Nah."

We laugh again.

"Kidding. I get along with my family. Most of the time. Well, some of the time. But I like being on my own. I'd miss my sister, though." I tilt my head and look up at the stars.

"Yeah, I could see that. If I went to Iowa, I'd miss my brothers."

"You're so lucky you have brothers. I wish I had a brother."

He grimaces, and I realize my glaring faux pas. I should *not* have mentioned the word *brother*. What was I thinking, bringing up Will?

"Rachel, I have a question for you," he says.

Heart. Beating. Quickly. "Yes?"

"You're not . . . Do you still have feelings for Will?"

"What? No!" No, no, no. Here's my chance. To get it all out in the open. "Actually . . . I wanted to tell you, Raf—

149

that I shouldn't have dated Will. After what happened with us. It must have been really weird for you."

He adjusts himself on the bleachers, leaning back on his elbows. "Yeah, you could say that. But it's not your fault. I should have told him it bugged me."

It bugged him? Yay!

"I should have explained to you about my dad's wedding," I say in a rush. "Why I had to miss Spring Fling. I should have—"

He shakes his head, waving my words away. "I should have been more understanding. I'm sure you were going through a rough time with your dad remarrying."

I was! He's so smart.

We're both quiet for a minute, and then he smiles and says, "I wish I had a sister."

"Really?" Better topic. It was getting a bit heavy there for a second.

"Sure. It'd be cute. Your sister's a cutie."

"Thanks."

"She always seems so serious. Like she's contemplating the fate of the world."

Poor Miri. "She kind of is."

"Does she like camp?"

"She's getting used to it."

He gives me a lazy smile. "Do you like it?"

I think about the lake, the stars, the fresh air. The coziness of my cabin. The fun of wearing my pajamas to flagpole and staying up late laughing with my bunkmates. "I love it."

"Do you think you'll come back next year?"

My left knee is only about a foot away from his right knee. "As a CIT, you mean? Definitely. You?"

"For sure. I'm coming back until I get to be head staff."

"Like Mitch?"

"Better than Mitch. I don't know how they put him in charge of anything."

"Oh, come on, I see him with his kids. He's fun! They love him."

And then there's silence. Now would be a perfect time for us to kiss.

Okay. Now.

Now.

"So," he says.

"So."

We're both quiet. Blood rushes up, and I'm light-headed.

He turns to look at me. His eyes are like brown paint. His fingertips lightly graze mine, and my hand is on fire. He leans in close and—

Bam! Owwwwwwwwwwwwwwwwwwwwwww!

Something hits me in the forehead. I might have screamed out loud, because Raf jumps up and says, "Are you okay?"

"I don't know," I say, head spinning. "What was that? Have I been shot?"

He bends down and rolls something off the seat and into his hand. "A soccer ball."

"That's what hit me?"

"Yeah. That was so weird. It came out of nowhere. I don't

think anyone's even around." He looks into the distance. "Hello?" he shouts. "Anyone there? Someone has to be there!"

No answer.

Not that I'm surprised. Because I know the truth. I did it. I did it again. I jinxed myself. What is wrong with me? I touch my palm to my throbbing forehead. "I don't feel so good."

He places his hand on top of mine. "It must have really hurt. Let me take you to the infirmary."

No! Not the infirmary! "That place is right out of a horror movie."

He laughs. "Dr. Dina is cool. Don't worry, I won't leave you."

"Promise?"

"Promise. I'll protect you from the bogeyman."

It's not the bogeyman I'm scared of. It's an out-of-control witch.

Me.

"*O thus be it ever, when free men shall stand* . . ."

Alison pats me on the head during the national anthem. "Poor Rachel."

"Poor me," I echo. Woe is me. It's the next morning, and I'm standing at flagpole with a massive bluish bruise on my forehead. "I'm hideous."

"You are not. You can barely see it. We'll cover it with some makeup, and presto, it'll be gone."

"I've already covered it with makeup. This *is* post-makeup." Sob.

"Then conquer we must, when our cause it is just . . ."

The only silver lining in this misadventure was that Raf proved to be a total sweetheart when the going got tough. He paged Dr. Dina for me, then sat with me for forty-five minutes before I was told that I was concussion-free. I spot him across the circle and give him a tiny my-head-still-hurts wave.

He makes a sad face and waves back.

"Did you get the kiss at least?" Alison asks.

I'd shake my head, but it hurts too much. "No."

"O'er the land of the free and the home of the brave!"

"I've never seen any two people have so many problems hooking up," she says. "You guys are cursed!"

"Walk, don't run, to the dining hall!" Anthony orders.

And I'm the one doing the cursing.

153

I spend the next few days pressing ice packs against my fore-head and practicing my megels. I even practice megeling the ice pack but stop after I accidentally drop it on my forehead, which gives me another headache. But despite the ice pack–dropping, I'm getting better at it. Really. Miri thinks I'm getting better too.

We agree to meet at two in the morning, this time in the mess hall.

"Why here?" Miri asks when I show up ten minutes late.

"More places to hide if we have to."

She yawns. "We should do this during the day."

Get with the program, missy. "We can't meet during the day. We'll be seen."

She rests her cheek against the table. "So? Big deal?"

Is she crazy? "Hello? Do you want the entire world to know you're a witch?"

"What's the difference?"

"People will treat you like a freak."

She closes her eyes. "They already treat me like a freak."

My heart breaks a little. "Still?"

"I don't care if they like me or not. It's not like I'm Miss Popularity in the city. But the girls in my bunk are so obnoxious. Whatever. They're really not worth my time."

"Maybe you should put a like spell on them or something."

"I don't like playing with people's feelings. You know that." She snaps her eyes open and sits up straight. "But if they knew I was a witch, they wouldn't mess with me. They wouldn't dare! They'd be too scared of me."

Her eyes glow in the dark.

At the moment, I'm a little scared of her too.

"Obviously you need to find someplace even more secluded," Alison says. She lobs the tennis ball over the net.

I would love to hit it back to her, but unfortunately I can't get my racket to connect with the ball. I also can't get my lips to connect with Raf's. In the past few days, despite my attractive purple forehead, Raf has wanted to spend time with me. But even so, we can't seem to make the lip connection. For instance, there was the time we were swimming in

GS, and as soon as he made the lean, a humungous wave knocked him over.

Where does a wave come from? We were in a lake!

"Go to the lookout!" Poodles screams from one court over, where she's playing with Carly.

I bend down to pick up the ball and try to position my-self the way that Lenny, the tennis instructor, showed me. "Where's the lookout?"

Alison approaches the net and points to the path be-hind the tennis shack. "About halfway up the mountain. Just follow that path. It's like a ten-minute walk."

"It's private and really romantic," Poodles tells us, then hits her ball into the net. "Damn! What's wrong with me today?"

Carly waves her racket over her head. "Why don't you try concentrating on the game?"

155

"Rachel," Poodles continues, "just tell him you heard it's nice and ask him to show you the way."

Wait a sec. "You think he already knows where it is? Who exactly has he been going up there with?"

Alison laughs. "Oh, relax. We all used to go up there as kids."

I just don't know if I can try again. I mean, why do I have to keep setting it up? If he likes me, shouldn't he try to set it up too?

"Oscar! Oscar! Oscar!"

Oscar steps out of the kitchen and bows to his cheering fans in the dining hall.

"Oscar! Oscar! Oscar!"

Apparently, every time the camp chef makes his famous lasagna for dinner, we give him a standing ovation.

"Oscar! Oscar! Oscar!"

He waves to the adoring crowd and then disappears back into the kitchen.

What can I say? The lasagna is delicious. I help myself to a third serving.

"Hey, Rache," says Raf, strolling up to our table. "Do you want to go on a hike during free play?"

"Hike? I'm not much of a hiker."

Poodles kicks me under the table. "Where are you going to hike?"

Raf's cheeks turn red. "I was thinking about the lookout."

Aha! The lookout! Yes! He wants to make out! It's about time.

"Sounds fun," I say. The make-out part, anyway. Not the hiking part. Maybe tonight will be the lucky night?

"Great. I'll swing by your bunk to get you."

Yes!

"You stack, Rachel!" everyone screams.

Huh? I look up to see fingers on noses.

Damn. Missed the ball on that one. Not bad, though. My record is pretty good. I've stacked only seven times all summer. Morgan's at twenty-three. Poodles has never stacked. She's, like, the world's best freezer, and she's always the first one to spot pig.

After a watermelon dessert, I quickly toss the plates and then rush back to my bunk to prepare. First I brush my teeth. (Oscar is quite liberal with the garlic in his lasagna.) Then

156

I rush past Cece into the cubby room and debate. What does one wear on a make-out hike? Do I aim for cute or athletic?

I put on my shortest black shorts and a bright green top. Then I temporarily remove my top and put on another layer of deodorant, just in case. Not too sure about making out, but I know that hiking can get vigorous.

I model for Alison, who's lying in her bed. "How do I look?"

"Spectacular. Did you put on your bug spray?"

"Not tonight. I need to smell delicious, not like eau de Off!"

"Well, hike 'em dead!"

"Thanks! You okay?" Her face looks kind of pale.

"Yeah," she says, rubbing her temples. "I have a tiny headache."

"You'd better rest up. I heard that tonight's evening activity is capture the flag."

157

"Will do." She pulls her covers over her shoulders. "Have fun."

I pass Morgan on the porch, and she wishes me good luck.

From the steps, I watch Raf climb the hill. "Ready?" he asks.

"Let's go."

Side by side, we walk to the tennis courts and then toward the shack.

"There are steps right behind here," he says.

"Great."

We chitchat up the hill. Maybe hiking isn't such a good idea. I'm already all sweaty. Even my hands are sweaty. Or maybe that's just nerves. I almost trip over a rock, but Raf catches my arm and steadies me.

We keep walking.

Are we there yet?

We walk some more.

Now are we there yet? I don't ask, since I don't want to be the annoying kid in the back of the car. This is the longest ten-minute walk I've ever been on.

"Want some water?" Raf asks, waving a bottle.

Finally, our mouths shall make contact! Though indirectly via a water bottle. I take a sip and pass it back to him. "Thanks."

We walk a few more minutes before he gestures to a ledge and announces, "Here it is."

Whoa! I knew we were coming to a lookout, but I didn't realize how much of one. I look down from the ledge. The entire camp is laid out below us like an oil painting. The bunks, the lake, the mountains, the woods . . . And the sun is setting over the lake, turning it a fiery shade of red. Wow.

"Nice, huh?"

"Beautiful."

He reaches over and takes my hand.

This is perfect. I'm so glad this will be the spot for our first real kiss. So what if I'm sweaty and my hands are clammy? It's beautiful, and we're alone, and there's a sunset!

He turns away from the view to look at me. And then, still holding my hand, he leans toward me.

Now! Now! Now! He closes his eyes. I close my eyes and feel his breath on my face.

And that's when I hear the buzzing.

What the—

Bzz! Bzz! Bzz! I open my eyes to see . . . a cluster of bees above our heads.

You've *got* to be kidding.

Raf's eyes flutter open and then widen to the size of tennis balls when he sees the tornado of insects around our heads.

We jump apart. He starts swatting the air, which can't be a good idea. They start stinging. Ouch! Ouch! Ouch! My neck, my arms, my legs . . . Raf's neck, Raf's arms, Raf's legs . . .

What did I do? How did I manage that? I need the bees to stop! Stop! Stop! They're not stopping. I knew the woods were dangerous! I need a spell. Yes, a spell! I scream:

"Stupid, annoying bees,
It's time for you to freeze!"

It suddenly gets cold, the buzzing comes to a halt, and the bees fly away.

159

Ow, ow, ow. Don't cry in front of Raf, don't cry in front of Raf. . . .

"That was so weird," he says, his face white. "And painful. Did they get you?"

I lift my swollen arms and swallow my tears. "Yeah."

He lifts *his* swollen arms. "Me too. What did you say to those bees?"

"Huh?" Oh, no! My hands get even sweatier. This could be bad. Really bad. What if he figures out I'm a witch? Or even worse, what if he thinks I'm a weirdo who talks to insects?

"You screamed something at the bees about them being annoying, but I couldn't hear too well because of that buzzing."

Phewf. "I was just scared, that's all," I say, and the next thing I know, I start crying.

"Aw, poor Rachel," he says, putting his arm around me. "This sucks, huh? I think they got my earlobes, too."

As the tears pour down my cheeks, I see that his adorable earlobes now resemble oversize cherries.

I start laughing. I can't help it. It's too ridiculous. And now Raf is laughing too.

And I know just what will make our pain go away. A kiss. A big fat juicy—

"And one of the bastards nailed my lip," he adds.

Of course it did. Kiss postponed . . . yet again.

Raf and I return to the infirmary.

This is the second time in a week that I've been here. Witchcraft can be hazardous, that's for sure. While we're sitting on the bench outside, waiting for Dr. Dina, I declare that I should just move in.

"Ow, stop making me laugh," Raf says. "It hurts."

"It hurts to move." My hands and arms are already starting to look like I've got a bad case of chicken pox. The only good thing about this bee disaster is that it's kind of like announcing to the whole camp that we're an item. You can't get any more obvious than matching bee stings from the lookout. Tee hee! It's like getting matching tattoos or hickeys or—dare I say?—wedding rings.

If only we *were* an item. Now I have to wait for his lip to heal before we can seal the deal. Hello, annoying. I wonder if there's a heal-and-seal spell in Miri's A^2.

"Have you ever been stung before?" I ask.

"No. You?"

"Yes. It hurt this time too."

He laughs. "Ow. I told you to stop doing that."

"Attenthion all camperth and counthlorth! Attenthion all camperth and counthlorth! It ith now the end of free play. Pleathe protheed to your evening activity. Koalath to Upper Field. Monkeyth to the rec hall, and Lionth to the gym."

"We're going to miss the activity," I say.

"It's okay. Someone will tell them where we are."

A few minutes later, Dr. Dina pokes her head out the door. She looks surprised to see us. "You again?"

"Me again."

"I might insist that you start wearing a helmet."

Hardy har har.

"And you, too?" she asks Raf.

"Yup."

She studies our stings. "They got you good. What did you do, kick a hive?"

"Not exactly."

"Sure looks like it. I've never seen so many stings. Good thing you're not allergic."

Raf sighs. "Lucky us."

After scraping out the stingers with a scary-looking metal blade, Dr. Dina washes the affected areas, gives us each ibuprofen and ice packs, and then asks us if we want to call our parents.

We both nod. Now that I'm in pain, I kind of miss my mom. She'd know how to make it stop. She'd at least know a spell that would make it stop.

I go first.

Ring, ring, ring.

"Hi! You've reached Carol, Rachel, and Miri. We can't come to the phone right now . . ."

I hang up. I don't want to leave a message. It will just worry her.

"Can I try my dad?" I ask Dr. Dina.

"Of course," she says.

My dad doesn't answer either. I try to swallow the lump that's lodged itself in the back of my throat.

My parents aren't exactly at home pining for us, are they?

Raf goes next, and of course his parents are home and thrilled to hear from him, bee stings and all.

For the first time all summer, I feel a wave of homesickness. I miss my mom. And my dad. My room. My nonlumpy bed. I even miss my mom's cooking. Okay, not really, but I do miss the sound of her voice.

Once Raf is done, the doctor sends us on our way. Our slow way, since we can barely walk.

Halfway up the hill, we bump into Mitch. "I was just looking for you," he says.

"Me?" Raf asks. "Why? Everything's okay. I just spoke to mom and dad."

"Not you. Rachel. Her counselors are wondering where she is." He notices our ailments. "What happened to you guys? Why did you call the 'rents?"

"We had a run-in with some bees," Raf says.

"Ouch. Listen, Rachel, you'd better head straight to your bunk."

"Why? What about capture the flag?"

Raf raises his swollen arm. "I don't think we're playing capture the anything in our condition," he says.

"Forget capture the flag," Mitch says. "Go to your bunk. I just came from an emergency head staff meeting."

"What happened?"

"One of the girls in your bunk is being sent home."

"What?" I scream. "Who? Why?"

He shakes his head. "The tall one."

The tall one? That's all he can tell me? Oh, no. Oh, no. It must have been Poodles. She got caught with Harris! I ignore my aching body and, clinging to my ice packs, sprint back to my bunk, hoping with all my heart it's not true.

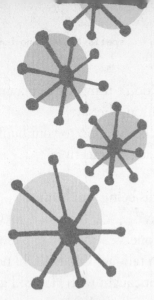

12
SMOKE SCREEN

By the time I reach my cabin, I'm out of breath. My entire bunk is standing on the porch with Deb. No, not my entire bunk. Morgan, Carly, and . . . Poodles? It's Poodles! Wait a second. Where's Alison?

"Guys? What's going on?"

Poodles runs down the steps and throws her arms around me.

Ow, ow, ow. I'm in no shape to be hugged. "I don't understand," I say.

"Alison got kicked out of camp!" she wails.

"I don't understand," I repeat.

"She's with Janice in the office right now. Her parents are coming to get her tonight!"

"But why?" What could Alison have done to merit getting kicked out of camp?

"She got caught smoking in the bathroom," Morgan says.

What? Impossible!

"That doesn't make any sense," I say. "She doesn't smoke."

"Apparently she does," Morgan says.

"No, she doesn't," I say adamantly. "She thinks smoking is disgusting! Where would she get cigarettes? It makes no sense."

"We have to do something," Poodles says. "Let's protest."

Deb shakes her head. "There's nothing you can do. It's too late. Rose caught her red-handed during free play."

"How?" I ask. What reason could the head of waterfront have to be in our bunk?

"She was outside the cabin and smelled smoke," Morgan recounts, as though watching the scene on a screen inside her head. "She stormed into our bunk and ordered Alison to open the door. When she did, the stall reeked of smoke, and Alison had a pack of cigarettes with her. I heard the whole thing. I smelled the smoke, too."

"If you smelled smoke, why didn't you make her stop?" I shriek.

Morgan shrugs. "Hey, don't yell at *me*. I wasn't the one smoking."

"So she was smoking in the bunk," Poodles says, her voice catching. "Big deal."

Deb puts her hand on my shoulder. "You know what Anthony said. Any camper caught with cigarettes will be sent home immediately. No exceptions. It's dangerous. Bunks are flammable."

165

"What about flatirons and kettles? People use those in the bunk and don't get booted out of camp," Poodles argues.

"You shouldn't," Deb says. "You're not supposed to."

Someone has a flatiron here?

"Girls, you know it's not up to me," Deb continues. "I'm just as devastated about this as you are. But rules are rules. There's nothing I can do."

"Talk to Anthony!" I say, choking up. "He's your boyfriend, isn't he?"

Deb turns bright pink. "What gave you that idea?"

Um, I saw you making out in the CL? I know that a counselor dating the head counselor is probably not allowed, but there's no time for lying. "This is crazy," I say instead. "Can't she get a warning?"

"I'm sorry," Deb says, tears welling in her eyes.

I can't stop my tears from rolling down my bee-stung cheeks. "Don't we even get a chance to say good-bye?"

"Everyone said good-bye," Carly says. "We helped her pack. Where were you?"

"In the infirmary."

"Are you sick?" Morgan asks. "You look like you have measles."

Poodles pats my shoulder. "Does it hurt?"

"I'm not sick; I'm stung." At the moment, I'm too upset to feel the pain. "Can't I go say good-bye?"

"I'm sorry," Deb says. "They told me to keep you all here."

I don't know what else to say. I don't know what to do. I want to scream and yell. I just don't believe it. I *know*

Alison. At least, I think I know Alison. And the Alison I know wouldn't smoke in the bathroom. She just wouldn't.

"This is so depressing." Poodles is writing our names on the wall in permanent marker. She said she wants to make sure that Alison remains a part of the bunk forever. Or at least until they repaint.

The rest of us are in bed, quiet. The girls of fifteen are laughing and talking, not even caring that their old friend was sent home, but we're too miserable to speak.

"I wish they'd shut up," Carly squeaks in her high-pitched teddy bear voice.

My bunk bed feels lonely with only me in it. Alison's bed has been stripped bare. Her cubby, too.

167

If only I hadn't gone hiking with Raf. I could have made Alison put out her cigarette as soon as I smelled the smoke. I would have made it rain on her if she didn't open the bathroom door. Hell, I made it rain once before. I can do it again. At least I could have warned her that Rose was coming. Or wished Rose out of the bunk.

If only I was a powerful enough witch to turn back time.

"Hey, why don't you take the lower bunk?" Morgan suggests.

"How can you even suggest that!" I snap. "That would be sacrilegious!" I flip over, trying to get comfortable. "What was Rose doing near our bunk, anyway? She never comes around here."

Poodles drops her marker and it clangs on the floor. "Do you think someone told on her?"

I try to remember if any of them were in the cabin when I left with Raf. I might have seen Cece . . . but she wouldn't have done it. Shaving cream is one thing, but getting an old friend kicked out of camp?

I know Morgan was here, but she wouldn't have ratted Alison out.

Just my luck that I find a camp BFF and she gets kicked out.

I'm the one who feels kicked. Kicked in the butt.

168

We sulk through flagpole. We sulk through breakfast. We sulk through cleanup. Today I have sweep as well as Alison's dustpan, since Morgan, who's chore-free, claims she's too depressed to help. Sheesh. It's not easy doing both jobs. It's like playing softball and being expected to pitch and catch simultaneously.

Speaking of softball, we're scheduled for a game against bunk fifteen. Since it's the four of us against the six of them, it's not much of a game.

"One of your girls should play for our team," Deb tells Penelope.

"Any of you willing to switch over?" Penelope asks her bunk.

"We don't need any help," says Poodles.

"We're fine on our own," says Carly.

Exactly. We can do it. I can do it. With a little help from my magic.

The bases are loaded. Liana's playing first base, Cece's on second, Natalie's on third, Kristin's catcher, and Molly's in the field. Trishelle, the pitcher, narrows her heavily lined eyes, purses her lips, and rolls her arm back and tosses the softball at me.

Now, the thing is, I am not a good hitter. And my seven thousand bee stings aren't going to help. But I don't care. I'm getting a home run. Now.

I focus all my raw will and—

Kabam! The ball soars over all their heads, way over the roof of bunk three.

The girls of both fourteen and fifteen gasp. Deb whistles.

169

Morgan, Carly, and Poodles run home while Deb hollers her heart out.

I slide into home, accidentally knocking over Kristin.

"My earring!" she screams. "I lost one of my earrings!"

I'm too excited to care. Go, Team Glinda! We're going to win in honor of Alison!

My home run euphoria is short-lived. First we have to spend twenty minutes sifting through the dugout for Kristin's precious pearl, and then Liana and Trishelle switch positions, and Liana strikes us all out.

Meanness must be stronger than magic. That's the only

explanation I can think of. Either that, or my megeling just hasn't been working.

In the next inning, all of fifteen's balls fly directly into wide-open spaces. Deb insists that both she and Penelope jump into the game to even it out, but it doesn't help. The balls start coming directly at me, and I keep dropping them. I try to use my magic to help me catch them, but nothing works.

They win nineteen to four.

We're silent during lunch. When Deb calls "freeze," we ignore her, and each of us cleans up after herself.

Carly hangs her head. "I can't believe Alison is really gone. This is the worst summer ever."

I'm starting to agree. I can't believe it. This was supposed to be the best summer of my life. It started out as the best summer of my life, so what happened?

The lunch meat loaf is burnt and tasteless, reflecting our mood.

"Cheer up, girls," Deb tells us. "Tomorrow will be a better day."

It can't get worse, can it?

Unfortunately, it can. And does. After lunch, it gets much, much worse.

It's rest hour, and Deb is handing out the mail.

"Morgan!" She tosses a beige envelope to Morgan. "Poodles and Rachel, you both got packages."

Poodles gets her copies of *Entertainment Weekly* and

People. I get a box of something called Summer Rain from Jennifer.

Huh?

Is it possible that this time Jennifer got me something normal, like perfume?

I read the label: *For feminine cleansing. A douche.*

Ew, ew, ew. What is wrong with her? She obviously doesn't want us to be friends if she's trying to humiliate me in front of my bunkmates.

Directly into the garbage it goes.

After Deb is done distributing, she announces, "Bunk meeting!"

I'm lying on my stomach, writing Alison a letter. Or trying to. I don't know exactly how to start or what to say. *Dear Alison, What were you thinking? Why didn't you tell me you smoked? Are you an idiot? You ruined my summer.* I sigh, put down my pen, and roll onto my side to face Deb.

171

Carly takes a break from her sit-ups, and Morgan stops tweezing her eyebrows. Poodles continues flipping through her magazine and asks, "What now? Gonna send another one of us home?"

"Come on, girls," Deb says. "Cheer up."

"Whatever," Carly says.

Liana is silently standing by the door, her arms folded across her chest. What is she doing here? Eavesdropping again?

"I have some news that I think you're all going to be excited about," Deb says.

"You're bringing Alison back?" I ask, my eyes lingering on Liana.

Deb shakes her head. "No, we can't do that. By now she's—"

"Probably grounded for life," Morgan mutters.

Poor Alison.

"Back home," says Deb. "Anyway, Janice was concerned about the small number of girls in this bunk, so she asked if anyone in fifteen would consider moving over to this side—and Liana volunteered!" Deb finishes.

You've got to be kidding. We're all silent.

Liana flips her hair.

Un-friggin'-believable. Why does she want to be on this side, anyway? We're practically at war with her and her friends!

Deb waves the intruder over. "Liana, welcome to your new home! You're going to love it on this side of the world. Why don't you bring your blankets over and make your new bed?" she suggests, and then points to—no, don't do it!—the bottom of my bunk.

Noooooooooooo. Why didn't I take it when I had the chance? Though honestly, I think it would be worse to have Liana on top, always climbing over me whenever she wants to get up to her bed. Knowing her, I think she'd purposely step on my face.

I'll show her. I'll toss and turn and turn and toss, so that she never gets a good night's sleep.

Liana moves right in. By the end of rest hour, she's made her satin purple bed and set up her section of the shelf. She has more makeup than the pharmacy in there, as well as a heavy-looking antique jewelry box. What kind of person brings something so fancy to camp? What if it gets broken? And what kind of jewelry does she have inside, anyway? I never see her wearing any of it.

The rest of the girls are watching her with curiosity. I'm watching her with a whole lot of suspicion.

I pull Poodles over during basketball drills on Lower Field to share my thoughts: "Something is up with Liana."

Poodles' blue eyes widen. "What do you mean?"

I bounce my ball to her. "I don't know. But why would she ask to be switched when she's BFF with her whole bunk? It's not like she's friends with any of us."

She bounces the ball back to me. "That is a good point. She could be up to something. We'll keep an eye on her. I'll tell the others."

The next day, all four of us watch and treat her suspiciously. We are a unit and Liana is the outsider, and we display this during second period at soccer. Liana is now on our team—not that you could tell. None of us passes her the ball. There's no way I'm going to believe she'd actually play against her buddies from fifteen.

After ten minutes of running around, Morgan is gasping. "Does anyone have water? I could have sworn I brought mine, but I don't know where it went."

Liana appears next to her with a full bottle. "You can have some of mine," she says sweetly.

Morgan steps back in surprise. After a moment's hesitation, she takes a long sip from Liana's bottle. "Thanks," she says, smacking her lips.

Liana smiles. "Happy to help."

After that, Morgan passes Liana the ball. And Liana doesn't waste it. She kicks it directly into fifteen's net.

"Go, Liana!" Morgan cheers.

Go away, maybe.

So she scored a point for our team. So what? She's obviously up to something. But what?

After soccer, Morgan seems to have either forgotten or dismissed our Proceed with Caution plan. Suddenly, Morgan and Liana are BFFs. They sit together at lunch. They pick each other as partners for tennis.

Part of me is not entirely surprised. I like Morgan, but sometimes she's a little obnoxious, not to mention crude.

"There's something off about her," Poodles says after tennis, as we pick up our stray balls. "But I can't put my finger on it."

"I never did trust Morgan a hundred percent," I say.

Poodles looks at me funny. "Why are you backstabbing Morgan? I'm talking about Liana. I don't trust her at all."

My face burns. I feel chastised, and even angrier at Liana. Look what she's turning me into! A backstabbing bunkmate. "I don't trust Liana either," I say. "Or like her."

We look up and catch Liana glaring at me. Then she whispers something to Morgan and the two of them crack up.

Poodles tosses her ball into the air and then catches it. "The feeling is obviously mutual. She doesn't seem to like you, either."

Raf and I are in the playground, swinging side by side, enjoying our afternoon snack.

Everything about this moment is yummy to the power of three. One, instead of plain milk, there's surprise chocolate milk; two, I'm on a swing; and three . . . well, Raf.

"How do you like your new bunkmate?" he asks.

I kick my legs up to gain momentum. "There's something weird about her."

"What do you mean?"

"Just something," I say noncommittally. Recalling what Poodles said about backstabbing, I don't tell Raf all about why I don't like her. I don't want him to think I'm mean. Or paranoid.

"Hi, guys," I hear.

Speak of the devil. Liana is standing in front of us with Morgan. Morgan is wearing her typical itsy-bitsy bikini top and short swim shorts. Liana, on the other hand, is looking glamorous, as usual, in a tight white halter top and a long navy blue wrap skirt.

She really does have the best clothes—and a lot of them. Now that I think about it, I realize I've never seen her wear the same outfit twice. How is that possible? Her cubby is too neat to hold so many clothes. But I guess she has to keep it that way to keep track of them all.

I'd be happier right now if I weren't wearing a particularly grubby black T-shirt and gray shorts that I love to wear but keep forgetting to toss into my laundry bag.

Liana's eyes are on me. "Need a push?"

"No, thanks." Unless it involves pushing you out of the way.

She turns to my quasi boyfriend and smiles. "Raf, I'd love to give you a push."

The chocolate milk in my stomach curdles. I can't believe she said that. Who introduced them, anyway? She smiles at him sweetly. Why is she flirting with him? *Hands off*, I want to yell. *Step away from the swing!*

"I'm all right," he says.

"You know, Raf," she says, "you look so much like Will. Don't you think so, Rachel?"

Just where is she going with this? She doesn't know about us, does she? She can't know . . . unless Morgan told her.

"I think he looks like himself," I answer, and glare at the two girls.

"Really?" Liana purrs. "I think he looks just like Will. But better-looking."

If she doesn't stop hitting on my Raf, I'm going to . . . Before I can control myself, her chocolate milk leaps out of her glass and lands in a blob on her previously clean white halter.

She looks at her shirt in shocked silence. Then she looks up at me and scowls.

As if it's my fault.

Okay, it *is* my fault, but she has no way of knowing that.

I feel guilty for a half second, before Raf jumps off his swing and offers to get napkins from the kitchen. Liana follows him, giving me a nasty smile.

Morgan spots Will and runs off to shake her boobs.

Thanks, Liana, for killing my romantic moment by the swings. Yeah, I know it's my fault for letting my magic get the best of me, but it wouldn't have happened if she hadn't flirted with my guy.

As I sit on the swing by myself, I decide that I might need to make another visit to Miri tonight. It's becoming apparent that I need something stronger than megels.

Deb, Poodles, Carly, and I decide to work on our tans during GS, while Liana and Morgan and all of bunk fifteen splash around in whale.

"I can't believe they're BFFs all of a sudden," Carly says while reapplying suntan lotion to her legs.

"Girls, be nice," Deb says. "She's not that bad. Sure, she's a little high-strung, but—"

"You *have* to be nice," Poodles snorts.

I spot Miri alone in her bunk line. The rest of her bunk is in the water. I wave her over. "What were you doing?"

She spreads out her towel next to mine. "Thinking."

"Why aren't you swimming?"

She shrugs.

"Want me to go swimming with you?"

"No, thanks."

"Why not?"

"I'm not wearing a bathing suit."

"Miri, you have to wear a bathing suit on the beach."

"I didn't think I'd have anyone to go swimming with."

"I'll swim with you."

"I don't have my suit on, remember?"

I sigh. "You should be socializing during GS, not just thinking."

177

"Raf isn't socializing."

I look at where she's pointing and spot Raf lying on his back, engrossed in a book. He's so cute when he's studious. "That's different. He's not socializing because he wants to read, not because he doesn't have any friends."

I swear I didn't mean for that to come out as awful as it sounded.

"Why are you so mean to me?" Miri snaps, turning bright red. She pushes herself off the sand, grabs her towel, and starts walking away. "I've made friends, by the way. Not that you would notice."

"Mir, stay. I'm sorry. Hang out with me."

For a second, I think she's going to keep walking, but then she sits back down. "Can we do some Glinda-ing tonight?" I ask. My code word for training.

She hesitates. "I can't."

"Why not?"

She plays with the lanyard bracelet on her wrist. "Because . . . because I'm exhausted. I didn't sleep well last night and I need to get some rest."

"Oh. Well, fine. Tomorrow night?"

"Maybe."

"Good. And I like your bracelet. Great stitching. Very impressed that you learned square."

A long shadow cuts across my upper torso. Liana is blocking my sun.

"Hi, Rachel." She gives Miri a big smile. "Hi, Miri."

Excuse me? First Raf and now Miri? "How do you know my sister?"

Liana kneels down on my sister's towel, and Morgan sits beside her. "Mir and I are old friends."

"Oh, really?" Mir? Is she kidding me?

"We're taking tennis together," Miri explains hurriedly. "As an elective."

Liana takes a big drink of her water. "Deb, you look kind of dehydrated. You'd better drink some water."

"What? Oh, thanks." Deb takes a gulp, then hands the bottle back.

"Poodles, do you want any? You're also looking kind of red."

"No, thanks."

Liana shrugs. "Carly?"

Carly shakes her head.

Gee, thanks. She offers it to everyone but me and my sister. Not that I want any. We don't need any Liana cooties.

"Your sister is fantastic, Rachel," Liana says. "Her serve is deadly."

Miri beams. "That means so much coming from you. Did you know that Liana is an internationally ranked player?"

Oh, please. She is such a liar.

Morgan whistles. "Wow."

Liana brushes the compliment away with the back of her slender hand. "No big deal."

"That will look totally cool on college applications," Morgan says.

Deb eyes Liana's muscled legs. "Is that how you stay in such great shape?"

One point Liana. But the game isn't over yet.

The next few days pass by in a blur. Visiting day is on Sunday, so people are preparing for their parents' arrival. I can't believe that summer is half over. I can't believe that summer is half over and Raf and I still haven't kissed.

I can't seem to get any time alone with him. Every time it's just the two of us, someone pops up. Raf and I are sitting on the porch at night; Morgan joins us. We're swimming at GS; Trishelle splashes us. We're sitting together at evening activity; Liana sits next to us.

He would totally kiss me if he had the chance. Right?

Unless he hasn't kissed me because he doesn't like me. No. That can't be! He likes me! He broke up with Melissa because he likes someone else. But what if it's not me? He tried to kiss me (several times, to no avail), so it *has* to be me. What if it was me but now he's changed his mind? What if he's still weirded out about me and Will? No. He still likes me, or else he would have given up by now. I just need time alone with him. Time alone to cement the deal. To cement our lips. Together.

Funny, I can't seem to get any time alone with Miri, either.

I stop by her bunk at supper washup, but she's not there. I can't find her at free play, either. I finally corner her the next day at SI. "What do you mean you're still tired?" I ask her. It's Thursday morning, three days before visiting day. We're sitting on the bench at the top of the beach, waiting for the period to start.

"I need more sleep."

"What about at free play? We'll use the invisibility umbrella."

"I'm busy at free play."

"With what?"

"Stuff."

"Miri, come on." I close my eyes and let the sun warm my cheeks.

"No. What about after evening activity, before curfew?" she suggests.

"That's not a good time for me," I say.

"No, you're too busy with Raf then."

True. "If I'm not with him, then he can't kiss me."

"You're choosing Raf over me," she says.

"You're choosing sleep over me!"

"Anyway, you don't need me to practice your megels."

"But, Miri, I think I'm ready to—"

"Have you perfected your megels yet?"

"No. . . ."

"Then you don't need me. None of you need me."

My eyes shoot open and I turn to look at her. "What are you talking about?"

Her face is flushed and it's not from the sun. "Huh?"

"What do you mean nobody needs you?"

"How many letters has Mom written you?"

"Um, I don't know. About two per week." I lean over, pick up a few grains of sand, and roll them between my fingers.

Miri pales. "Oh."

" 'Oh' what? How many has she written you?"

"None."

"What?"

181

"She hasn't written me once."

"That's impossible."

She shrugs. "It's true."

"They probably got lost."

"Why would your letters find you but mine get lost?"

Good question. "Hey, are you getting weirdo packages from Jennifer?"

"Yes! What is up with that? This week I got a box of tampons. What's wrong with her?"

"Better than what I got this week—a tube of Preparation H."

She snickers. "That *is* worse."

"Mir, you're getting Dad's e-mails, right?"

"Yeah. Dad, who only has time to write us joint e-mails."

Her not getting any mail from Mom still doesn't make sense to me. "Hey, Mir, maybe Mom has your bunk number wrong, and Stef is sending them to the wrong cabin. Next time you write her, make sure to tell her the right one."

"Forget it. I'm not writing her if she can't be bothered to write me."

"Miri, I'm sure that's not it. . . ."

"She's too busy with Lex. You have Raf, and Mom has Lex. Hey, you don't think he's coming for visiting day, do you?"

"I don't know. Probably not."

"What about Jennifer?"

"Yeah, she's probably coming. Dad wrote that they're driving up with Prissy and then leaving her here."

"I wonder how he's getting away with that since starter camp begins the day *after* visiting day."

"He probably paid them a little extra to take Prissy a day early."

"See? He doesn't care about any of us either."

"Miri!"

She scoops up a pile of sand with her hand and lets it sift through her fingers. "It's true. All he cares about is Jennifer and having a new baby with her. That's why we're at camp to begin with."

She's not completely wrong. I mean, that is how going to camp came about, but I don't think that Dad doesn't care about us. He loves us, and so does Mom. They're just busy with their own lives.

"Miri!" I say, smacking my bare knee with my hand. "I just realized that Mom and Dad are both coming to visiting day! Both of them! In the same place! How uncomfy will that be?"

"I don't care," she says. "It's their mess. Let them worry about it."

183

Unfortunately, my psyche doesn't work that way. I almost wish they weren't coming. Now I have to spend the next few days worrying about whether my mom and Jennifer will talk to each other, whether seeing my dad will hurt my mom's feelings, and whether they both realize that the other one's going to be here. . . . I can't help getting annoyed at them. The past month has been parental-issue free.

Rose blows her whistle, interrupting my children-of-divorce daydream. "There should be a name for bad daydreams," I say to Miri. "For nightmares during the day."

"Daymares?" Miri suggests, taking off her shorts.

"Everyone in the water!" Rose orders. "Hustle, hustle."

Oh, right, there's already a name. It's *swimming lessons*.

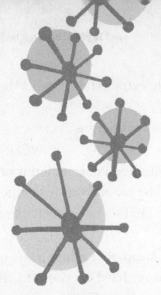

13
HELLO, MUDDAH.
HELLO, FADDAH.

"Ten, nine, eight, theven, thix, five, four, three, two—"

All the girls of fourteen and fifteen are waiting on the porch for two o'clock, ready to pounce. Today is visiting day, and our parents are currently gathering in Upper Field, which has been turned into a temporary parking lot. Campers are not allowed off their porches until Stef says so.

"One!"

She blows her whistle and we all take off. Since our bunk is one of the closest to Upper Field, we'll probably be the first ones there.

We run down the hill, and that's when we see the stampede of parents. There are hundreds of them, all smiling and clutching packages, on a mission to find their kids. I jump back to get out of their path. I think I'll just wait till my parents come this way. No reason to fight the tide.

About ten minutes later, I hear a high-pitched voice: "Am I going to sleep here, Mommy? Here? What about there?"

It's Prissy! A warm rush of emotion washes over me. How about that? I didn't even realize that I missed her until this second. Who'd have thought? What the heck—I run against the crowd to find them. And there they are! Prissy is trying to walk while twirling in her white sundress (which will get filthy in about five seconds; I hope Jennifer packed her some more appropriate camp clothing). Jennifer is wearing a trendy knee-length jean skirt and a silky purple sleeveless top. Her blond hair is pulled back in a tight ponytail, and her eyes are shaded with big sunglasses. My dad looks as badly dressed as always. He's wearing beige shorts that show off his skinny, hairy legs and a striped tucked-in golf shirt. But it's so good to see him!

"Hi!" I scream, trying to throw my arms around all of them. The familiar smell of their lemony fabric softener brings unexpected tears to my eyes.

185

"Hello, honey!" my dad says, squeezing me tightly.

I reach up to pat his bald spot. "I missed you guys!"

"You look so nice and tanned," Jennifer says. "And your hair got so long and beautiful!"

I pick Prissy up and spin her around. "Ready for camp?"

"Yup! I packed my flip-flops and my bathing suits and my princess doll and my teddy bear and my—"

An anxious mother pushes her way past us and I nearly trip.

"Sorry," she says sheepishly. "Trying to find my kids!"

"No worries," I say, à la Poodles.

"Have you been getting my packages?" Jennifer asks.

"Oh yeah. Um, thanks."

"My pleasure! Hope you enjoy!"

Alrighty.

My dad peers down the road. "Where's your sister?"

"I'm sure she'll show up in a sec. My bunk is right up there. Why don't we get out of everyone's way?" They follow me up the hill to my cabin.

My dad leans against the railing. "So this is where you live?"

"This is it." I keep a lookout for my mom and Miri. They'll be coming from different directions, but I should be able to spot them both on the road.

"Can I live here too?" Prissy asks, and then sticks her finger into her nose.

Jennifer knocks her hand away. "Sweetheart, we talked about that, didn't we? Fingers don't go anywhere near your face. Got it?"

"But what if I have food in my teeth?"

"I packed your dental floss. It's in your pink princess cosmetic bag."

"But I don't like to floss! It hurts my hands."

Within the next ten minutes, most of the parental traffic has subsided. I finally spot Miri making her way up the road. "Mir! We're over here."

She scowls. "Why didn't you come to my bunk? I was waiting for you."

"And hello to you, too," my dad says. He puts his arms out and waits for Miri to walk up the hill and give him a hug.

186

"Hi," Miri says quietly, backing out of my father's hold. "Hi, Jennifer. Hi, Prissy. Is Mom here?"

"Not yet," I say. What is wrong with her? A little enthusiasm, maybe? And where *is* Mom? It's two-fifteen! All the other parents have been camping out since one-thirty. She gets only three hours with us, and she's wasting them!

Miri shrugs. "She probably forgot."

"She wouldn't forget," I snap. Why is she making Mom look bad in front of Dad and Jennifer? I try to give her a "shut up" look, but she's too busy staring at her sneakers to notice.

"I'm sure she'll be here," Jennifer chirps. "She probably got stuck in traffic. How is she getting here, anyway? She doesn't have a car. Daniel, why didn't you think to offer her a lift?"

Now that would have been interesting.

"Can I see my bunk now?" Prissy asks.

"Not yet, honey. We're waiting for Rachel's mom."

"Rachel and Miri's mom," Miri says.

"What, honey?" my dad asks.

My sister crosses her arms in front of her chest. "Miri. Me. Does anyone remember me?"

"Of course, dear. We're here to *see* you."

"No, you're here to drop Prissy off."

"What's wrong with you?" Dad asks. "We just got here and you're already picking a fight? We haven't seen you in almost a month."

"Sorry," Miri grumbles.

"Why don't we walk to Upper Field?" I say extra brightly, trying to instill some cheerfulness. What is Miri's problem? "Mom might not know where to go." I lead the way to Upper Field and immediately spot my mother crossing the parking lot. At least, I think it's my mother.

It looks like her. Kind of. But she's slimmer and smiling, and she has short hair the color of Morgan's.

"Is that Mom?" Miri asks incredulously.

"Where?" asks Jennifer. "I don't see her."

When the redhead—aka Mom—sees us, she starts waving her hand like a crazy woman.

"She looks great," Dad says. "Who is that with her?"

I was too shocked by Mom's new do to notice Lex at first, but there he is, holding her hand. Do they have to do that in front of my dad?

I look at my dad to see if he's weirded out.

His features look frozen, like he's been Botoxed, and he immediately reaches for Jennifer's hand. Yeah, you could say he's weirded out. True, he's the one who dumped my mom, so it's not like he has a right to be, but I guess it's strange to see your ex with someone new, no matter what.

"It's Lex," Miri says. "I can't believe she brought him."

"He *is* her boyfriend," I say.

"This isn't Take Your Boyfriend to Work Day," Miri snaps, kicking the ground with the toe of her shoe. "It's Spend Time with Your Kids Day."

My mom is still waving her free hand. I run up to give her a hug. "Hi!" I squeal. "You look great."

"Thanks, so do you."

"A little help from your fairy godmother?" I whisper in her ear.

"A little help from a salon in SoHo. You like?"

"I love. You look ten years younger!" I check out her new svelteness. "Have you been working out?"

"Lex and I have taken up jogging."

If Lex can get my mom to stay healthy, then he's worthy of being upgraded to hug status. I pull away from my mom and give him a quick squeeze. "Very impressive, Lex. You got her off the couch."

He tips his cowboy hat. "She outruns me every time."

"That's because you're a hundred." Miri mumbles this from a few feet away, but I hear her.

My mother does too. "Miri!"

"What? I'm kidding. Hi, Mom." Miri gives her a millisecond-long hug and pulls away. "You're late."

189

"We got a little lost," Mom admits.

"She's not that late," I say quickly. "Do you want to see my bunk?"

"That sounds great," Lex says. He tips his cowboy hat at my dad. "You must be Daniel."

My mom's cheeks turn pink. "Lex, meet Daniel. And Jennifer. And Prissy. Everyone, meet Lex, my friend."

They all shake hands while I die of uncomfortableness.

"I love your hair color," Jennifer says to my mom.

My mom fluffs her new hair. "Thank you."

"It's so much fun. Maybe I'll become a redhead too. It's so feisty. What do you think, Daniel?"

I think I want to hide in Lex's car. "Follow me," I say,

leading the pack back to bunk fourteen. What am I going to do with them for the next two and a half hours? I really don't want to hang out and discuss feisty hair colors. I push open the door and wave them all in.

Poodles' bed is covered in packages. Carly is showing her parents, who both look like her, around the bunk. I introduce my parents to her parents.

Liana is nowhere to be found, which suits me just fine. Having my mom and dad both in the same place at the same time is stress enough for one day.

After about five seconds, Miri says, "When are we going to *my* bunk?"

Sigh. "Fine, let's go now," I say. "There's nothing more to see here, anyway."

"Um, where's your little girls' room?" my mother asks.

"The bathroom is just past the cubby room," I answer, motioning with my chin. "But trust me, you don't want to go there." Even though we cleaned extra hard for visiting day, I don't think parents should be subjected to our graffiti, never mind the doll-sized toilets.

"Trust me, I do. I had four cups of coffee this morning." She laughs and makes a run for it.

"You guys go on ahead," I say. "I'll wait for Mom."

"I'll wait with you," Lex says, looking uncomfortable.

He probably doesn't want to go with Dad and Jennifer, I think as I watch the others leave. Not that I blame him. Talk about awkward.

"Hello, Rachel," says Liana in her nasal voice. She's perched on her bed, her legs crossed and ladylike.

Huh? Where did she come from? She's so sneaky. "Hello, Liana," I say through clenched teeth. "Where's your family?"

"They're traveling for the summer, so I told them not to bother."

"Oh. Okay. Have a nice day."

"I'm dying to meet your family."

You already stalk my quasi boyfriend and my sister, so I'd rather not. "You're too late."

"Pity." The next thing I know, she's on her feet, shaking hands with my mother's boyfriend. "Hello, Lex. It's such a pleasure to meet you. I love your shirt."

Such a pleasure? What a pleasure it would be if she jumped out a window. Why is it a pleasure to meet Lex, anyhow? Why does she care? And what's up with the "I love your shirt"? Is there a bucket I can throw up in?

Come to think of it, how exactly does she know his name? Ah. Miri. Why is Miri feeding Liana background on our family? I make a mental note to ask her later. To interrogate her, actually. What the heck is going on with my sister?

Lex tips his hat. "It's a pleasure to meet you, too. And you are?"

The bathroom door opens and slams. We turn to see my mother, who's readjusting her outfit. "Those stalls are tiny," she says.

I turn back around, but Liana is gone. How rude.

"Where did she go?" Lex asks.

"Who knows?" Hopefully far, far away.

"Who are you talking about?" my mother asks.

"One of my bunkmates," I say. "Um, can we please go now?" The last thing I want to do is talk about Liana.

We head to Miri's bunk and meet up with the others. Prissy is hopping from foot to foot, looking bored out of her mind. "Can we go see my bunk now?"

"I want to show them the tennis courts," Miri says.

"Why don't we stop by Prissy's bunk first, and then we'll go to the courts?" Jennifer says.

So we all head to bunk one, Prissy's bunk. My mom and Lex decide to wait on the porch, but the rest of us go inside.

"Look, honey, here you are!" Jennifer says, pointing to a photograph on the bed near the window. "That's the picture we sent in last month, remember? And look, they wrote your name inside a big red heart. Later, Daniel will get your bags from the car, and we'll get you all settled. How does that sound?"

At first Prissy looks excited, but then she says, "Am I the only girl in the bunk?"

"No, the other five girls are coming tomorrow," says a tall brunette. "I'm Tilly, your counselor."

"Oh, hello!" Jennifer says excitedly. "So nice to meet you. Prissy, say hello to Tilly."

Prissy suddenly gets shy and buries her face in her mother's legs. Then she pulls away, looks around the bunk, and announces, "I want to go home."

"What are you talking about, sweetheart? You've been counting down the days until camp."

Prissy stamps her leather sandal on the ground. "I want my bed."

"This is your bed for two whole weeks," Jennifer says.

192

"I don't like this bed. It smells like pee."

"You'll like it, I promise. Rachel, won't she like it?"

"Yes, Prissy, you will," I say, sitting down on one of the bare mattresses. "You're going to have so much fun!"

She considers this for a moment, then asks, "Why will I have fun?"

I'm too tired for this. "Because . . . because you can go sailing."

"I don't want to go sailing."

"She probably can't go sailing," Miri says. "You can only go sailing if you have your dolphin."

Prissy's face crumples. "But I want to go sailing!"

I shoot Miri a dirty look. "Prissy, you can go swimming."

"I don't know how to swim."

"You'll learn," says my dad.

"I don't want to learn." She starts crying and then sobbing, but then she notices my lanyard bracelets, stops abruptly, and points. "Did you get those here?"

I roll one around my wrist. "I made it here. You can make one too."

"Can I make it now?"

"I think A&C is open," I say.

"I thought we were going to the tennis courts," Miri whines.

"Let's just get her some lanterns first," Jennifer says.

"Lanyards," I say. "Look, why don't Mom and Lex go with Miri to the tennis courts, and I'll take you guys to A&C and we'll meet them there when we're done?"

We find Mom and Lex making out on the porch steps.

"Yuck!" screams Prissy.

193

I'm too mortified to talk. There are parents roaming around all over this place. Children, too. Little children, who will be scarred for life.

Mom and Lex pull away from each other and at least have the decency to look embarrassed.

"Forget it," Miri says, scowling. "I don't want to be alone with these two. Let's all go to A&C first."

After our stop at the A&C, Stef announces snack time over the loudspeaker ("What did she say?" Prissy screams at the top of her lungs. "What's a *thnack*?"), so we go to the picnic tables and pile Danishes and cantaloupe on our paper plates. I introduce my mom and dad to all the other kids. And then the kids introduce my parents to their parents. I feel my face flush when I introduce them to Raf's parents, because the last time I saw his parents, I was on a date with Will.

194

Then we get Prissy's stuff from my dad's car and set her up. Then we check out the lake, and my dad decides he wants to go rowboating, and then all of us—oh yes, the whole clan—get fitted for life jackets by Harris (Jennifer, my mom, and Prissy giggle and bat their lashes), and we pile onto the lake.

Can you say *awkward*? I can't help counting the minutes until it's time for all the parents to go home.

When we get back to shore, the head staff is handing out Popsicles. Stef returns to the loudspeaker and announces, "Vithiting Day will be over in ten minuteth. Would all parenth thay their good-byeth and thtart making their way to Upper Field?"

When our parents drive off—separately, of course—and Prissy is clinging to my hand, blinking away tears, I realize that Miri never showed them the tennis courts. "Why didn't you remind us?" I ask. I realize that I forgot about something else, too—I meant to ask my mom if she's been sending her letters to Miri to the right bunk. Oops.

"Because no one cared," she answers.

"That's not true."

"Yeah, it is."

"What's gotten into you lately?"

"What's gotten into *you*?"

Prissy tugs me toward the A&C. "Can I get more lanyard?"

"Let's go find Tilly," I tell her.

"I'm going back to my bunk," Miri says.

After depositing Prissy with Tilly, I stop by Miri's bunk to try to talk to her again.

"She's not here," says one of her bunkmates, a scrawny girl in full headgear paraphernalia. This is one of the girls who's picking on Miri? Please.

195

"Do you know where she is?"

She shrugs.

I check the tennis courts but don't find her there, either.

I finally see Miri at dinner, but she's uncommunicative. Prissy, on the other hand, won't stop talking.

"I got more lanyard, and Tilly showed me how to do butterfly but I'm not so good at it, so I braided them instead and then I got to help make the other girls' beds, and their names are Mandy and Candy and Dahlia and Caprice, and they're all coming for two weeks just like me, except Mandy and Candy and Dahlia are seven and Caprice is six like me—"

"That's great, Prissy, but I have to get back to my table, 'kay?"

She's still talking as I make my way across the mess hall.

"You looked like you wanted to kill your family today," Poodles says to me.

"I did. It was so uncomfortable. It was the first time my mom, her boyfriend, my dad, and his wife were all together. It was awful. So embarrassing. Carly, pass the spaghetti?"

Liana, who's sitting next to Carly, grabs the pasta and serves herself. "Rachel, tell us. Why was it so awful?"

"What do you mean? It just was. When your parents are divorced, you don't want them in the same room."

"Seems immature to me. If they don't care, why should you?"

"Because I do." Why's it her business, anyway?

"Where was your family?" Carly asks Liana.

"They're way too busy to come here," she huffs. "They're yachting in France. With some Greek prince."

Morgan's eyes widen into saucers. "Really? A prince?"

"That is so cool," Deb says. "Have you met the prince?"

"Of course I have," Liana says with extra haughtiness.

I don't buy any of this. "Oh, come on."

"Don't believe me if you don't want to. Unlike you, I don't care about what other people think."

I'm about to tell her where to get off when Deb yells, "Freeze!" at the top of her lungs.

My nose is tickling. I think I'm going to—

No! "Achoo!"

"You stack, Rachel," Deb says.

That sneeze came out of nowhere. I hope I'm not getting sick.

"Whoops," Liana says as she dribbles tomato sauce

across the table. "Hope you don't get all dirty when you clean up. Sorry about that, Rache."

No, she's not.

The only thing around here making me sick is her.

Evening activity is charades in the rec hall. Unfortunately, it's interrupted by Tilly, who finds me and asks me to go with her. "Prissy wants you. She's seriously homesick."

"Sure," I say, grabbing my sweatshirt. "See you later?" I ask Raf.

"Okay."

Miri, who's sitting two rows up, turns around. "Where are you going?"

"To check on Prissy. She's homesick."

"Do you want me to come?"

"Who are you?" Tilly asks.

"I'm her sister."

"I thought Rachel was her sister."

"She has two sisters."

"Oh," says the counselor. "No, you can stay. She just asked for Rachel."

Miri's face clouds.

"Why don't we both go?" I say.

"Never mind, I don't want to go," Miri says, and whips her head back around.

"Miri, come on," I say, but she ignores me.

Why is my entire family so crazy?

I follow Tilly all the way across camp to bunk one, wave

hello to the on-duty counselor on the porch, and enter Prissy's cabin.

"Hey, kiddo," I say.

She jumps off her bed and throws her arms around me.

"There are ghosts under the beds," she wails. "Stay with me?"

"Of course."

She wraps her arms more tightly around my waist.

Two seconds of silence and then: "I want to go hooooooooooooooooooooome."

"Prissy, you're only here for two weeks."

"I don't like it. The water is cold. I want warm water. And I want my bath!"

"No baths at camp, Priss."

"I want one."

"Come on, Prissy, let's get into your bed and I'll tell you a story."

"I don't want a story."

"Well, what do you want?"

"Lanyard?"

"Fine, we'll do lanyard."

I spend the next twenty minutes making a bracelet for her. It's already nine-thirty, which is way, way past her bedtime. Evening activity should be ending. If I leave now, I'll still have time to spend with Raf.

"Sleep with me?"

"I have to sleep in my own bunk, Priss."

"Pleeeeeeeeeeeeeeease?"

"I can't, Prissy."

She starts to blubber again.

"I'll stay until you fall asleep, okay?"

She immediately stops crying. "Okay."

It takes her hours to fall asleep. Okay, fine, more like forty minutes, but it feels like hours.

I slowly extract myself from Prissy's iron grip and tiptoe across the cabin. I carefully open the door, trying hard not to let it creak, and say good-bye to the on-duty counselor. Then I cross Lower Field, passing the mess hall and the beach. I notice with hope that some older campers are still milling around. Maybe I'll see Raf. But no Raf. Maybe he'll be waiting for me on my porch.

I hurry along the road, wanting to get there as fast as possible, so that we can make use of the last few minutes before curfew. I turn left, toward the hill that leads to my bunk.

Someone is standing on the steps. It's a guy! It must be Raf.

Nah, it can't be Raf. The guy is leaning in to kiss someone.

They're kissing! Anthony and Deb, maybe? Hello, gossip!

It doesn't look like Anthony and Deb.

I take a few steps closer. My heart turns to ice.

It can't be.

It can't be, but it is. It's Raf.

And he's kissing Liana.

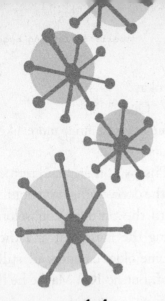

14
THE BOYFRIEND-STEALER

I can't move. My shoes are stuck to the gravel. Or perhaps my feet are too heavy because my heart has sunk to the bottom of my toes. I can't do anything but watch.

They're kissing. My quasi boyfriend is kissing another girl. Not peck-peck, nice-to-see-you-dear kissing but real, heavy-duty frenching. Their heads are rolling from side to side and I want to yell at them to stop, but no words come out.

I think I'm going to be sick.

Eventually, Liana pulls away. She turns to face me and smiles.

Raf's eyes pop wide open. "Rachel, hi!" he says. Either he's not as bright as I thought he was, or he thinks I'm blind, because the next thing I know, he's asking, "What's wrong?"

At first I'm speechless. Finally, words flow from my mouth. "You just swallowed Liana's tongue."

"Hi, Rachel," Liana purrs. "Raf, you should probably go back to your bunk now."

"I—I don't understand," Raf stammers.

The raw will is brewing inside me. My legs and toes and arms and fingers are trembling. I want to do something terrible. Something awful. I want to yank Raf and Liana up and hurl them into the lake. I want to drop them headfirst onto the tennis courts. I want to turn Raf into a six-legged toad and Liana into a turkey—just before Thanksgiving.

Raf chose Liana over me.

Raf never really liked me.

But I was his swimming buddy, wasn't I?

I feel like I've swallowed a fifty-pound beach ball. Yeah, I was his buddy, all right. I was his . . . friend.

The towels on the railings of the porch start to quiver. I take a deep breath. I'm not going to let my magic get out of control. I need to calm down before I accidentally blow up the camp. Think megels, I order myself. Harness that energy! Concentrate!

The towels lie still. I back away from the porch.

If there's ever been a time when I needed Miri, it's now. Not because she's a witch. Because she's my sister.

I run across camp, past the gawking campers, up the stairs to her bunk, and over to her bed. She's already in it, under her covers, reading her spell book. I climb up her ladder and slither under the sheet beside her. "Mir, I have to talk to you."

"What are you doing here?" she asks.

The other girls perk up in their beds.

"Somewhere private," I whisper.

201

She pulls out a small bag filled with a green and black concoction, sprinkles some of it into the air, and whispers:

"As the day is short and the night is long,
Your sense of sound will now be gone."

"What was that?"

"A new spell I learned. They won't hear you for the rest of the night. They won't hear *anything* for the rest of the night."

That sounds kind of mean. "When did you learn that?"

"I do have a life beyond you, you know."

So she keeps telling me. "Mir, something awful happened."

"What?"

"When I left Prissy's, I went back to my bunk and saw Raf and Liana kissing!"

Her mouth drops open. "No way."

"Way. I swear, I saw it with my own eyes."

"Honestly, Rachel, I don't think Liana would do that. She's not interested in Raf."

I narrow my eyes. "How would you know?"

"I know. Liana and I are friends."

"Liana isn't your friend, Miri. She's a horrible person."

Miri hugs her pillow to her chest. "She is not! I will not let you bad-mouth her like that."

My mouth is drier than a beach full of sand. "You can't be friends with someone who tried to steal my boyfriend!"

"Raf isn't your boyfriend."

Tears spring to my eyes. "He kind of is."

"It's not all about you, Rachel."

I feel like I've been slapped. "What are you talking about?"

"You can't have everything," she snaps.

"I *don't* have everything."

She flips her hair, like she's Liana. "You act like you think you deserve everything. Like you're owed."

"What has gotten into you?"

"You know what? I don't want to talk to you anymore."

"But I want to talk to you," I plead. I don't understand why she's being so mean to me.

"You don't get to make all the decisions, and I don't want to listen." She dips her hand back into her bag, sprinkles the green and black powder again, and chants:

"As the day is short and the night is long,
My sense of sound will now be gone."

"Are you kidding me?" I scream.

She turns her back on me. "Sorry, can't hear you."

203

My hands are shaking with anger. I storm out of her bunk, slamming the door with a bang—not that anyone can hear it.

I walk aimlessly around camp for the next few hours. When I finally return to my bunk, Deb is waiting on the porch.

"Where have you been?" she asks, glaring at me.

"Around," I say. I don't feel like dealing with her now. My head is pounding and I just want to go to sleep. Maybe I'll wake up and this whole mess will have been a dream.

"I don't know who you think you are," Deb says. "You can't just wander around by yourself for over three hours."

"I'm sorry," I say listlessly.

"Sorry isn't good enough," Deb says. "You're zapped."

Yes, I am. Miri just zapped me in the heart.

"For a week," Deb adds.

I open the door and stagger into fourteen. All the girls are already in bed, including Liana. She's the only one awake.

"Everything all right, Rachel?" she asks.

"Shut up, Liana."

I don't even bother getting washed. I climb up my ladder and try to sleep, but I keep hearing Liana's voice in my head: *Everything all right, Rachel?* What a phony.

"My sense of Liana now be gone," I whisper to the darkness.

If only she were a mosquito and I could poof her into oblivion.

Raf approaches me at flagpole. "Can we talk?"

I ignore him.

"Please, Rache, I don't understand why you're ignoring me."

You've got to be kidding. I can't believe I was so wrong about him for so long. I've liked him since *September*. That's eleven months! What a waste of time. What a waste of energy.

What a jerk-off.

I tell Poodles the story as we walk to the mess hall.

"I can't believe it," she says, shaking her head. "I'm going to kill her. And him. How could he do that to you? We'll boycott her. No worries. I'll tell Carly and Morgan the plan." She puts her arm around me and squeezes me tightly. "He's not good enough for you."

She's the best. "Hey, Poodles, what exactly does *zapping* entail?"

"Ouch, when did that happen?"

"Last night."

"It means you can't leave the bunk for free play and you have to go straight back to the bunk after evening activity."

"Deb zapped me for a week."

"No way! That was harsh. I wonder what's up with her. She's never zapped anyone for that long. Last year I got zapped for one night, but that's it."

Whatever. It's not like I have anyone outside my bunk to hang out with.

"Rachel," Deb says, hands on her hips, "isn't it your job to do the porch today?"

It's cleanup, and I'm in bed, trying to sleep off my pain and avoid Liana simultaneously. "It might be."

"I'd appreciate it if you did it," she says. "It's a mess; there are towels all over the place."

"She's right," Liana coos while sweeping next to our bed. "It's embarrassing. I can't ask boys over here if it's going to look like that."

Boys? She's cheating on my Raf already? Omigod. How can she be so horrible?

"I agree," Morgan says. "It's not right."

I can't believe that Morgan is being nasty to me when my heart is broken. I climb down the ladder and head to the porch. At least out there I won't have to listen to her.

Or face Liana.

We have pottery with bunk fifteen after cleanup. I use the period to enjoy pounding the clay between my hands, trying to look threatening. The others are making bowls.

Poodles, a troubled expression on her face, pulls me to the sink. "Bad news," she says, turning on the water so that no one can hear us.

"What is it?"

"Liana is claiming that the kiss never happened. That you made it up to turn us against her."

"*What?*"

"She says you've had it in for her from day one."

I storm right over to Liana, Poodles following close behind. "You are such a liar," I say. "I *saw* you."

Liana shakes her head, all innocent-eyed. "I don't know why you hate me so much, Rachel. I've never done anything to you."

"Yes, you did! You stole my boyfriend!" I scan the room for a piece of hardened clay I can throw at her.

She shakes her glossy hair from side to side. "I don't know what you're talking about."

"Really," says Poodles icily. Then she turns to me. "Why don't we just ask Raf? I'm sure *he* knows what you're talking about. We'll get him to admit the truth."

Oh God. I can't think of anything more embarrassing. What does she intend to do, march right up to him and say, "So, Raf, I hear you've been cheating on Rachel, who's so crazy about you that she can't see straight and is now

206

devastated for life"? I know that Poodles means well, but . . .
"Um, I don't think that's such a good idea, Poodles."

Liana smirks. "Go ahead, ask him. He'll back me up."

Big talker. She knows I'd rather be boiled in oil than go
through the humiliation of confronting Raf. She's bluffing.

Isn't she?

Of course she is. I mean, why would he deny it? It wasn't
like he was trying to hide what he was doing. He was making
out on the front porch in broad daylight. Broad moonlight,
that is, but still.

The smell of clay starts to make me sick—or maybe it's
the state of my life. "I think I need some air," I say, and head
out of the pottery room.

Poodles follows me outside. "I don't know why everyone
loves Liana so much."

Laughter erupts from the pottery room. "Liana, you are
so right!" Morgan squeals.

Nothing feels right anymore.

"Can I talk to you?" Raf asks, sneaking up behind me on my
way out of the mess hall after lunch.

"No."

"Rachel, please."

I stomp down the stairs, pretending he isn't behind me.

"I can't stand that you're mad at me," he says.

"Well, do you blame me?" So much for not confronting
him. But hey, he was the one who brought it up.

And then I have a thought. A small happy thought.

What if *she* kissed *him*? What if he was on the porch waiting for me, and then she attacked him or something, and he was just about to push her away when I came along and misinterpreted? It happens on TV all the time.

I wave him over to the picnic table and I sit on the bench. "Go ahead," I say, unable to mask the hope that's crept into my voice. "Talk."

He follows me like a puppy with its tail between its legs. "I like you, Rachel," he begins. "A lot."

I wait for him to say, *And Liana attacked me.* I stare into his eyes and wonder if I can forgive him. I think I can. If she came on to him, I mean. And if he was about to pull away.

"And I don't understand why you're mad at me."

What? Is he insane? "You kissed Liana," I say. "Is that a good enough reason?"

He shakes his head. "Why would you think that?"

"Because I saw!"

He looks like he's been slapped. "You couldn't have! It never happened!"

Is this some kind of plot that he and Liana concocted to make me think I'm going crazy? I might be a little unnerved, but I'm not ready for the funny farm just yet. "You're a liar, Raf. An awful liar. You make me sick."

His face pales. "How could you say something like that?"

"I. Saw. You." I can barely speak. The lump in my throat is so large that I can't even swallow. I can't see, either, because my eyes are brimming with tears. First he kisses her and then he lies to me?

"I don't know what you're talking about."

"You're a complete jerk! I can't believe I was so wrong about you! I don't want to speak to you ever again." Saying these words breaks my heart in two, but what else can I do?

I turn away and see Miri and Liana walking out of the mess hall together, laughing and deep in conversation.

I look from Raf to Miri and then back to Raf.

Who is this Liana, and why is she stealing my life?

At least I have Poodles and Carly. For the next few days, they're the only people I hang out with. Liana and Morgan have formed a tight little twosome, essentially ripping our bunk in half.

And I won't even look at Raf. I keep expecting to see him and Liana together acting all couple-y, but it doesn't happen. He spends all his time with Anderson, Blume, and Colton and with Will's bunk. It's almost as if Liana was never interested in a relationship with him to begin with. All she wanted was to ruin what I had with him.

209

Miri and I still aren't speaking. I'm too hurt to talk to her, and she hasn't made even a tiny effort to apologize to me. She can go hang out with her new friend, Liana, for all I care. I have another sister at camp. An adorable, cheerful sister.

Prissy is having a blast. At any hour of the day, she and her five starter camp bunkmates can be found laughing, jumping, and cheering, "We're bunk one, and we like to have fun! We're as sweet as a flower, but we don't like to shower!"

Her arms are weighed down with dozens of lanyard bracelets, her princess white dresses and outfits are caked with dirt, her hair looks like a bird's nest, and I'm pretty sure she has yet to crack open her toothpaste, but she's having a ball, so what the heck?

I take lots of pictures to freak out Jennifer with when I get home. They'll be my payback for all the embarrassing packages. This week I got foot deodorant spray. I mean, hello? It's camp; our feet are supposed to smell.

Since I'm zapped, I spend all my free time in the bathroom, practicing my megels. By the end of the week, I am much improved. I mean really improved. I can lift and lower that toilet paper roll with my eyes closed and one hand behind my back. Not that I need both hands to do it, but it's a neat trick. It might be useful the next time I'm in a public bathroom and the person in the next stall reaches under and asks for some paper.

The Saturday after visiting day is a scorcher. Head staff calls for an afternoon sun and swim, which means that the entire camp gets to hang out at the beach in lieu of participating in indoor activities. We can swim, we can go boating, or we can tan.

Poodles, Carly, and I are lying on our towels, trying to relax. *Trying* being the operative word. How can I possibly relax when Liana and Miri are together in the middle of the lake in a paddleboat?

I don't understand why Liana wants to hang out with my sister. It makes no sense.

"Did any of you see the way Liana told Morgan what to wear today?" Carly asks. "She's so bossy."

"Morgan has been acting like an android," Poodles says. "It's like she's under Liana's spell. And bunk fifteen is no better. They still follow Liana around, and they're not even in the same bunk anymore."

They do act kind of . . . bewitched.

Miri.

No.

You think?

My own little sister a traitor? A Benedict Arnold?

But why?

I gaze at the paddleboat. Liana is laughing at something Miri is saying.

Liana is why. I shift uneasily on the sand. What if Miri told Liana she's a witch, and now, eager for the attention, she's doing whatever Liana asks her to? Miri told me she didn't care if anyone found out. Unfortunately, it was Liana, someone who'd just love to get her greedy little hands on all that power.

Poodles adjusts her towel. "If I have to hear about her glamorous life in Switzerland one more time, I might have to shoot her. And why is she so obsessed with her water bottle? She's constantly trying to get us to drink from it."

"Maybe it's spiked." Carly laughs. "Maybe she's trying to get you drunk."

Why *is* Liana so obsessed with that water bottle? Come to think of it, Morgan drank from it. So did all of bunk fifteen, during soccer, way back on the third day. Deb drank from it too. Poodles, Carly, and I haven't.

A spell?

No—impossible. Miri wouldn't do such a thing.

211

Goose bumps cover my body.

Maybe I'm wrong about Miri. Maybe there's another explanation.

Funny how Liana has so many clothes and yet her cubby is so sparse.

Funny how Alison doesn't smoke yet was caught smoking—by Rose, who just happened to appear in our neck of the woods.

Funny how Raf can't remember that he was kissing Liana. (Well, not so funny.)

My heart hammers harder and harder until I'm afraid I might explode. "I have to go," I say, yanking on my shirt and shorts and stuffing my feet into my flip-flops.

"Go where?"

"To the bunk. To the bathroom. I, um, don't feel so well. Can you tell Deb I'm leaving?" Without waiting for an answer, I take off. I run all the way up the hill to the bunk and head straight for Liana's bed.

I need to find proof. I rifle through the stuff on her shelf. A brush. A hand mirror. Lipstick. Mascara. And then I spot her jewelry box. I know it's a long shot, but anything is better than thinking my sister is a traitor. I grab Liana's baby powder, sprinkle it on the box, and recite:

"From a caterpillar, a butterfly you became,

Now let this powder absorb your change!"

As soon as the powder hits the box, the box begins to morph, the month-old-milk smell becoming more and more pungent.

The jewelry box becomes a copy of A^2.

Liana's a witch.

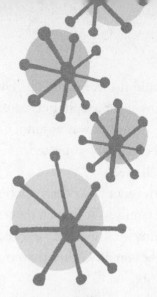

15
THE TRUTH IS OUT THERE (IN THE MIDDLE OF THE LAKE)

I open her spell book to the first page and read *Property of Liana Graff*.

How come everyone has a spell book but me? No fair.

I pace the length of the bunk. Liana's a witch. *Liana's a witch!* How could it have taken me so long to realize this? You'd think a witch would be able to spot another witch in a crowd. Where was my witch radar?

Miri is going to be so excited that we have someone else to talk witchcraft to.

Unless Miri already knows.

I continue pacing, looping through fifteen, the cubby room, and the bathroom, then back into the cubby room and then back through fourteen, trying to make sense of this situation. Miri and Liana have been best buddies lately, so it's possible Miri knows. But how would it have come up? Did Liana spot Miri doing a spell, get my sister to spill her secret, and then share her own? Or was it the other way around? Or maybe Miri just blurted it out, as I originally suspected.

If Miri knew, why didn't she tell me?

I mean, this is huge. We haven't met any other witches besides those in our immediate family. We haven't even heard of any other witches. I mean, we knew they existed, but we've never been given specifics on any other than our departed grandmother and our aunt.

I heave the spell book into my knapsack (it peeks out on top but I don't care), throw it onto my back, and run to the beach. My plan is to take out a canoe, find them in the middle of the lake, and confront them.

For someone who hates confrontations, I'm sure having my share of them.

I change my plan when I spot them tying their boat to the dock. I grab a life jacket, hurry down the dock, and jump into the boat before they can get out. "Pedal," I order.

"What are you doing?" Liana demands.

"Joining you. We're going to have a little talk."

"About what?" Miri asks.

I pull Liana's spell book from my knapsack and lift it in the air. "This."

Miri gasps. I'm not sure if she's gasping because she didn't know that Liana was a witch or because she thinks my bringing an A^2 to the beach violates some sort of witchy code of ethics.

"Careful!" Liana says, and starts pedaling.

Since the paddleboat has only two seats, I'm forced to lie across the container area in the back. When we reach the middle of the lake, they stop pedaling and turn to face me. "So," says Liana, staring into my eyes.

"You're a witch," I say matter-of-factly.

She doesn't break our gaze. "Yes."

I blink a few times and turn to my sister. "Did you know?"

Miri's face breaks into a wide smile. "Isn't it amazing?"

Huh. So she did know. A pang of something unpleasant (neglect? resentment? jealousy?) shoots through me like an arrow. "Why didn't you guys tell me?"

"We were going to," Miri says. "I swear."

"When? Next summer?" I kick the side of the boat in annoyance.

"There's more," Miri says, her eyes gleaming. She squeezes Liana's arm. "Should I tell her, or do you want to?"

More? What more could there be? I'm not sure how much more my brain can take. "Tell me what?"

Liana cocks her head to the side. "You go ahead."

Miri takes a deep breath and then shrieks, "She's our cousin!"

And that's when my head explodes. Okay, not really, but it feels like it. "*What?*"

"Liana"—Miri pauses for effect—"is Aunt Sasha's daughter."

I look from Miri to Liana and back to Miri. Liana is the daughter of my mother's only sister? The aunt I don't remember? Mom says I saw her only once, when I was a year old. "What are you talking about?"

215

"Aunt Sasha has a daughter. Liana. Who you must have met when you were a baby."

"But why wouldn't Mom tell us we had a cousin?"

"Who knows? After the fight, she didn't want us to have anything to do with that side of the family."

A million different emotions are tugging and pushing inside me. On one hand, yay! A cousin! I've always wanted a cousin my own age. How much fun is that? It's like having a twin but you don't have to share a room or identical DNA. On the other hand, of all the people who could be my cousin, does it have to be Liana, my new nemesis?

Not that I'm totally convinced she really is my cousin.

"Don't you think she looks like us?" Miri asks.

Her hair is darker and straighter than ours. More witchy. But her eyes and chin are kind of the same shape, I guess.

216

And she does have our genetic predisposition.

I suppose it's possible. . . .

"I look a lot like my mother," Liana says. "That's why I couldn't let your mother see me on visiting day. She hasn't seen me since the fight, but why take a chance?"

"How do you know about their fight?" I ask her. Their big *secret* fight.

Miri laughs. "Liana was the one who brought it up. And that's how I knew she really was our cousin!" She gives Liana an adoring look. "Not that I thought you weren't."

"But how did you know we were your cousins?" I ask.

"My mom didn't keep your existence a secret. I knew that I had two cousins, Rachel and Miri Weinstein, but she wouldn't let me contact you."

It's so unfair that her mom told her about us while

my mom kept her a secret. "Do you know what the fight was about?" Finally, the skeleton gets to come out of the closet!

Liana shrugs. "My mom never told me."

Oh well. It's back to the closet for Ol' Bones.

"Isn't this incredible?" Miri continues excitedly. "After the fight, our mothers never spoke to each other again, and then we randomly meet at camp thirteen and a half years later! It's like a movie."

Yeah, a movie I've seen twice, *The Parent Trap* and then its remake. I don't know what to say. I don't know what to think. "It's kind of unbelievable," I say finally. How did we possibly end up at the same camp? "How did you hear about Wood Lake?"

Liana smooths her hair back and smiles at my sister. "I wanted to go away for the summer and I read about it on the Internet. As soon as I saw it, I just knew. I felt that this was the place I needed to be."

217

"It's destiny," my sister says. "It has to be."

Sounds suspicious to me. Wait a sec. "Mir, how long have you known about this?"

She flushes and stares at her bitten fingers. "A few weeks."

"What? Since before visiting day? Mom was here, and you didn't tell her that her niece was here too?" I stare at Miri in astonishment.

"I . . . we were afraid Mom would pull me out of camp if she knew. You know how she feels about Aunt Sasha. She doesn't want anything to do with her. I . . . we were afraid that the banishment would extend to Liana, too."

"But I thought you wanted to leave camp," I say. "This would have been your ticket out."

"That was before." She smiles at our cousin.

That pang of neglect/resentment/jealousy strikes me again. "You could have at least told *me*."

"I wanted to, but Liana said not to. She said you didn't like her."

True, I didn't and still don't. She kissed my boyfriend! Why would my cousin try to steal my boyfriend, anyway? But more important, why would my sister keep a secret from me?

Liana takes her arm.

Ah. Of course. Miri finally had someone all to herself, and she didn't want to share her.

"You weren't very nice to her," Miri persists. "Like when you told your friends not to trust her after she moved into your bunk."

"How do you know that?" I ask.

"News travels fast in this place," Liana says.

"See?" Miri continues. "You started rumors about her for no reason. Liana's never been anything but nice to you."

Is she kidding me? "Liana, you stole my boyfriend!"

She widens her eyes innocently. "Honestly, Rachel, I don't know what you're talking about. I swear, I never kissed Raf."

"I saw you!"

"You couldn't have. You must have imagined it. New witches sometimes have hallucinations when their powers are just kicking in."

Miri nods. "It happens to a lot of witches, so don't get upset."

"Miri told me all about your problem," Liana says. "So I forgive you for making up rumors about me."

First of all, I can't believe that Miri told her about my problem. I take a moment to give Miri a good glare. Second, I did not hallucinate the kiss. Did I? "I don't know what to think."

"I'm sorry, Rachel. Jealousy can often trigger the hallucinations. So I forgive you. Sometimes I think my looks are a curse. Sometimes I wish I looked more like you, Rachel."

Gee, thanks. Is it possible? Did I imagine the whole thing? Raf has been denying it. . . . And my magic has been a bit fickle.

My newfound cousin is conceited, obnoxious, and manipulative, but—sigh—she's still my cousin.

219

"You have to believe her," Miri says. "Give her the benefit of the doubt! She's our cousin!"

I look at Liana. "All right." I'll give her a chance. I do like her version of events—the version in which Raf doesn't kiss her. Yay! Now I wish I hadn't gotten so angry at him. . . .

"You guys are going to love each other!" my sister gushes. "You just need to spend some quality time together. I bet you played together as babies."

Rose's whistle echoes over the lake. "All boats in!" she screams.

"Guess this is the end of our little chat," Liana says. "Miri, pedal backward and I'll turn us around."

Miri complies happily.

There's that pang again.

Liana might be her cousin, but I'm her sister. Who does this girl think she is, telling my sister what to do?

That's *my* job.

"Oh, say can you see . . ."

Instead of singing, I study all the campers and counselors at flagpole. If Liana is a witch, are other people at camp witches too?

Deb? Tilly? Will?

Raf?

I catch Raf looking at me and quickly look away. I'm so *embarrassed* about everything I said to him. I haven't quite figured out how to apologize for my crazy accusations.

I watch as Rose pulls a Koala boy out of line and yells at him to be quiet. Ha. If anyone else here is a witch, it's probably her.

Or maybe she didn't actually yell at the kid. Maybe I just imagined it. Maybe the kid yelled at her.

I keep looking around the circle. Prissy is singing at the top of her lungs in pig Latin. *"O'erway ethay andlay ofway ethay eefray andway ethay omehay . . ."* Speaking in pig Latin is Prissy's new favorite activity. "Ymay amenay isway Issypray" is how she now introduces herself. After she finishes the song, she sticks her finger into her nose, then wipes it on Tilly's sleeve.

For Tilly's sake, I hope I'm hallucinating.

While Carly stacks (her left arm wobbled during freeze), Deb stands at the head of our table, clapping. "Guess what, girls!" she squeals.

"What?" we say in unison.

"Break out your Camp Wood Lake T-shirts! Tomorrow morning we leave for an overnight canoe trip!"

Two days of being on a boat? I've tried canoeing only twice at camp, and I wasn't very good. And that's a lot of quality time with Liana. Intense quality time. I do want to get to know her better, but . . . well, she hasn't exactly made an effort to get to know *me*. I was already here when she came, and she chose a spot at the other end of the table.

221

I wasn't sure whether we were spilling the cousin-beans to the rest of the bunk, but since she didn't mention it, I decided I shouldn't either—which is fine with me. I mean, I have only two friends left in the bunk. Two friends who aren't too crazy about Liana. I wouldn't want to alienate them with my nepotism.

I wonder if anyone has an extra T-shirt to lend me, so that I won't have to wear my Oodle Wamp Ack.

"Just the five of us?" Morgan asks. "Or is fifteen coming too?"

"Bunk fifteen is coming too," Deb says. "And me. And a leader."

Poodles' ears perk up.

"Who's the leader?" I ask for Poodles' sake. "Is it Harris?"

"No, Harris only goes with the guys' bunks. Rose is coming with us."

We all boo.

"Come on, girls," Deb says. "She's not that bad."

"Yes, she is," Poodles says. She's obviously disappointed for other reasons.

"Where are we going?" Carly asks.

Deb gives us a thumbs-up. "Harbor Point."

"That's supposed to be nice," Carly says. "My sister went there two years ago and loved it."

I don't totally understand what a canoe trip is. Do we sleep in the canoes?

"Where exactly do we sleep?" Liana asks.

Omigod, she was totally reading my mind! How cousinly!

"In tents," Deb says.

I'm not crazy about tents. I imagine there are lots of spiders in tents. And what if it rains? Are tents waterproof? I don't want to get all wet. "Who puts up the tents?" I wonder aloud.

"We do," Deb says.

We do? "And where do we go to the bathroom?"

Poodles laughs.

"In the WC," Morgan says. "Wooden can. Or you pee near a tree. Or under a branch toilet if you need to get formal."

I am from Manhattan. I do not pee in the woods.

"I hate canoe trips," Carly whines. "Do we have to go?"

"Yes!" says Deb.

"It could be fun," says my cousin the suck-up.

"Now, that's the spirit," Deb says. "We pack tonight instead of going to evening activity, and we leave from the dock at nine. Tomorrow we canoe till about one and then we hang out at Harbor Point. We leave the next morning."

I wonder how many rolls of toilet paper we should take. I suppose I can always megel some more all the way from camp. I've got that particular megel down pat. Too bad it's the only thing about my life that seems to be working.

"So you really think Liana is a good witch?" I wouldn't want to have to drop a house on her or anything. It's free play, and Miri and I are leaving the mess hall and walking to the Upper Field bleachers.

"Definitely. She's taught me so many fun spells! Like automatic bed-making and sweeping. And some advanced ones too, like communicating with animals. I'm going to test them out on Tigger and Goldie when we get home."

223

I can understand trying to communicate with our cat— after all, cats are supposed to be mediums for witches—but our goldfish? This I have to see.

"Did you know she knows tons of other witches? They all hang out together in Switzerland. They go to boarding school and everything."

I raise my eyebrows. "What, she goes to Hogwarts?"

"No, Rachel, don't be dumb. It's more of an underground thing. We are so lucky to have such an in-the-know witch for a cousin," Miri says, all googly-eyed.

If you want to know the truth, it's nauseating. "I think she's a little strange," I say.

"I think she's amazing."

Gag me, please. "Miri, isn't it a bit weird that she wants to spend so much time with you?"

Miri stops in her tracks. "No, Rachel, it isn't. Some people like spending time with me. Not everyone sees me as a nuisance."

Hello, drama queen. "I know that, but Liana is two years older than you. I wonder why she went out of her way to be friends with you and not me, that's all."

"Is it so impossible for you to believe that someone would prefer me to you?"

"That's not what I meant."

"It is too. Yes, Liana would rather spend time with me than with you. And you know what? I would rather spend time with Liana than with you. She actually respects me and enjoys hanging out with me. She cares about important stuff, things more important than popularity, straight hair, and boys who don't even like *her*!"

I gasp. "I can't believe you just said that."

"Well, I did. It's true. I can't take how completely self-involved you are."

"I am not! You'd better apologize," I say to her.

"Why? Are you going to turn me into a roll of toilet paper if I don't?"

I'm so angry that I take off at full speed and leave her standing on the road. "I'm not speaking to you until you apologize," I call over my shoulder.

"I don't care. I have someone better to talk to!"

Sucker. With Liana and me away on our canoe trip, the only person who will speak to her is Prissy.

I hope Miri knows pig Latin.

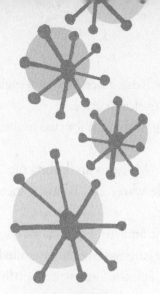

16
TENTS AND OTHER DISASTERS

"Knuckles facing out, Rachel, knuckles facing out," Carly says.

Unfortunately, I'm still not a very good canoeist. Which is surprising, considering it's so boringly simple. In-out, in-out, repeat process a million times.

Carly is in the stern, behind me, because that's where the best canoeist is supposed to be. Poodles called dibs on the bow. I'm in the crappy middle, the only spot that doesn't have a seat and requires painful kneeling.

"Did somebody fart?" Carly asks.

"Gross, no," Poodles says.

"Well, I smell something."

"Whoever smelt it dealt it," I tell Carly.

"Maybe it's the turkey sandwiches," she says.

"Turkey doesn't smell," I say. Our lunches are packed in our canoe. Dinner (hot dogs), tomorrow's breakfast, and a scary-looking vegetarian option Rose refers to as veggie paste are in the cooler in the counselors' canoe.

"It does when it's been boiling in the sun for two hours," Carly says.

"Can we take a break?" I beg. "My arms are killing me."

We lift our paddles out of the water and balance them across the boat. Ah. That's better.

Also in our canoe are the tent and three plastic garbage bags (to keep stuff dry). Inside my garbage bag are my rolled-up sleeping bag, a towel, a change of clothes, and water bottles.

Cece, Liana, and Morgan are right behind us.

Poodles turns to face us. "Rachel, you're burning up. Did you put on sunscreen?"

"Yeah, but it doesn't seem to be working. You're bright red too."

Carly passes us the bottle and we reapply.

I dip my hand into the calm water. "How much longer, do you think?"

"It's only eleven, so two more hours," Carly replies.

"Isn't it beautiful?" Poodles says, admiring the mountainous scenery.

I gaze around. "Like I'm living in a postcard. If only it weren't so hot. I wish I could jump in."

"Don't," says Carly. "You'll never be able to get back on the boat without tipping us."

"I know, I know," I grumble.

Poodles cups her hand, scoops up some water, and dribbles it on her forehead. "Try that."

I lean over and make my hand a cup and—

We rock to the right. Uh-oh.

We rock to the left. Uh-oh again.

"Careful, Rachel!" Carly screams.

We rock back to the left, and into the water we go.

Splash!

I land facedown in the lake, and the railing of the canoe smacks me on the calf. "Ow!" I wail. How in the world did I manage to do that? I didn't lean over any more than Poodles did!

Laughter echoes from a few yards away.

I lift my head above the freezing-cold water to see the girls in Liana's boat howling.

Did she do that? No . . . she wouldn't. She's my cousin. She wants us to be friends.

"They are so obnoxious," a dripping-wet Carly grumbles, slamming her fists into the water. "Liana'd better not come back next year." Her teeth chatter. "God, this lake is like the Arctic."

"Damn, my paddle is floating away," Poodles says, swimming after it.

Unfortunately, Liana is laughing the loudest, which makes me think, Whoever smelt it dealt it. Don't assume the worst, I tell myself. She had no reason to tip my boat. She wants to get along with me as much as I want to get along with her.

So why is she still laughing?

As I tread water, Miri's voice nags in my brain, telling me to give Liana the benefit of the doubt.

Carly grabs hold of her garbage bag and tries to keep it above the surface. She giggles. "You're such a klutz."

"No worries," says Poodles, floating on her back. "That was refreshing."

"Help me flip the canoe back over," Carly says, swimming to the boat.

We gather around and manage to turn it over while climbing in.

As we carefully reach over to pull in our stuff, I look across at Liana's boat.

Sorry, Liana mouths, smiling nastily.

The nerve! She did that!

Who does she think she's playing with? I'm a megel expert these days. I'll show her. Help me out, raw will! My fingers start to tingle. Raw will, don't let me down! I whisper:

"You're not so innocent, I'll bet.

It's your turn to get all wet!"

My arms feel rubbery and cold, and then I eagerly watch as Liana's boat sways to the right, then to the left, then back to the right—

Come on, come on, tip over!

—and then steadies itself.

Crapola.

Liana looks up at me and purses her lips, and the next thing I know, I'm back in the water.

"You've got to be kidding me," Carly grumbles.

Some expert. Liana's the professional, and I don't even qualify for the PeeWees.

After two hours, we finally arrive at Harbor Point. We pull our canoes onto the beach, toss off our life jackets, and drag our stuff to a clearing a few yards away. Before setting up, we cool ourselves off in the water and then get ready to unpack our lunches.

Where are our lunches?

The food from our canoe has disappeared.

"You probably left it in the lake," Rose says with a loud sigh. "You're lucky I packed extra veggie paste."

Why do I have the feeling that Liana is responsible for this as well?

"Did you lose your drinks, too?" Liana asks. She reaches into her garbage bag and passes her water bottle to Carly. "You can have some of mine."

"Don't drink it," I say, my heart pounding.

Carly hesitates.

"Look, you want some or not?"

Carly shrugs and makes the reach.

"No, don't!" I shout, but it's too late. She's already guzzled half of it.

Carly blinks and then blinks again.

Then she looks at me with narrowed eyes. "What's your problem? I'm thirsty. Why shouldn't I drink from her bottle?"

That was fast.

"Yes, Rachel," Liana purrs. "Why shouldn't she?"

"Because . . . because . . ." Because you've poisoned her into being your friend and hating me? "Because I saw a bug fly in."

"I didn't see it," Liana says. "Rachel, you're probably imagining things. Again."

Carly laughs and my heart sinks. Forget my fly excuse; it's like *Lord of the Flies* around here. I'm losing people by the second!

"Here, Poodles, you can have some too," Liana says, and offers her bottle to my last remaining friend.

Please say no, please say no!

"Nah," Poodles says, giving Liana a pointed look. "I'm not into insects."

After lunch, Poodles tries to talk me through peeing in the woods.

"Pretend you're on a toilet," she says, her back to me.

"But I'm not on a toilet." Instead of concentrating on getting the job done, I'm wondering if I should tell Poodles the truth. The *whole* truth, that is.

"Squat like you're in a public bathroom and you don't want your butt to touch the seat."

Nah, I probably shouldn't. Tell her, that is, not squat. What if she tells someone? What if she mentions it to Harris? What if she thinks I'm crazy? My mom never told anyone—not even my dad. How can I blurt it out to someone I've known only a month? Instead, I say, "What if it goes all over my shorts?"

"It shouldn't if you're squatting properly."

"But what if it does?"

"So take them off."

I step out of my shorts and my bikini bottom and squat over the root of a tree. And then I try to pee. And I try again. "It's not coming."

"Concentrate!"

This is harder than a megel.

It takes me about five minutes, but I finally get it. "That was disgusting," I say. "Thank goodness for indoor plumbing."

When I put my shorts back on, I notice they have a big ugly grass stain—right where the sun don't shine.

She couldn't have. Could she? I look around, but I don't see Liana. But that's no proof. Maybe she brought her own invisibility umbrella.

Next we tackle putting up the tent, which is no easy feat, especially since Carly has switched teams and is now insisting on sleeping with Liana, Morgan, and Cece, even though they have only a three-person tent.

"Why would you do that?" Poodles asks, thoroughly confused.

"Because I'd rather hang out with them," Carly explains.

"But you hated them this morning."

"That's not true," Carly huffs.

"Let her go," I say. I know there's no hope. "More room for us. Let the other girls make space for her sit-ups."

Two hours later, we're finally finished. I didn't think it would be a promenade in the park, but we take ten times longer than Liana's group. That was to be expected, since Liana totally used her superpowers to help her. Not that I'm surprised. Just envious because my powers aren't as developed.

When we finally do get our tent to stand upright, we discover a dinner plate–sized hole in the tippy-top.

"How on earth did that happen?" Rose asks. "I checked them all before we left."

That's a question I know the answer to. What I'm wondering is why.

I corner Liana while she's taking a swim. "Why?"

She leans her head back to wet her hair. "Why what?"

"Why are you trying to make my life miserable? I thought we were going to be friends."

"You mean why did I tip your canoe, steal your friends, stain your shorts, and give your tent a big fat hole?"

She's not even going to try to deny it? "Yeah, that."

"Because I don't like you."

"Are you kidding me?"

"No. That's the reason. You asked and I answered. Now get out of my way." She strolls out of the lake like she doesn't have a care in the world.

I'm too shocked to respond. If she doesn't like me, then she could have zapped Raf into kissing her and then zapped the memory out of his mind just to ruin my life. What am I going to do? I take a few moments in the lake to compose myself. (Okay, that's a lie. I take a few moments in the lake because I'm afraid of the woods and I have to pee again, but that can be our little secret.)

It rains all night.

Now I understand the hole in the tent.

By the next morning, Poodles and I are both cold and shivering and not in the mood to paddle the four hours back to camp. Especially since the two of us are the worst paddlers ever and Carly seems determined to return with the others.

"Carly, we let you sleep in the other tent, but you *have* to canoe back with Rachel and Poodles," Rose says, snapping on her life jacket. "They're not strong enough without you."

"But there's room for me in Liana's boat!"

Rose puts on her I-mean-business face, which is the same as her mean face. "Tough."

Ha! I silently apologize to the powers that be for every nasty thing I've ever thought about Rose. Carly is a top-notch canoeist and we need her. Unfortunately for us, as mean as Rose was, Carly is now meaner.

"Slide the blade in, Rachel, don't smash it. You keep splashing me."

"I'm trying, I'm sorry." Trust me, I want to do my best here. I'm dying to get back to camp as quickly as possible for several reasons. One, Liana is a witch. Two, Liana is evil. Three, I've thought long and hard about the Raf situation, and although I'm not sure whether I hallucinated the kiss, if I didn't, I'm sure that Liana is responsible. Either way, Raf thinks I'm acting crazy, so I have to apologize. Beg for forgiveness. Tell him I had a fever that night and was delirious.

233

Why did I even doubt him? That was what got me into trouble at the Spring Fling.

"Knuckles facing out, Rachel, knuckles facing out!"

I'm going to knuckle her in the forehead if she keeps this up.

"Can we take a break?" I ask an hour later, exhausted. "My arms are killing me."

"I don't know why," Carly snaps. "It's not like they're doing anything."

I ram my paddle into the water, sending a spray up behind me. That one *was* on purpose.

As we approach the camp, I hear the lunch announcement on the loudspeaker. Perfect. In the mess hall, I'll be able to talk to Raf. Or kiss him. If I'm forgiven.

After dumping my stuff onto my bed, I run to the mess hall and head straight to Raf's table—Raf's empty table.

"They just left on their canoe trip," Poodles tells me.

"Are you kidding me?"

" 'Fraid not. Harris went with them. He left me a note."

My shoulders sag in disappointment. "That sucks." Now I'll have to wait another day before I talk to him. "At least they'll be back in the morning."

Poodles shakes her head. "They went on a three-nighter. They won't be back until Thursday."

"That is so incredibly sexist," I cry. "They get to go for three nights, and we only go for one?"

"Did you want to stay longer?"

I shudder. "Not a chance."

But three more nights in a Rafless world . . . I don't know how much more I can take.

After lunch, Rose lets us use the pool showers while bunk fifteen goes to Upper Field. I'm not sure if she's being nice 'cause she thinks we bonded during the canoe trip or if she just can't stand the smell of us, but who's complaining?

Liana, Morgan, and Carly go first, while Poodles and I wait on the pool bleachers.

Morgan and Liana are done first, and Poodles and I take our turn. I hang my bathrobe on the hook outside the stall and step under the burning water. Ah. Feels good. The hot water beats against my back and arms. When I'm done, I reach for my bathrobe.

And reach.

Where's my bathrobe? I push aside the curtain to find the hook empty. "Poodles!" I scream. "Poodles!"

"What? Do you need conditioner?"

"I need my bathrobe!"

"It's not there?"

"If it was, I wouldn't need it, would I?"

"Hold on, I'm almost done," she says, and turns off the water. Through my peephole, I watch her inspect the pool area. "You're right. It's gone."

235

"Liana," I say. She is obviously responsible.

"That is so evil," Poodles says, shaking her head. By now Carly is long gone too. It's just the two of us. "Stay here. I'll run back to the bunk and get you a towel."

Poodles takes off, and I stand there shivering. While I wait, I summon my raw will and try to zap up a bathrobe. I squeeze my eyes shut and try to envision terry cloth. I feel something on my toes, and my eyes pop open. It's a face-cloth. A teeny-weeny facecloth, not even large enough to hide my smaller boob.

I turn on the hot water to keep warm. I'm going to kill Liana. Kill her. Or at least get revenge. Don't get mad, get even, right?

After ten minutes, I think I hear a faint knocking at the door and quickly turn off the water. Actually, I have no choice. The water's gone cold.

I stick my head out the shower curtain and hear Poodles shout, "The door locked! You have to let me in!"

She's got to be kidding. Here goes nothing. I check the windowed pool walls to make sure the coast is clear, run to the door, pull it open, grab the towel, and wrap it around myself all in one swift move.

I can't believe I pulled that off.

Or not. From my new position, I see that I had a blind spot from the shower. Prissy and five of her starter camp friends are gaping at me through the window.

Could have been worse. Could have been the starter camp boys.

236

Even worse, the Lion boys.

"I know you took it." I'm standing by our bunk bed, still in my towel, jabbing my finger at my cousin.

She looks up from *Vogue* and bats her lashes. "I don't know what you're talking about."

"Yes, you do."

"She didn't take your precious bathrobe," Morgan says. "We were right there. We would have seen her."

"One of you took it," Poodles says. "It didn't just disappear on its own."

More than likely it did.

That's it. I've had it. I can't sit back and take this

anymore. No more fooling around. I need to get my magic up to speed ASAP. Fire needs to be fought with fire, not pathetic matchsticks.

This is no longer revenge; this is war!

I need Miri's help. Unfortunately, Miri still isn't speaking to me. I need a plan B.

"Why are you bringing an umbrella?" Poodles asks me the next day as we head to the beach for sailing. "It's not raining."

"That cloud looks pretty threatening." I put a hand on my stomach and groan. "You know what, Poodles? I'm not feeling well. I'm going to stop by the infirmary to see Dr. Dina. Tell the sailing people where I am, okay? And Deb, if I don't make it to GS." Next stop, the Oscars!

I hurry up the road, but instead of going to the infirmary, I sneak into Miri's empty bunk. I aim right for her shelf and quickly rifle through her things until I find what I'm looking for: her faux pencil case.

I brought my own baby powder.

I sneak into the mess hall, break open the invisibility shield umbrella, sprinkle the powder on the pencil case, and spend the afternoon studying.

It's time for a crash course in revenge.

"Omigod!" Carly screams, pointing.

We've just returned from dinner, and as we turn up the hill, a skunk pushes out through the bunk's front door, runs down the stairs, and darts into the woods.

All five of us hurry into the cabin to see what the damage is. We follow the scent into the cubby room.

Carly is close to tears. "Which one did it get?"

Trishelle purses her lips and points to the cubby in the corner—the perfect cubby that looks like it's never been touched.

Liana's face is whiter than my sheets.

"That is such a shame," I purr. "Really, Liana, I wonder why it chose yours?"

She clenches her fists. "I wonder why too. I can tell you one thing. That skunk is going to be sorry."

Bring. It. On.

238 "Wake up, everyone, wake up!" Janice says, storming through our bunk the next morning.

I roll over in bed.

Itch. Scratch.

Scratch, scratch.

My head is itchy. Why is my head itchy?

I scratch again and slowly move my hand in front of my eyes.

A small reddish brown bug scurries down my finger. Lice.

I scream and scream and then scream some more.

"Liana, there's something on your arm," I hear Carly say. "And your other arm. And on your legs."

They just got back from the showers and are in the cubby room changing. I didn't join them in the showers because I already spent half a day in the infirmary showers with a bottle of Nix. I spent the other half sitting on the infirmary bench with the nurse and a nit comb. Since my sheets and comforter are still being fumigated, I've been lying on my sleeping bag.

"It's red," Carly says.

"It's ugly," Morgan says.

"It's poison ivy," Liana hisses.

Damn straight.

"I want my pencil case. Now!" Miri screams, hands firmly on her small hips.

239

"Oh, *now* you're talking to me." I put my surely winning hand facedown on the porch. It's free play, and Poodles and I are in the middle of a gin rummy game.

"I'm not talking to you," Miri snaps. "I'm yelling at you."

"I'll be right back," I tell Poodles as my sister drags me by the arm into the bunk. I pick up Miri's book and toss it at her. "Here you go."

"Outside!" she barks. I follow her behind the cabin.

Her eyes are popping out of her head like Slinky toys. "Did you give Liana poison ivy?"

"Miri, calm down—"

"Don't tell me to calm down. Just tell me the truth!"

Fine. "Yes."

She gasps and then chokes on her own gasp. "And you used my spell book to help you?"

"Yes."

A moment of quiet and then she explodes again: "How could you do that to my best friend!"

"Your best friend"—I cannot believe she just called that evil witch her best friend!—"gave me lice!"

"She did not. I'm sure you got it from Prissy or one of her dirty friends."

"Prissy does not have lice. Did Liana tell you that?"

"Yes, she did."

Now I'm furious. "And you believe her? That's just great, Mir. You take the word of someone you've known for five weeks over your own sister's?"

"At least she keeps her promises."

"You're a gullible idiot."

"I'm sick of you!" Miri screams, kicking the green wall. "You're always putting me down! Everything is about you! It's been like that since I was born!"

"If you hate me so much, then go live with another family!"

"I'm planning to," she says slowly. "Liana wants me to go to boarding school with her in Switzerland, and I'm going."

That is the most ridiculous thing I have ever heard. "You can't go to boarding school," I scoff. "Mom would never let you."

"Well, I have news for you, Rachel. She can't stop me."

"Of course she can! You're twelve!"

"She has no say in what I do. Did you know that witches

believe that a girl becomes an adult when she turns twelve? It's just like Judaism."

"That may be, but you still won't be allowed to go."

"She isn't the boss of me."

"Uh, yeah, she is, Mir. And I'm going to tell her what you're planning."

"Go ahead. She'll find out eventually."

"I'm writing her right now."

"Too bad she's away. And you can forget about instant messaging or e-mailing. Liana's already concocted a blocking spell. By the time Mom gets back, I'll be gone."

"Oh, really? When exactly are you planning on leaving?"

"Saturday night. Liana and I don't see a reason to stay at camp any longer. It's kind of a waste of our time. Liana cares about the same things I do. We're going to spend the last few weeks of summer doing something real. We're going to use our powers to help people. And then we're starting school at the end of the month."

"You can't leave. Mom gave you that location anklet to keep you from taking off." So there!

Miri waves my words away. "Liana is a brilliant witch. She knows how to get rid of it."

Liana this, Liana that. "May I ask how you're planning on paying for this school?"

"I'm a witch, Rachel. I'll zap up some money. I'll zap up permission forms. I can do it; I'm an incredibly powerful witch, you know." She fiddles with the lanyard bracelet on her arm. "Liana says I'm one of the most powerful witches she's ever seen. Even more powerful than Mom."

241

Nice big head she's got there. "They'll search for you. They'll drag you home."

"No, they won't. They won't care. It's not like Mom will even notice I'm gone."

I sigh. "Oh, Miri, of course she will."

"No, she won't! No one will. Mom is busy with Lex, and Dad is busy with Jennifer and Prissy, and he'll be even busier with a new baby. And you're . . . well, you're always busy with your friends and your boyfriends."

Is that how she really feels? "Mir, you know that's not true." Not lately, anyway, since I'm down to one camp friend and zero boyfriends. Guilt creeps through me. It's true. I have been a little preoccupied. But I'm a teenager! We're supposed to be preoccupied!

She nibbles her fingers as she talks. "You ignored me all summer. You only cared about me when you needed me. When you needed my magical powers. Now that you have your own, you won't need me for anything. But Liana cares about me."

I grab her tightly by the shoulder. "Miri, I care about you. I would do *anything* for you."

She's looking at the ground instead of into my eyes. "No one at school will notice. It's not like I have any friends."

"Because you don't make an effort!"

She shakes her head. "You know I never fit in. Not like you. And Liana knows tons of teen witches around the world. Girls just like me."

"I'm not going to let you go."

"You don't have a choice. And neither does Mom. I'm a

much more powerful witch than her, and with Liana's power as backup, nothing can stop me."

That's when I realize she really can pull this off. We might end up like Mom and Aunt Sasha, and I might never see her again. Why can't I make her listen? "Please don't do this," I say, my voice cracking. And then, softly, "I . . . I'll miss you."

She hesitates.

"What?" I ask.

She looks up at me with big hopeful eyes. "If you care about me so much, come with me."

I take a step back. "I can't just take off!" Can I? Sure, my parents are crazy. Sure, I live in a cramped apartment with one bathroom, and I have only one close friend at school. But you can't just run away when the going gets tough. Your problems just come with you. "No," I say. "That's no solution."

243

"See?" she says softly. "You're a liar. You *wouldn't* do anything for me."

And with that, she walks away and doesn't look back.

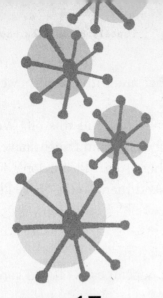

17
LET'S MAKE A DEAL

After bedtime, I climb down my ladder and stand by our bed. "We need to talk."

The late-night moonlight slinks through the window, illuminating her nasty smile. "I'd be delighted to."

"Let's go somewhere private. The CL?"

"The nighttime make-out center? That's hardly private. I prefer the lookout."

"I'm not quite in the mood for hiking." Or bees, for that matter.

"Please," Liana snorts. "What kind of witch do you take me for?" With a snap of her fingers, the bunk's broom rises from its spot near the door, soars across the room, and lands in her hand. "Let's go."

I wish I had my helmet.

We take off from the porch and zoom up to the lookout in thirty seconds flat.

I slide off the broom to safety as soon as my tiptoes touch the ground.

"So," she says, twirling the broom in her hand like a baton, "what do you want to talk about?"

"You are not taking Miri with you to boarding school," I say, arms shivering. It's colder up here than I thought it would be.

"I don't think it's up to you," she says calmly.

"She's not acting like herself at all. Did you put her under a spell?" I'm sure that she did.

Liana laughs. "You have to accept the fact that your sister *likes* me. She would rather be with *me*. I can teach her things you'd never be able to. You have to consider what's best for her, Rachel. It's about time you thought about someone other than yourself."

I try to clear my mind by looking at the star-filled sky. Am I being selfish? Is Miri better off with Liana?

No. What would Liana teach Miri? How to be evil? And Miri is way too young to be on her own. "You're crazy if you think I'm letting you take her."

She laughs—cackles—again. "You're crazy if you think you can stop me."

She does have a point. How could I stop her? Her magic is eons more advanced than mine. Trying to fight it would be like challenging her to a tennis match, a newbie against a pro. I need to go at this another way—by begging. "Please, Liana. Tell Miri this is a bad idea. You can still spend time with her. You can spend next summer with her if you want. You don't have to kidnap her. Think about how devastated my parents will be."

She tilts her head to the side, as though considering this. "Well, when you put it like that . . ."

My heart races. It's working! The begging is working! Who knew that begging was so effective? I should have begged Raf for a kiss from day one. No, forget that. A girl has to have some pride, after all. But when a sister is at stake, pride be gone! "And how would I explain it to my dad?" I press on. "He doesn't even know we're witches!"

"There is one other option," Liana says, nodding. "It will be more up to you than Miri."

I pause. "What is it?"

She stares me dead in the eyes. "I won't take Miri with me to boarding school if you'll switch psyches with me."

Huh? "What are you talking about?"

"There's a swapping spell, where two people can switch psyches without anyone knowing," she explains in a rush.

Why would the wonderful and glamorous Liana want to change places with boring old me? "But why would you want to be me?" I ask. It makes no sense. I can't believe she'd switch places with me just so Miri can be with her. Something else is brewing in her evil little mind. I'm sure of it.

She shrugs. "It's just a really cool spell, and I've always wanted to try it. Once swapped, you see the other person's memories and everything." She crosses her arms in front of her chest. "Look, do you want to try it or not?"

"How long would we have to switch for?" I ask, my suspicion mounting.

She looks away. "Whatever. Not long."

"How long?" I repeat.

She hesitates before answering. "Until we both want to switch back."

Chills creep down my spine. What if Liana never wants to switch back? Sure, my life may have its issues, but you know what? In spite of all my issues, I'm happy being me. "I don't really like this idea," I say. I like her even less. She's the last person I'd ever want to be.

"Come on, Rachel. You whine about your life constantly. About how annoying your family is. About how the guy you like won't kiss you. About how you have no friends at home. Wouldn't you *kill* to be me?"

247

"I never whine about—" I stop. She's right. I do whine. But like I said, I may have issues, but I wouldn't trade my life for anything, not even for a pair of perfectly matched boobs. "No," I say. "Absolutely not."

"Then it's back to option one," she says. "I'm taking Miri."

"That's blackmail!" I cry. "You can't do that!"

If the situation weren't so terrifying, I'd laugh. If Liana had come to me with this idea in the first place, before she started getting all nasty, I might have agreed. Hey, I like a good practical joke as well as the next person. I mean, it might even be fun for a while, like maybe a day or two, or even a week. And I'd get to whip some butts in tennis. But now she's using it to blackmail me.

The question is, why does she want my life? I don't believe for a moment that she cares one iota about Miri.

She throws her leg over the broom and raises a foot off the ground. "I can do whatever I want. Don't you get it, Rachel? I always get my way."

With that, she flies off, leaving me in the dark. And if that's not bad enough, now I have to hike all the way back.

On the trek down, I have a full-blown panic attack. First of all, I swear I hear howling in the distance. Just wonderful. To top off a perfect night, I'm going to get eaten by a wolf.

But even worse: what am I going to do? I need to find a way to stop Liana, to beat her at her own game.

If only I could get in touch with my mother. But Miri said Liana cast a blocking spell. All I need to do is unblock the block, and for that I need to get my hands on Liana's spell book. Right, and then you can crown me queen of England.

I swat a mosquito out of my hair.

I have to try. What choice do I have? I creep into my bunk to find my enemy fast asleep. Ha! Fool. And I thought she was smarter than that. I'll just take her jewelry box and . . .

Where's her jewelry box?

Her jewelry box is gone. Did she hide it, or did she morph her spell book into something else? Maybe a comb? A bottle of suntan lotion? I look around at all our belongings. She could have morphed the spell book into anything.

I grab my baby powder and begin sprinkling it, first on Liana's stuff and then liberally around the room, all the while chanting the appropriate spell under my breath.

Nothing morphs. Instead, it looks like it snowed in here. Either that or someone has really bad dandruff.

"Penguin Bear's all white!" Carly cries, waking me up.

Liana's laughter echoes through the room.

I cover my head with my comforter. This isn't over yet. Not by a long shot.

Yay! Raf's coming back today! Not that I have the energy to deal with that at the moment. I mean, come on. I currently have a little more on my mind than apologizing to and sealing the deal with my quasi boyfriend.

Though maybe if I can get one part of my life in order, the rest will fall into place. Like with a math problem when you start with the brackets and the rest of the equation begins to make sense.

The boys aren't scheduled to return until fourish, which is smack in the middle of GS. Poodles and I wait on our beach towels, eyes peeled for any signs of incoming boats on the lake. I'm going to walk right up to Raf and plant one on his lips. Then I'll apologize. I don't care who sees, either. This is happening today. Now. As soon as he lands his canoe. (Not sure if you *land* a canoe, but it sounds right, since you're

249

bringing it to land.) Maybe the sight will shock my sister, who is ignoring me and reading a book on the other side of the beach, into changing her mind.

"I miss Harris so much," Poodles says, fiddling with her hair. "Do I look okay?"

"You look gorgeous as usual." I, on the other hand, am beyond caring what I look like. Raf has already seen me in my pj's, with a ginormous bruise on my head, and covered in bee stings. I doubt smoothing my hair will tip the scales. I just want to kiss him already! "You know you can't kiss Harris in public, right? He's still staff."

She sighs. "I know. But I just want to see him. I know I said this was just a summer fling for me, but I think I'm falling for him."

"But you live across the country."

Her eyes are shining. "We still have two weeks of camp left. And maybe he'd consider transferring to UCLA."

"Oh, isn't that sweet?" Liana says, making herself comfortable next to us on the sand.

"This has nothing to do with you," I tell her.

"Seriously, Liana," Poodles says, smoothing her hair again. "Get lost."

Liana smiles. "Everything has to do with me. Haven't you realized that yet, Rache?"

"There they are!" Poodles shrieks, scrambling to her feet. "I'm going to wait on the dock."

The four canoes are now in view, pulling up to the camp. Harris is in the stern of the first boat; Raf is in the bow of the second. "I'll be there in a sec!" I call to Poodles as she runs down the beach.

"No, you won't," Liana says.

I glare at her. "Yes, I will."

"Silly Rachel. When are you going to learn that I'm the one calling the shots?" She lets out an exaggerated sigh. "I've given this some thought and here's how the game is going to be played. See, you surprised me yesterday. I expected you to agree to my plan right off. I thought you would jump at the chance to spend time in my shoes. It should have been an easy choice for you. Your sister comes with me, or you become me. But instead you're forcing me to make this far more difficult than it needed to be."

"What are you talking about?"

"Shut up and listen," she orders, her voice icy cold. "We *are* going to switch places. Don't you get it? That's why I'm here. That's why I came to camp in the first place."

Excuse me?

251

Liana's eyes flicker over the beach. "The question is, how far do I have to go to get what I want?"

The spine chills are back. "What are you going to do?"

She fixes her gaze on Poodles. "It's sweet that she has such strong feelings for Harris, don't you think?"

Poodles waves to Harris and runs toward him.

"Leave her alone," I say.

Liana ignores me.

"Don't!" I shout, and then, helpless, I feel a gust of cold and watch as Poodles throws her arms around Harris and kisses him right on the mouth.

Unfortunately, I'm not the only witness. Deb sees it. Anthony, Abby, Mitch, Janice, Houser, and Rose all see it too.

That can't be good.

Liana sighs. "Say bye-bye to Harris. I'll bet he'll be asked to leave camp immediately. Poodles might have to leave too. A shame. Two whole weeks early."

Nausea overwhelms me. "You're crazy," I say.

"No, I just know what I want. Ready to switch yet?"

I don't answer.

Her eyes are on the dock. "Look at Raf in his canoe. Doesn't he look like he's having a good time?" she asks.

I feel another gust of cold, and with a flick of Liana's wrist, Blume, paddle still in his hands, spins around and knocks Raf over the side of the dock. Raf lands headfirst in the water and comes up coughing.

"Leave Raf alone!" I cry.

"I will if you switch with me."

At least Raf's okay. I watch as he pulls himself onto the dock. "No," I say clearly. "I'm not going to let you bully me. I will not switch places with you."

Her cheeks flush with anger. She purses her lips and takes another look around the beach, then spots my sister, who is still sitting by herself, reading. "You know, Rachel, traveling through Europe can be dangerous for a twelve-year-old. Really dangerous. It would be so easy for something to happen to her. For her to just disappear. Don't you think?" She smiles sadly. "I've always wanted a little sister. Someone just like Miri." Her smile fades. "Too bad."

Fear slices through me. I gaze at my sister, who is obliviously reading her book and looking so sweet and helpless. I watch her for a moment before I turn back to Liana.

I've lost. If I don't do what she wants, I could lose Miri—forever. Tears sting my eyes. "I'll switch, okay? But if I do this, you have to promise you'll never hurt Miri. Ever."

"I'm not such a monster, you know. I really don't want to hurt anyone."

What a crock. That's all she's been doing since she arrived at camp. "Promise me."

Her face hardens. "I promise."

I know I have no reason to trust her, but what choice do I have? And anyway, maybe I can still outsmart her . . . somehow. "All right."

She stands up and wipes the sand off her shorts. "Come on, let's get this show on the road." She smiles sweetly. "And then I have to go make up with *my* sister, which will be a piece of cake. Let's just say your sister is very malleable. She's soon going to realize that I'm the nasty person you always said I was, and that you really are wonderful. Don't look so glum, Rachel. Isn't that what you wanted?"

I swallow the rock in my throat and follow her up the beach. I take one last look at Raf. The next time I see him, it will be through Liana's eyes. The next time he sees me, I won't be me.

Then I look at Miri. I don't know why Liana's doing this. All I know is that I have to save my sister. I try to will Miri to look back at me, but she goes on reading. After Liana gets through with her, Miri will never want to set eyes on me again.

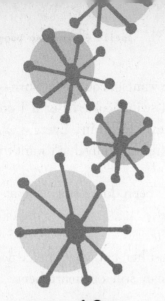

18
THE BIG SWITCHEROO

Switching is a trip.

We do it at the lookout. We have to sit facing each other with our legs out, bare feet touching.

Liana passes me a black candle and a book of matches. "When I count to three, we're going to light our candles. Ready?"

As ready as I'll ever be, I suppose. I want to run down the hill, but what's the point? If I don't do this, she could hurt Miri . . . not to mention Raf, Prissy, and everyone else I care about.

"One, two, three!" she shouts, and lights her candle.

I scratch my match against the box, and the flame leaps to life in my right hand. I pick up my candle with my left and light it. "Now what?"

She extends her candle over the center of our circle. "Our flames have to become one," she says.

Here goes nothing. Or everything. I lean over and let my candle's flame touch hers.

As they interweave into one, Liana tells me to repeat after her. "As this flame burns through the night . . ."

I hesitate.

"Say it!" she barks.

"As this flame burns through the night . . . ," I whimper.

"Please listen to our plight," she says.

"Please listen to our plight," I repeat.

"Let our two souls switch . . . ," she continues.

"Let our two souls switch . . . ," I repeat.

Liana: "With absolute perfect pitch."

Me: "Because you're a total bitch."

Liana scowls and then says the line again: "With absolute perfect pitch."

255

Me, also scowling: "With absolute perfect pitch."

Liana: "Let she be me . . ."

Me: "Let she be me . . ."

Liana: "And me be she."

"And me"—I hesitate and she kicks my foot—"be she."

It starts with sinus pressure. At first it feels like I have a bad cold on an airplane. But then the pressure gets more and more intense, like a nail is being rammed into my brain, trying to knock something out, which I guess is what it's doing—trying to knock me out.

The next thing I know, the pain is gone. Just like that. There's no pain at all, just peace. In fact, I feel great, like I'm a cloud, or a gas, floating above the lookout. It's like I'm dreaming.

Then I'm feeling that ramming again—but this time,

I'm the nail being rammed. A square nail being slammed into a round hole. And then the headache stops and I open my eyes.

Omigod.

I'm staring at myself. It worked! It actually worked! I'm sitting across from myself! You know what? I'm cuter than I thought. My hair might be wavy, but it has a nice fullness. I have really good skin, and my lips aren't too thin. What was I always whining about? Why did I think I was so plain? You know what else? Don't trust mirrors. Or even photos. There's nothing like looking at yourself through someone else's eyes. This is the real thing. This is really me. And I'm adorable!

The Rachel across from me is staring at me with as much amazement as I'm looking at her with. Er, at me with.

I look down at my hands (these are not my hands!) and then at my legs (these are not my legs!) and then at my boobs (these are—unfortunately—not my boobs!), then run my not-mine hands through my not-mine hair. My super-glossy not-mine hair.

My super-glossy hair that Liana permanently straightened before camp.

Huh, how did I know that?

Millions of images download into my head at the same time.

Whoa. I have access to Liana's past. All of it.

Maybe I can find something in her, some kind of spell, that will return me to my own body—while at the same time making sure she doesn't hurt anyone.

I close my eyes and let the memories wash over me. It's

like I'm watching a movie about someone's life. Except it's not a biography. It's now an autobiography. . . .

I've just turned five and I'm on a broom with my mom, Sasha. Her long brown hair is tied tightly in a low ponytail and it keeps brushing my face.

"This is going to be so much fun," my mom tells me. "You're going to love it in Paris. You're going to learn to speak French."

"But I don't want to learn French. I want to go back to London," I say, "where Imogene is."

Imogene has been my best friend for the past four months, as long as I've been living in the United Kingdom. Before that I was in Rome, before that in Vancouver, and before that I don't remember. All the cities have blurred together like overexposed pictures.

"You'll make new friends," my mother tells me.

My tears drip off my cheeks and into the clouds, but my mother doesn't notice.

"Can I have a sister?" I ask. We're on a yacht in the Red Sea. I've been playing checkers by myself for the past hour and I'm totally bored.

My mom and her gentleman friend, whose boat we're on, laugh.

"Please? I want someone to play with."

"Liana, you're doing just fine on your own."

"But a sister would be so much fun! Or a brother. I'd take a brother, too."

"Sasha barely knows what to do with you," the awful man says.

My mom nods. "One kid gets in the way enough."

My powers finally kick in when I turn ten. I'm in a hotel in San Francisco, watching another movie on pay-per-view TV, when I manage to change the channel without the remote. I'm bubbling with excitement about telling my mom. She's going to be so proud of me! I wait eagerly by the elevator (I'm not allowed to leave the floor when she's out, but she lets me run up and down the hallway) and wait and wait and wait. When she finally returns from her date, I run to her, yapping a mile a minute. "I did it! I'm a witch too! Just like you! Now we can train together and I can come with you everywhere and—"

She shushes me with a flick of her hand. "Not tonight. I have a headache."

I cry myself to sleep.

My mom and I fight about everything.

How I should wear my hair. How I should dress. How I don't want to keep moving. "I just want a normal life," I plead.

"We're never going to be normal. You're a witch. Go study your spell book."

"I don't want to study anymore!" I scream. And then: "I wish I could live with my father!"

My mother never talks about my father. I must have pushed her too far, because she yells, "You don't have a father!"

"I must have had one at some point. I wasn't hatched." Not even witchcraft can manage that. "Who is he? I have a right to know!"

"You did have a father, but when you were six months old, I caught him with another woman."

Even before I ask the next question, I'm dreading her answer. "What did you do?"

"I turned him into a mouse. And her into a cat. And that was the end of that."

259

I spend the night throwing up in the hotel bathroom.

I meet a girl named Joanna in the park. She tells me my teeth are long and look like carrots.

I turn her into a rabbit.

Then I feel bad and turn her back into a girl. But I leave her with really floppy ears.

I'm so lonely I want to die.

Then I develop a crush on a boy named Matthew.

He says he likes me as a friend and he has a girlfriend named Ellen.

I put a love spell on him and give Ellen chicken pox.

"Where are we going?" I ask my mom. She's zapping our clothes into two big Louis Vuitton trunks.

"I'm meeting some friends down in Rio. You're going to Switzerland."

"Why?"

"You're going to Miss Rally's Hall for Girls. It's one of the top boarding schools in the world."

"I don't want to go to boarding school!"

"It's not up to you," my mom says.

"But I want to stay with you."

"Liana, it's for the best. You need to be in school, and I have some traveling I need to do on my own."

"But you can't just desert me!"

"I'm not deserting you. I'm sending you away to school. Other girls would give their eyeteeth to be in your situation. You'll love it at Miss Rally's. There are even some other witches there, so you'll finally be able to make some real friends."

"Girls don't like me," I say.

"Because you're always putting spells on them. Give it a chance. For me?"

I agree. I want to make her happy.

There's a snake in my bed. Again. I want to take it and wrap it around the throat of my new archenemy, Olivia.

Although this isn't a school for witches per se, Miss Rally herself is a witch. And that's why mothers who can't be bothered with their witch daughters like to send us here. There are at least six or seven of us here at one time, and Miss Rally keeps an extra-special eye on us.

The other girls have no clue.

Bunch of idiots. Don't they wonder why we always get the nicest rooms? The best food? The easiest chores?

Not that it makes living here desirable. Not for me, anyway.

I hate Miss Rally. I also hate the other witches, especially Olivia, who sleeps in the room next to mine and whose personal project is to make my life a living hell.

At Thanksgiving break, I beg my mom not to send me back. "Please," I say. "I hate it there." I would run away, but my mother has shackled me with a location anklet that won't let me leave without her permission. It's like a magnet I just can't shake. I'm going to be stuck there for the next four years.

"Liana, you just have to get used to it. You'll be fine. You can't stay with me. I'm way too busy."

"With what?"

"I met a wonderful man named Micha." She goes on and on about the wonderful Micha until I want to jump off a bridge.

I already knew about Macho Micha. I found a spell to create a virtual crystal ball, and although it can't predict the future, it can show me what other people are doing.

"Will I get to meet him at Christmas?" I can't wait for Christmas break. A whole month off from the school from hell!

"Oh, about Christmas . . ." She pauses. "Micha and I are going to spend a week in Tahiti. I spoke to Miss Rally and she said that your staying there is no problem."

I want out. I search through my spell book for a way to break my invisible anklet, but there isn't one. Instead, I discover a five-broomer spell that allows two people to switch places.

If I switch places with someone, she'll live in Miserable Hell (my pet name for Miss Rally's Hall), and I'll be free.

All I have to do is find someone to switch with. My choices are limited, since she has to be related by blood. So I start by consulting my crystal ball.

And that's when I discover Rachel, the daughter of my mother's sister, Carol. I knew there was a huge fight years ago, but I didn't know I had a cousin! A cousin my age. A cousin who has everything I ever wanted. According to what I see in the crystal ball, she has the perfect life, but she doesn't appreciate it. Why is she always whining? She makes me so angry that I can't look at her without my arms shaking and my teeth chattering.

First of all, she doesn't have to move all the time. She gets to stay in one place, and I'm not talking about boarding school. She has a normal life. A wonderful life. Friends. A mother who loves her. A father who adores her. But what makes me the most envious is that she has a sister. Two, actually. Two sisters who adore her. Who worship her. But the one she lives with is the one I'm interested in. Rachel is so obsessed with being popular and stupid fashion shows and stupid boys that she ignores her. As far as I'm concerned, Miri is ripe for the taking. For making her *my* sister.

Rachel is the perfect candidate for me to switch with.

I want Rachel's life. I want to be Rachel.

But how? I watch her talking about camp in the crystal ball, and a plan unfolds in my head. If I go to camp too, I can make the switch. Convincing my mom to let me go will be a snap. She doesn't want me hanging around with her and Macho Micha all summer.

The snag is that I have to get Rachel to agree to the switch. She's not all that happy with her life, but is that enough to make her want to do it? The annoying thing is that I can't put an obedience spell on her. She has to agree to it out of pure and free will.

263

Of course, there's no rule that says I can't make her miserable. Make her detest her life even more. Provide her with the straw that breaks the camel's back.

Make her beg me to do the switch.

I remember turning on the lights in the CL.

I remember launching a soccer ball at Rachel's head.

I remember giving all of bunk fifteen, Deb, Morgan, and Carly my enchanted water.

I remember attacking Raf and Rachel on the lookout with a flock of bees.

I remember bewitching Alison into smoking in the bathroom.

I remember bewitching Raf into kissing me. And then wiping his memory away.

I remember making Miri's mail disappear.

I remember turning Jennifer's care packages of lip glosses and bubble gum into the most embarrassing gifts possible.

I remember giving Miri an amplifying charm disguised as a lanyard bracelet. The seeds of Miri's anger were already there. All I had to do was help bring them out.

I remember convincing Miri that I could take off her location anklet. As if! If I knew how to do that, I wouldn't be in this mess in the first place. But I needed her to believe that I was going to take her with me. I needed her and Rachel to buy my bluff, to buy into my plan.

264

I open my eyes. I—the fake version of me—am still sitting in front of me, watching me. "Having fun?" Liana asks nonchalantly.

"I'd feel bad for you if you weren't so awful." *I'm* feeling awful—because I should have known that Miri wouldn't just desert her family without some magical assistance. But . . . her unhappiness didn't come from nowhere, I think guiltily. She really did feel unloved and unwanted at home.

"Whatever. Have fun in hell. Hope you're not afraid of snakes."

"So this is it? I'm stuck like this?" The sickening truth hits me. She's never going to switch back. I can't believe I fell for her entire plan.

She shrugs. "I'll see how I like being you. Maybe I'll switch back when you graduate."

I can't believe this is happening. I can't believe I let Liana get away with this. I want my life back! I want to be me again!

But even if I could switch back, how could I risk hurting my sister?

"Of course," Liana says, "there's no way I'm going to change back until Miri is completely mine—without the aid of amplification. You're a fool, Rachel. Look what you gave up. And I'm not just talking about sisterly love. I'm talking about power. Sisterly power. The combined power of blood-related witches. There'll be no stopping us now. No stopping me, that is, because I'll control every move Miri makes."

Instead of feeling even sicker, I'm elated. Liana has just given me the solution. Part of it, anyway. Together, Miri and I can overtake her. Together, we can stop her from hurting either of us or anyone else we care about.

The question is, how do I switch back?

Miri and I can figure it out together. If not, she'll just have to get used to my new appearance. (I kind of like my new chest, anyway.) At least we'll be together.

I just have to get to her before Liana does. I slowly stand up, not wanting Liana to guess what my plan is.

"I don't think so," she says, cackling, and then, with a snap of her fingers, a broom appears in her hand and she takes off.

Where did she go? How did she/I do that? I stop for a second and think. If I have access to all Liana's memories, do I also have access to all her advanced witchcraft skills? I snap my fingers and wish for a flying broom.

Nada. Guess not. That is so unfair! I get her crappy life and memories but none of her expertise. Where's the fun in that?

265

I arrive at Miri's bunk about ten minutes later, huffing and puffing. Miri and the fake me are waiting for me on the porch. "Miri," I say, "I have to tell you what happened."

"I don't want to talk to you," she says, waving her lanyard bracelet in the air. "I can't believe you would do that to me, Liana. You must think I'm the biggest idiot."

I shake my head. "You have to listen to me."

"No, I don't. You make me sick. How did you think you could get away with putting an amplifying spell on me?"

"What? I didn't! She did!" I point at my conniving cousin.

"Rachel told me all about it. You tried to get me to dump my whole family! And I almost let you! At first I didn't even believe my sister, but she told me to take off the bracelet—and *poof*, no more amplification."

I want to cry. "No, you don't understand! I'm Rachel! I'm not Liana! She made me switch places!"

"Save it. You're sick, Liana. Sick in the head. I will never believe anything you say ever again."

I need to prove the truth to her! What can I do? "Ask me something about our past. You'll see that I know the answer!"

"Of course you do; you've been spying on me all year with your crystal ball. I don't want you coming near me."

"Liana," the fake me says to me, "you'd better stay away from my sister. We found a restraining spell."

Miri picks up a Styrofoam cup that's sitting next to her, tosses its contents at me, and chants:

"With this magic restraining order,
Fifty feet will be your border!"

Suddenly, I'm forty-five feet in the air. I land on my butt (in a sandpile, thank goodness) near Lower Field. I try to push my way back to my sister's bunk, but an invisible wall won't let me through. "You can't do this!" I yell.

But there's no point. She can't even hear me.

For everyone else at camp, the last two weeks are the best.

The weather is sunny and beautiful, the rules have melted away, and everyone is hooking up left, right, and center.

Anthony is breaking his own rules by dating Deb, so he can't exactly fire Harris. Instead, he and Deb go public with their relationship and tell Harris and Poodles that they can continue dating as long as Poodles' parents approve, which they happily do.

Anderson finally makes a move on Carly, and judging by Carly's stories, not even Morgan can call her a prude.

Speaking of Morgan . . . she gets over Will and hooks up with Blume, rumored spit crust be damned.

Even Prissy is having the time of her life. "No, I don't want to go!" she cried, kicking and screaming when her two-week starter program was up. Her counselors let her call Jennifer, who, after listening to much howling, finally agreed to let her stay the remaining week and a half.

There's color war (Angels versus Devils), there are pool parties, there are more campfires. There're the camp lip-synching contest, the camp play, the camp dance show.

Everyone has a blast. Everyone except me.

I'm miserable. First of all, every time I get fifty feet from Miri, the invisible wall knocks me down like I'm some sort of human bowling pin. I have huge noninvisible bruises all over my body, and no one knows where they're coming from.

Second, I finally get together with Raf. I apologize for my hallucinations, and Raf forgives me almost immediately. Every night after evening activity, we share big juicy kisses on the bunk porch. Unfortunately, I'm not there to appreciate them, since I'm no longer Rachel.

"I'm so happy you two finally hooked up," Carly says to the fake me.

Liana has reversed her poisonous friendship spells, so Carly, Morgan, and Deb love me again. The fake me. And they've all gone back to hating Liana, aka the real me. So now everyone hates me, including Poodles, who was never bewitched in the first place.

The only person who will even talk to me is Prissy. She calls me Ianalay and I let her braid my hair.

"It's the prettiest hair in the whole world. Long and smooth and pretty, just like Belle's from *Beauty and the Beast*," she tells me when I visit her bunk.

I've never been happier to have a six-year-old friend.

It's the last day of camp, and everyone is crying.

Big babies, I think. What do they have to cry about? They're not living in someone else's body.

I pack Liana's stuff into her duffel bags.

"Here's what you're going to do," she tells me. "I'll shrink the restraining spell to ten feet so you can take the bus back to Manhattan with us. Then you'll grab a cab to JFK and take your flight back to Zurich. I'm sure you don't have the skill for a broom yet, so I cast you up a flight reservation. Wasn't that nice of me?"

"Isn't your mom going to pick me up at the bus stop?"

She snorts. "Yeah, right. I'm sure she and Micha are going to cut short their trip to Antarctica to come get you. You're on your own, cuz. Your new mother doesn't give a crap about you, so you'd better get used to it."

I lug my way through the final banquet (taking a moment to enjoy Oscar's lasagna), the slide show, the final campfire (by now I know the words to the camp song but have no one to sing it with), and then the social. Since I can't go to the dance (Miri's inside and I'll get wall-slapped), I stand outside the rec hall and peek through the window.

My whole bunk is having a blast doing the Sweep, the Soccer Player, and the Brushing Your Teeth.

Then I watch myself slow dance with Raf.

I can't believe it. After a full year of dreaming and hoping that I would one day go to a dance with Raf, my wish finally comes true.

269

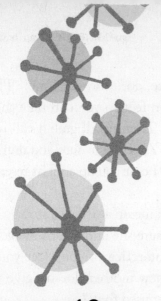

19
FAMILY REUNION

Through the front-seat window of the bus, I can see my mother and Lex waiting at the drop-off point on Fifth Avenue. They're holding hands, gazing into each other's eyes.

This is my last chance. If I can reach my mother before Miri gets within fifty feet of her, maybe she'll see my resemblance to her sister and listen to me. Maybe she'll believe me.

The bus stops and I squeeze my way toward the door.

"Not so fast," Liana whispers into my ear when I'm stuck waiting for the door to open. Before I realize what she's up to, she rubs some sort of jelly onto my neck and whispers:

"Till the next moon has come around,
You have lost the use of sound."

I open my mouth to yell at her, but I can't speak.

This was my last chance! What now? If only my dad

were here and not at the Long Island stop picking up Prissy . . . I step off the bus and get pushed to the side as Miri and her invisible wall (now back to fifty feet from her) disappear from my life. There's nothing I can do but watch helplessly from farther down the street. I have to tell them the truth! But how?

Through the crowd of parents, returning campers, and tourists, I watch my mom hug Fake Me first. Fake Me looks flushed with happiness. Then Mom hugs Miri. My sister holds on to her longer than she ever has before. I guess the whole run-away plan really freaked her out. I can see their mouths moving, but they're too far away for me to hear what they're saying. So I summon my raw will and think:

Bounce their words against the cloud,

To make these words ten times as loud!

Yes, I know it's not my best rhyme, but what do you want? I'm under major pressure here!

"Let me help you with your knapsacks," Lex says.

I can hear him! Wahoo!

"Thanks so much," Fake Me coos. "You're such a doll."

I try to make out my sister's face for a reaction. Come on, Miri! Would I ever call Lex a doll? No! No, I wouldn't!

Unless I was calling him an antique doll.

Miri looks at my fake face for a split second longer than necessary but then looks away and continues walking.

No, Miri, no!

I try to hurry after them, but I smash into the wall. I settle for following at my fifty-foot distance while listening to their conversation.

Miri and Fake Me are trailing slightly behind Mom and

271

Lex, walking to the corner of the street. "Mom's going to be so impressed with how good your magic's gotten," my sister says.

Tell me about it. It's almost as though I've been a witch for years.

My mom and Lex wait for Fake Me and Miri to catch up. "I have an announcement," my mom says.

Omigod. She's engaged. Is she engaged? I squint, trying to see if she's wearing an engagement ring.

"What?" Miri asks.

"I told Lex . . . about us."

She did?

"You did?" my sister asks. "Wow. I can't believe it. That's, like, huge."

"I wanted to do it right this time. A clean slate. I wanted to be honest. With myself and with Lex."

"You're the best, Mom," Fake Me says. "And honesty is so important."

Liar, liar, pants on fire.

"I'm glad you didn't get scared away," Miri says to Lex.

Lex laughs. "Scared of her? Never. But I have to admit, I thought she was, well, a little off when she first told me. I mean, witchcraft? Gimme a break. But she proved it to me, and I came to terms with it."

"How did she prove it to you?" Miri asks.

Lex winks. "Let's just say it involved a dozen roses."

My mother giggles. "It's not unusual anymore for a woman to give a man flowers."

"It was when I watched them grow out of my living room carpet," he says.

272

"I can't believe you did that!" Miri squeals.

"Now, don't get carried away," my mom says. The light changes and they all cross the street, with me following as closely as I can. "I'm still a nonpracticing witch." She takes Lex's hand. "Most of the time."

"You're good for my mom," Miri says to Lex, then adds, "I was pretty nasty on visiting day. I want to say I'm sorry. I was having some issues."

"Don't worry about it," he replies. "Clean slate for us, too."

"You'd better watch out," pipes up Fake Me. "If you're not nice to my mom, I might turn you into a mouse."

My mom wags her finger. "Rachel! We will do no such thing."

Fake Me turns bright red. "I was just kidding."

Mom puts her arm around Fake Me. "And how's your Glinda going?"

273

"It's getting good," Fake Me says.

"She's gotten *really* good, Mom," Miri says.

"Great," my mom says as she steps onto the curb and pulls Fake Me into a hug. "I'm so proud of you, honey."

Fake Me's smile has lit up my entire fake face.

I can't believe I'm watching all this family bonding from fifty feet away. I love family bonding! I'm the queen of family bonding!

This is a new low.

"You realize, of course," my mom says, "that you still have a lot of work ahead of you. Control, control, control!"

"Are we taking a taxi?" Fake Me asks.

"No, Lex drove. We're parked in a lot just on Madison."

"Thanks for picking us up," Miri says.

"No problem. I'm just glad the bags get delivered."

I hurry behind them as they make their way to the south side of the street and then down a driveway into an underground lot.

The restraining spell won't let me follow them down the driveway. But from my angle, I can still see them if I squat. Lex opens the trunk of the car and stuffs our two knapsacks into it. Then Miri and Fake Me climb into the car.

This is it. They're going. What should I do? Do I just stand here? Do I follow them in a cab? Liana will probably put a restraining spell on the entire apartment. On the entire school. On all Manhattan. And any day now, I'm going to get sucked back to Switzerland because of Liana's ankle magnet.

I watch as Lex opens the passenger door for my mom, then closes it.

He walks over to the parking lot attendant to pay and gets the keys.

He opens his car door. Gets into his seat. Starts the car.

My life is officially over.

"Thanks, sweetie," my mom says, rolling down her window. "How much do I owe you for parking?"

"Nothing," Lex says with a smile. "It was free."

"Oh, come on, tell me. It must have been a fortune. The girls were so late."

"Really?" Miri asks. "How long were you waiting?"

"We got here at twelve-thirty, because you were supposed to arrive at one," she says while rifling through her wallet. "It's now one-forty-five. Lex, tell me what I owe you."

"One kiss."

"Rachel, help me out here," Mom says, pointing to the price list on the wall. "It was eight dollars for the first half hour, and four-sixty for each additional half hour. How much do I owe him?"

Seventeen-twenty, I think but don't say, because I can't talk.

"Excuse me?" Fake Me asks.

"How much do I owe Lex?" my mom asks. "You know I'm no good with numbers."

Fake Me hesitates. "Um, I don't know."

Ha! But I bet she knows she *should* know. After all, she knows everything about me, right? Too bad our expertise isn't transferable.

My sister does a double take. "What do you mean you don't know? You should know."

"Of course I know. It's, um . . . um . . ."

"Are you counting on your fingers?" Miri asks in disbelief.

"No! Why would I do that?"

As they pull out of the driveway onto the street, I hear my sister scream, "Stop the car! This isn't Rachel!"

Wahoo to the power of a billion!

Lex slams on the brakes. "Excuse me?"

"She's an impostor!" Miri cries. "It's Liana in disguise!"

Phewf. What can I say? It's about time.

Lex drops us off at the apartment. He kisses my mother (still gross, but I'm learning to live with it) and says, "Have fun, ladies."

275

"Chicken," my mother gently teases. But I know she's relieved. This is a hen roost. No roosters allowed.

After my family realized the truth, Liana admitted to the silence and restraining spells, which my sister immediately undid. I then ran toward them, waving my arms and blubbering like a five-year-old. Miri—also blubbering—threw her arms around me and would not let go.

Now the four of us—my mom, Miri, the fake me, and the real me—are sitting in the living room. Unfortunately, my mom can't undo the switching spell. For that, both me's have to freely agree to swap back. And the fake me isn't being too agreeable.

"Tough," she keeps repeating. "You can't make me."

"There's no point in you staying Rachel if we all know it isn't really her," Miri wisely points out. She turns to me with a sheepish expression. "I'm still sorry. I should have believed you."

And I say, "I know, Miri, you've told me a hundred times." More like three hundred times, but who's counting? I keep telling her it wasn't her fault. I also keep reminding her that she's the one who saved me. If she hadn't picked up on the math thing, I would have been banished to Switzerland.

"I want to talk to your mother," my mom says to Liana, and we all gasp.

"What makes you think she wants to talk to you?" Liana asks snidely. "The two of you haven't spoken in over thirteen years!"

"Where is she, Liana? Tell me."

But Liana doesn't budge.

"Tell me where she is," my mother orders, this time infusing her command with a little bit of raw will.

Liana spits out the information.

"Are you going to fly over and get her?" I ask, loving the drama of it all.

"I was thinking I'd start with a phone call," my mom answers, and disappears into the kitchen.

Right.

Ticktock, ticktock. The tension in the air is thick. Who knows what's going to happen? What if there's another fight?

Suddenly, the smoke detector goes off.

"It's my mom," Fake Me says. "She likes to make a smoky entrance."

"She was always a drama queen," my mom says with a sad smile.

277

We run to the kitchen. As the smoke clears, a tall, thin figure appears by the stove. A tall, thin, dark-haired figure who looks like Mom, except she has a bigger chest and fewer wrinkles. Fewer wrinkles makes sense. She is the younger sister. "Hello, Carol," she says.

"Hello, Sasha," my mom says, walking over to her. "It's been a long time."

The two women are standing about a foot apart, staring at each other.

Nobody moves.

Nobody breathes.

Nobody—

"Achoo!" I sneeze.

"Quiet!" snaps the fake me.

"Gesundheit!" says my sister.

"So," Sasha says, now circling my mom.

"So," my mom says, standing her ground, arms folded across her chest.

"It has been a while," says Sasha.

"A long while."

Sasha looks her up and down. "Your hair's red."

"New look," says my mom. "You look exactly the same."

"I've aged well. Better than you."

"Which is it, plastic or magic?" Mom retorts.

"Nature, of course," says Aunt Sasha. She tears her eyes away from my mom and looks at the fake me. "You've grown."

Well, duh.

"Actually," my mom says, "you're looking at your own daughter. She's in my daughter, and vice versa."

Sasha looks at the fake me, then at the real me, and then back at the fake me. "Are you sure? My daughter would never wear her hair that frizzy."

"Mom!" exclaims Fake Me. "I can't help it; it's her hair!"

Sasha frowns. "Liana, what do you think you're doing?"

Fake Me juts out her chin. "I'm not switching back."

"Yes, you are."

"No," Fake Me says. "And you can't make me. If I don't approve the switch, it can't happen."

And my mom thought *I* was a pain in the butt.

Sasha looks around helplessly. "What am I supposed to do with her? She's so difficult!"

My mother snaps to attention. "You're supposed to *parent* her. She's only fourteen years old. You're the mother."

"But she never listens!"

I can't help noticing the pain on Fake Me's face. I know how she feels. I can see her memories. I know what she wants more than anything in the world. "Why don't you try listening to *her*?" I suggest.

The kitchen is quiet.

"Now, there's an idea," my mom finally says.

"She doesn't care," Fake Me says. "She never has."

Her tough-girl act doesn't fool me for a second. Her lips are quivering and she looks like she's about to cry. "Tell her, Liana," I prod gently. "Tell her how lonely you are. Tell her how much you hate boarding school. Tell her how much you need her."

"What for?" Her voice breaks. "I've told her before, but she didn't listen. She *never* listens."

"I'm listening now, so talk," Sasha says impatiently.

"But you don't care! You don't care that I hate school. It's like you want me to be miserable. You don't care about me at all!"

"Of course I do."

If this were me and my mom, at this point we'd give each other a big hug, proclaim our love, and probably cry a little. But this isn't my family. Well, okay, maybe it is, but it's the wacko side of the family. (Every family has a wacko side, right?)

Fake Me stomps her heel into the carpet. "If you care about me, why don't you want to spend any time with me?"

Sasha closes her eyes. "Liana," she says slowly, "we both know that you're better off without me."

Fake Me throws her arms up in the air. "Are you crazy?"

"I could never be a good mother," Sasha continues. "I was never good at anything. Ask Carol."

My mother looks up in surprise. "What are you talking about?"

"About growing up. I was never good enough in school. I was never popular. I was never pretty."

"Of course you were!"

"No, I wasn't! Not naturally. Anything I wanted I had to use magic to get. I was never good at anything on my own. Not like you. You didn't need magic to make friends. To do well in school. To make men fall in love with you." She looks at me and Miri. "To be a good mother."

"You were always so insecure," my mom says, shaking her head. "I never understood why. The magic you were capable of even as a little kid . . . I was so envious."

"You were not!"

"Of course I was! But you refused to see that. It always amazed me that someone so powerful could have so little confidence."

"How could I have confidence when I had Miss Perfect as an older sister? Everyone always loved you best. Mom. Dad. People fell over themselves to be near you." She turns back to Liana. "You had the right idea, switching places with Rachel. You would have been better off with Carol as your mother."

"Maybe." Fake Me looks up at her mother and, her voice cracking, says, "But all I ever wanted was to spend time with you."

Sasha's eyes lock onto her daughter's. Then she nods. "Fine."

"Fine what?" Liana asks.

"If you hate it *that* much at Miss Rally's," Sasha says softly, "then we'll figure something else out."

As long as she doesn't appear as a JFK High sophomore, I'm a happy girl.

"Now, Liana, if you don't mind," my mom says, picking her nails, "can you switch back with my daughter, please?"

"No," Liana says, finally breaking the eye contact with her mother. "There are still other things I want."

What? She wants my soul? My room? My pink suede designer sneakers? *What?*

Liana leans against the kitchen counter, a determined look on her face. "No more trips," she says to her mother.

Sasha hesitates. "Not even with you?"

Liana half smiles. "Of course *with* me."

"What else?" Sasha asks.

"Um, can I have a sister?"

"No way."

Liana's face falls. Uh-oh. Is that the deal-breaker? "You can hang out with Prissy," I offer. Liana doesn't answer. "She loves to braid your hair," I say, "and this way you get the best of both worlds. You can return her to her parents whenever she gets whiny." I'm not sure how Dad and Jennifer would react to my bargaining off their daughter, though I'm pretty sure they'd appreciate the free babysitting.

"I'll think about it," Liana says, appearing to consider the offer.

281

Sasha takes her daughter's wrist. "Liana, you'll do it. How can I give real parenting a try if you're not in your own body?"

"All right," Liana says. "But only if you dissolve the prison anklet on my real body right now."

"As soon as we get home."

"No, now. Before I change."

"Fine," Sasha says. "Carol, do you happen to have any soy milk?" She opens her purse and takes out a packet of salt.

My mom points to the fridge. "Help yourself."

A few seconds and a de-ankling spell later, Sasha has freed Liana's body, aka me, and my cousin is appeased.

Phewf.

"Do we need one too?" Miri asks, looking down at her feet.

"I did yours last night before you left camp," my mom says.

Aw, Mom, so thoughtful.

"Now switch back, Liana," Sasha orders.

"Hold on," I say, raising my hand. "Now there's something I want." All heads turn toward me. I motion to my aunt and my mother. "Before we switch, I'd like to know what happened between the two of you."

"Yeah," says Miri. "Why don't you two speak to each other?"

My mom doesn't answer.

"A clean slate?" the real me reminds her.

"It's hard for me to talk about," my mom says.

Sasha dives right in. "Carol killed our mother," she says bluntly.

Oh. My. God.

"She had a stroke, Sasha," my mom says.

Sasha points a long red fingernail at her sister. "It was your one screwup, but it was a biggie. Mom had a stroke. And you could have saved her. You could have healed her. But you didn't."

"I couldn't," my mom says.

The red claw is still pointed at my mother. "Why?" Sasha asks, her voice full of contempt. "Because Miss Perfect thought that using witchcraft was beneath her? Please. You're only a nonpracticing witch when it suits you. When someone's life is at stake, you act, Carol. You do what you have to do. I will never forgive you for letting her die."

Miri grips my hand.

"Is it me you can't forgive?" my mom asks. "Or is it you? Let me remind you, you weren't here when it happened. You were in Paris with Liana's father. Or was it London? It's hard to keep track. You kept running off on us."

"I needed to be on my own," Sasha says, eyes flashing. "I needed to be someplace where everyone didn't always compare me to you."

"That's no excuse for the way you acted. Not telling us how to reach you! Why are you always so immature? By the time you came back, it was too late. She had been gone a year."

Sasha turns white. "Not a day goes by that I don't wish I'd been here. But I wasn't. I was a terrible daughter, and I admit it. But you!" she spits at my mother. "You were here, and you did nothing. You should have saved her."

Tears stream down my mother's cheeks. "You don't think I wanted to? Do you think I wanted her to die?"

My sister and I immediately move next to our mom and put our arms around her.

"But you're right," Mom says sadly. "I could have saved her. And I didn't."

I suppress a gasp. "Why not?"

My mother doesn't speak for a moment. She lowers her head into her hands, then slowly raises it and says, "To save a human life, another human life gets taken."

Whoa. Heavy.

"You should have cast the spell anyway!" Sasha screams.

"She wouldn't let me. She said she could never live with that kind of guilt. And she didn't want me to live with it either. Dad wouldn't let Mom use it on him when he was sick. We were young, but I remember. And Mom listened to him."

"Well, Mom was wrong. And so were you," Sasha says flatly. "You just let her die."

"I didn't know what to do. I hesitated and I hesitated and I hesitated. And then it was too late. She was gone."

Sasha shakes her head. "You should have done it."

"But, Mom," Fake Me says, looking up at her mother, "anyone could have died in her place. Someone you loved. Or what if it had been you?"

Sasha blinks twice. "And then you never would have been born."

If only we would have been so lucky. Kidding. Kind of.

We're all silent.

Sasha looks down at her hands. "I just miss her so much. Maybe I needed someone to blame."

My mom puts her hand on her sister's shoulder. "She missed Dad. She said that she was ready. That she was needed somewhere else. That he was waiting for her."

The lights flicker off and then on. And then they do it again.

We all look up.

"Who did that?" Sasha asks.

"Not me," says my mom.

"Not me," says Miri.

"Not me," says Fake Me.

"Don't look at me!" I say.

"Do you think . . . ?" Mom asks.

We look at one another in wonder.

"Hey, she was a witch," Miri says. "Anything is possible."

Liana jumps up, eyes blazing. "Maybe we can contact my dad."

285

"What happened to your father?" my mom asks.

"Aunt Sasha turned him into a mouse," I say.

"She did not!" my mother protests, shocked. "Sasha, you didn't!"

"She did," Fake Me says. "She told me."

"I never actually did that," Sasha admits. "But I wanted to."

"You mean my dad is alive?" Fake Me asks excitedly.

"Presumably," my aunt says with a shrug.

My mother shakes her head. "I can't believe you told your daughter that you turned her father into a rodent. Though Sasha was always obsessed with rodents," she tells Miri and me. "She used to have a pet mouse."

Sasha laughs. "I called him Mickey."

How original.

"Does he know about me?" Fake Me asks.

"He knows that you exist, but I wouldn't let him have anything to do with you."

"Did he know that you were a witch?" the real me asks.

Sasha sighs. "Yes. He's a wizard."

Fake Me squeals.

"Don't get too excited," Sasha says. "He's not a very good one."

Fake Me takes off for the door. "Let's go find him!"

My mother clears her throat. "Um, don't you think we should switch you back before you go gallivanting across the globe? You probably want your father to see the real you, right?"

"Oh, right." She looks down at my uneven chest. "I don't want him to think I'm deformed or anything."

Gee, thanks.

Good-bye, boobs; hello, me.

I hope it all works out for Liana; really I do.

Still, I feel pretty confident that I got the better end of the deal.

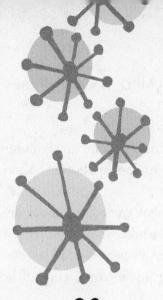

20
IT'S ABOUT TIME

"Is it wrong that I'm relieved they're gone?" Miri asks. The three of us are sprawled across the living room couch. Miri's head is resting on one end, mine is on the other, and our feet are meeting in the middle on our mother's legs. I love my feet. I also love my legs. And my head and my ocean hair and every single part of me that is mine, mine, mine.

"They were a little overbearing," my mom says. "I have to admit that I'm relieved too. You girls should appreciate how lucky you are that you get along so well."

My sister's eyes meet mine over our mother. "We do," she says. "Nothing will ever come between us again."

"New household rule," I say. "Miri will never worry that your family doesn't care about her."

"Accepted."

"Good one," says my mom.

"New household rule," says Miri. "Rachel will never take her sister for granted again."

"Or her mother," my mom adds.

"Accepted," I say. "I will also never complain about how much my life sucks. In fact, I am no longer allowed to complain at all."

"Especially now that you've got game," my mom says, giving me one of her big freakish winks.

I wink back. "You mean since I've got Glinda."

To illustrate my point, I zap us up three cups of hot chocolate.

My mom rubs her knuckles against the inside of my foot, making me giggle. "So tell me, Rachel. How exactly did your magic get so good when you weren't supposed to be practicing at camp?"

La, la, la. Distraction! Quick! "Omigod, Mom, did I tell you that I finally learned to swim?"

"It's true," Miri says, reading the SOS signal in my expression. "Isn't that exciting? And I learned to play tennis."

"I also learned to pee in the woods," I add.

My mom laughs. "You can pretend that Rachel didn't use her powers during the summer all you want, girls. I won't call you on it."

Phewf.

She stretches out her arms and pats our heads. "But I'm glad you brought up these new rules. Because I'm going to spend the rest of the year enforcing them."

I guess I walked right into that one. "No problem, Mom.

Rule away. But I need to know where you stand on one particular issue immediately."

"Oh yeah? Which one? Homework spells? Zapping up cupcakes? Broom flying?"

"No," I say with a smile. "Boyfriends."

First we call my dad's house.

"Are you both on the phone?" he asks.

"Miri's right beside me," I say.

"Hold on, let me get Jennifer."

There's a pause and muffled noise, and then "We have news!" my dad and Jennifer say simultaneously. "We're pregnant!"

Miri and I stare at each other. And I can see the kaleidoscope of my emotions—the delight, the excitement, and the fear—reflected in her face. Sure, we want a new sibling, and we're happy for them, but we can't help wondering how it'll affect our relationship with our dad. What if he doesn't have time for us anymore? What if he loves the new baby more than he loves us? What if I—

Deep breath.

"Congrats," I murmur. "Congrats!" I repeat with more enthusiasm.

"I can't believe it," Miri says, shaking her head. Then she grins. "I hope it's a girl."

"Me too." Would be a great excuse to break out those Barbies.

Next I call Tammy. "I missed you!" I shriek.

"I missed you! she shrieks.

"I missed you more!" I shriek.

After a half hour of discussing who missed whom more and making plans for the next day, I call Alison.

"I honestly don't know what came over me," she says. "I found matches and a pack of cigarettes on my shelf and I just took them to the bathroom and lit up. I have no excuse. No idea what I was thinking. I had a weird headache that day and I guess it made me act crazy. . . ."

"Did your parents ground you for life?" I ask her guiltily. Her getting kicked out of camp was—indirectly—my fault.

"At first," she says. "But then my brother got me a volunteer job at the hospital, and they started to loosen up."

"How was that?"

"Amazing. The best job ever," she gushes. "I'm sorry I haven't written, but they kept me so busy there! I got to help with all the patients. And you're not going to believe this, but I'm dating one of the other volunteers! He says he knows you. Jeffrey Zeigster? He went to JFK and was on student council last year. He's so smart and cute."

Smart? Yes. He was the only student council member chosen because of his GPA. Cute? Well . . . to each her own.

I invite her to hang out with me and Tammy the next day. I just know they'll get along great.

I'm about to make another call when Miri pops into my room. "Before you tie up the line, do you mind if I use it?"

"Sure." Wait a sec. Miri never uses the phone. "Why? We already spoke to Dad."

Her cheeks redden and she fiddles with her fingers. "I was going to give Ariella a call. You know? From school. I thought I'd see if she wanted to get together. Maybe."

I am speechless.

"Is that a dumb idea?" she asks, eyes wide with uncertainty.

"Actually," I say, struggling to keep my voice nonchalant while my insides scream, *Go, Miri, go,* "I think it's a great idea."

While Miri calls Ariella, I run to my mom's room and whisper to her about what's taking place.

"Really?" she asks excitedly. "She's making a friend?"

I shush her as Miri joins us.

"Mom?" Miri asks. "Is it okay if I go to Ariella's apartment? Some of the girls in my class are there and—"

"Yes!" my mom quickly exclaims.

"Yay!" I cheer.

"You guys are so embarrassing," Miri says, but the smile lighting up her face tells a different story.

Finally, I call Raf.

"Hey," I say. "What are you doing?"

"I was just about to call you."

Wahoo! "Wanna come over tonight?"

"Sure. Around nine?"

After he arrives and says hello to my mom and Miri, I take him up to the roof for some privacy. It's one of the best parts of the building. Its floor is Tarmac and it isn't fancy, but it has a great view of downtown, and at night, the city lights twinkle like stars in the sky.

"Can you believe we're starting school in a few weeks?" he asks.

Honk!

"Not really," I say, distracted. The scene is almost perfect, but something is missing.

Honk! Honk!

He takes my hand. "The summer went by so fast."

Honk! Honk! Honk!

"Too fast," I say.

"Do you ever think the honking sounds like music?" Raf asks.

Aha! Music! I close my eyes and make a wish:

For the moment to be just right,
Serenade us with a song tonight.

And then, as if from a loudspeaker in the sky, the beginning bars of Frank Sinatra's "New York, New York" ring through the late-night air.

But for some reason, Sinatra is singing, *"Thtart thpreading the newth. . . ."*

I never said my spells were perfect.

If Raf is surprised to hear music suddenly floating through the sky, he doesn't let on. Not that it's so unusual. After all, this is New York, the city that never sleeps. The city where dreams come true.

"Dance with me," he says.

Finally. The Spring Fling, prom, the camp social . . . I've

been waiting a long time for this moment. "I'd be happy to," I say.

He pulls me into his arms. But instead of dancing, he smiles and finally, finally kisses me. *Really* kisses me.

"Wow," he says, eyes widening. "That was amazing. Our best kiss ever."

Wow is right. "I should hope so," I say, since this time it's really me. I pull him in for round two.

And it's absolutely magical.

The magic continues in
***Parties & Potions,* coming December 2008!**
Turn the page for a sneak peek. . . .

So Many Outfits . . .
Only One First Day

Do I like red?

I pirouette before the mirror. Yes, the red shirt could work. Red makes my hair look super glossy and glamorous and goes great with my favorite jeans.

If I do say so myself.

The shirt has a scoop neck and adorable bubble sleeves. It's my back-to-school top for the big, *big* day tomorrow—the very first day of sophomore year! My BFF Tammy and I went shopping last week, since we absolutely needed new tops for the special occasion. I know I could have just zapped something up, but the first rule of witchcraft is that nothing comes from nothing. I didn't want to accidentally shoplift a new shirt from Bloomingdale's.

I like the red. It works with my complexion. But I don't know if it *truly* shows off my fabulous tan. Hmm. I touch the material grazing my collarbone and chant:

"Like new becomes old,
Like day becomes night,
Pretty back-to-school top,
Please become white!"

I've found that adding *please* to my spells really helps. The Powers That Be seem to appreciate when I'm polite.

A chill spreads through the room, sending goose bumps down my back, and then—*Zap!*—the spell takes effect. The red of my top quickly drains from the material, turning fuchsia, dark pink, pale pink, and finally as white as Liquid Paper.

Now we're talking! Yes. It should be white. White shows off my awesome summer tan.

My awesome *fake* summer tan. Obviously. It's not like I have a pool in downtown Manhattan to lounge by, and anyway, it's way too muggy and humid in this city to stay outside for more than twenty seconds, so how could I get a tan? Unfortunately, my camp tan is long gone. But is my fake tan a spray-on? Nope. Is it from one of those tanning booths that could pass for a medieval torture chamber? Again, nope.

What is it, then? Why, I call it the Perfect Golden Tan That Makes Me Look Like I Live in California Spell. Patent pending.

I made it up last week and it worked immediately. True, at first I looked like I had a rash, or perhaps a severe case of the measles, but by the following afternoon the color had settled into a golden glow. A golden glow that makes me look like a native Californian.

I am very in control of my powers these days. Ever since Miri taught me megel exercises (where you control the flow of your raw will by lifting and lowering inanimate objects such as books and pillows—not glasses. Don't try glasses. Trust me on this), my magic muscles have gotten much stronger.

I finally got my very own copy of A^2 (otherwise known as *The Authorized and Absolute Reference Handbook to Astonishing Spells, Astounding Potions, and History of Witchcraft Since the Beginning of Time*), but since I'm so good at making up my own spells it's not like I need it. If you know how to cook, do you need a recipe? I think not.

Yes, my top has to be white. Everyone knows white is the best color to wear when you're tan. Tomorrow, when I glide into JFK High School, they will say: "Who is that perfectly bronzed girl? Could that be Rachel Weinstein?" and "Did you hear? She's going out with the wonderful and gorgeous A-lister Raf Kosravi! Isn't she amazing?"

Yes, it's going to be a great year. The best year ever. I'm calling it the *Sophomore Spectacular*! My very own Broadway show. And tomorrow is opening day.

Nothing can go wrong because:

I am tanned, I have a boyfriend, and I have a groovalicious new haircut with lots of fabo layers. And I am a witch.

Yup, I'm a witch. Obviously. How else would I be able to change the color of my shirt over and over again without any type of dye? My mom and sister are witches too. We're broom-riding, spell-chanting, love-spell-casting magic machines. Well, Miri and I are magic machines. Mom is a mostly nonpracticing witch.

Luckily, I did not need a love spell to make Raf fall in love with me. Nope, he loves me all on his own. Not that he's said those three magic words. But he will eventually. Am I not lovable? I think I'm pretty lovable. He's definitely lovable.

He's my honey bunny.

Okay, I haven't actually called him that to his face. But I am auditioning potential terms of endearment in my head. Other options are Sweet Pea and Shmoopie.

Shmoopster?

Just Shmoo?

Even without the names, we make everyone sick. Not throwing-up sick, but yay-for-them sick. I think. Since we hooked up at camp, we've spent practically every day together. We hung in the park. We watched TV. We shopped (he bought this awesome-looking brown waffle shirt that brings out his brown eyes, olive skin, and broad shoulders, and every time he wears it I tell him how hot he is). We kissed (there was a lot of kissing. A ginormous amount of kissing. So much kissing I had to buy an extra-strength Chap Stick. But it tasted like wax paper, so I switched to extra-glossy cherry lip gloss. Yum. The problem is I love it so much I keep licking it off. Which just increases the chappedness of my lips. It's a vicious cycle).

As I was saying, I've never used a spell with Raf.

Okay, you got me, that's a bit of a lie. Last week I zapped up fresh breath after gorging on too many pieces of garlic bread. I didn't want him to have to hold his nose while doing tongue gymnastics. But that's it. I would never cast a love spell on him.

Okay, that's another lie. When Miri first got her powers, I tried one on him. (Yup, Miri, my two-years-younger sister, discovered she was a witch before I did. How unfair is that?) But we accidentally cast the spell on Raf's older brother, Will, instead, so no harm done. Well, not too much. Will and I dated but broke up at the prom when I realized he was really truly in love with my friend Kat.

Now, what was I doing? Oh, right. White!

I pretend my room is a catwalk and sashay away from the mirror and then back toward it. Here's the prob. Wearing white might be mega obvious, since everyone *knows* you wear white when you're trying to show off a tan. Also, for some reason, white is making my head look big. Do I have a big head? Is having a big head bad? Or does it mean I'm mega smart?

Perhaps I should try blue. Blue looks good on me. It brings out my brown eyes. Yes! I must bring out my eyes! I need a new spell! I clear my throat and say:

"*Like night becomes day,*
Like calm seas become wavy,
Pretty back-to-school top,
Please become navy!"

Cold! Zap! Poof!

Interesting. I twist for a side view. Not bad. But is it better than red? I mean, I could always wear blue eye shadow. Maybe my shirt *should* be red. Or white. Or maybe something shimmery? Gold?

"Like night becomes day,
Like new becomes old,
Pretty back-to-school top,
Please become gold!"

The top starts pulsating with color. It's yellow! It's red! It's blue! It's a rainbow of cloth!

"Rachel!" Miri bellows, throwing my door open and wagging her finger at me in the mirror. "Enough! You've been at it for forty-five minutes! Just choose a stupid color and get ready for tonight!"

Ah. The one annoying part of the day. My thirteen-year-old sister is insisting that instead of going out with Sweet Shmoopie tonight, I *must* accompany her to some weirdo Full Moon dinner. "I'm almost ready," I say. "But I want to lay out the perfect outfit for tomorrow. It's so hard! Do you think I have a big head?"

She laughs. "You? Full of yourself? Never!"

I cluck my tongue. "I mean, does my head look *physically* big?"

She plops down cross-legged on my pink carpet. It used to be orange, but when Tigger, our cat, had fleas, the exterminator's chemicals somehow turned it pink. Oh well. At least I like pink.

Maybe I should make my shirt pink?

"Your head is bigger than mine," she says. "But only slightly."

"Huh." My big head is my second major physical imperfection. The first is my uneven boobs. The left one is larger than the right. It's not ideal. "Do you think there's a color I could wear that would make my head look smaller?" I would use a spell, but my mom claims body-morphing spells can do serious damage. Like accidentally shrinking my brain or giving me a mustache.

Miri sighs. "Do you know that every time you choose a new shade, my bedspread changes color?"

"Really? Cool!" Like I said, in magic, nothing comes from nothing. If I zap myself new sandals, the shoes have to come from somewhere. If I zap myself up twenty bucks, someone's wallet just found itself twenty short. If my top turns navy, some piece of fabric just had its blue pigments zapped right out of it.

"Not cool!" she wails. "My bedspread is currently a hideous shade of pale puke."

I straighten the shirt and square my shoulders. "Miri, take one for the team."

"I'm *always* taking one for the team. Team Rachel. You better turn your shirt back to its original shade before bedtime."

Original shade? Like I can remember. "Or what?"

"Or . . ." She eyes my purse, focuses on it, and makes it slowly rise off its spot on my desk. "Or I'll spill your stuff all over the floor."

"Oooh, now I'm scared. Anyway, whose house are we going to for dinner tonight? Huh, huh?" She can't argue with me, because I am ridiculously in the right. "Wendaline is your fake friend, is she not? I would much rather be going out with my friends, thank you very much." Unfortunately, I agreed to this dinner before Raf invited me to a pre-back-to-school bash at Mick Lloyd's. I claimed I had a family function I couldn't get out of. Which is kind of true. I just didn't give the witchy specifics.

"She is. You're right." Miri met Wendaline on mywitchbook.com. It's a social network, kind of like Facebook or MySpace, but just for witches. It's enchanted, so no one else can access it. Liana, our cousin, my mom's sister's daughter, sent us both friend requests. I declined. Ever since she tried to steal my body at camp, I'm wary of all things Liana-related. Anyway, it's not like I have the time to friend surf. I'm way too busy with Shmoo Pea. And Tammy. And my other best friend, Alison, who does not go to my school but does go to my camp. I am way too busy for witch friends. Especially ones you meet over the Internet. Everyone knows that cyberfriends only count as a fourth of a real friend, anyway.

Miri, on the other hand, loves mywitchbook. She made three friends on her first day and is desperate to make more. Last week, on her thirteenth birthday, they all sent her e-brooms. Ha, ha. In real life she got a cell. We've been bugging Mom for practically the last decade to get us phones, so I'm ecstatic she finally caved. I'm not complaining about the fact that Miri got one and I didn't—yet—because it's my birthday on Thursday (four days away! Wahoo!) and I'm assuming I'll be receiving mine then. Although it's kind of annoying that my little sister got a cell, and magical powers and boobs, before I did. (And unlike mine, her boobs are a matching set.)

Anyway, one of Miri's e-broom-sending mywitch-book.com friends—Wendaline—lives right here in Manhattan and goes to JFK High with me. (Miri has one year to go in middle school.) Wendaline is the one who invited us to the Full Moon dinner at her house tonight. Whatever that is.

Miri is psyched.

I'm concerned Wendaline might be a *psycho*.

"What are you gonna wear?" Miri asks me now.

"Black pants and a T-shirt. And ruby slippers in case I have to urgently tap my heels to go home."

"Rachel, she is not a psycho! She's a witch!"

"Exactly. What if she's a bad witch? Like the one in 'Hansel and Gretel' who lures unsuspecting children with promises of food and then eats them?"

"She's not a cannibal. She's super-nice."

"Sure she is."

When Miri woke me earlier this week with the groundbreaking news that there was another witch at JFK, I feared the worst.

"Tell me who it is," I demanded, imagining the most evil person in my class. "Is it Melissa?" Melissa is my archenemy and Raf's ex-girlfriend, and she constantly tries to steal him away. Obviously she wasn't a witch last year, because then I would so be a frog by now. At the very least, she would have turned the whole school—no, the whole world—no, the whole universe—against me.

"My life is over!" I wailed, pulling the covers over my head. Sure, Miri didn't care; being in eighth grade will keep her safely hidden in another building.

"Why are you so such a nut?" Miri asked. "It's not Melissa."

"Oh. Good." I removed the covers.

"It's her first year at JFK. She's a freshman. Her name is Wendaline."

"Seriously?"

Miri's brow wrinkled in confusion. "Why not?"

"Wendy the Witch? Does that not sound familiar? From Casper the Friendly Ghost?"

"It's Wendaline. Not Wendy."

"She still sounds like a made-up character. Like Hannah Montana. Or Nate the Great. It's too much rhyming."

"Wendaline the Witch doesn't rhyme. It has alliteration."

"It still sounds made up."

"I'll make sure to tell her that."

Anyway, I'm meeting Wendaline tonight, at her Full Moon dinner. I still have no idea what Full Moon signifies. I am hoping it does not involve any kind of nudity. Mom seemed to think it was kind of like the

Jewish Shabbat, or Friday-night dinner, but for witches. And monthly instead of weekly.

'Cause a full moon happens once a month. I think.

"What's her last name?" Mom asked.

"Peaner."

"Hmm," said Mom, deep in thought. "Okay. You can go if you want to. It might be healthy for you to meet some nice"—read: non-body-snatching—"witches."

Yeah, I can't believe she's letting us go either. I mean, Internet witches? How much sketchier can you get?

"Are you ready?" Miri asks me impatiently, my purse still hovering above her head. "I don't want to be late. And your bag is getting heavy. Why do you have to carry so much stuff around with you?"

"I just do," I say, opening my closet. "I'll be two secs, I need to change."

"Why can't you just wear what you have on?"

"It's my back-to-school top! It needs to be fresh."

"Just zap it fresh tomorrow."

"Just hold your horses." I slip it over my head, hang it up, and put on a purple V-neck shirt. Then I change out of my jeans and into black pants. More appropriate for a family dinner, no? I check myself out in the mirror. Not bad. Good enough to meet she-whose-name-sounds-like-a-TV-character and her family.

Imagine if *I* were a TV character! My life is pretty fascinating. It would make a killer TV show. A comedy about two sister-witches in New York City? Who wouldn't watch? That's good television.

The premise could also work well as a reality show.

Omigod! I'd be famous! I'd get to go on all the talk shows! People would stop me in the street and ask to take my picture and I would smile modestly and murmur, "Anything for my fans."

Except then everyone would know I was a witch. Awkward.

Maybe I can still do it. In disguise. I'll wear a blond wig. Although then I'll be covering up my awesome new layers that make me look like I have real cheekbones. Not that I don't have cheekbones. Obviously I do. But I never noticed them before Este the hairstylist got her expert hands on me. Alison recommended Este after I showed up at her apartment with a bald spot. I had attempted to zap my own hair. Apparently I am no stylist.

I'm trying to convince Miri to pay Este a visit. She could use some cheekbones.

What was I thinking about? Right. Wigs. I'd have to wear one if I was on a reality show. Although technically, viewers would probably be able to figure out my identity from my Greenwich apartment, my high school, and my friends.

My friends would wonder why I was always being trailed by TV cameras. I'd have to tell them the truth. About the show . . . about my double life.

Imagine. If everyone knew.

In a way it would be a relief. I wouldn't have to keep my big secret squished down inside me like dirty clothes in the laundry hamper.

In the mirror, I watch as my still-airborne purse quivers and then lands with a thud on Miri's face. "Ouch," she whines.

Or maybe they'd think I was a freak. Or worry I'd cast love spells on them that accidentally bewitch their older brothers.

No, my secret must stay squashed. I shiver and sling my purse over my shoulder. "Let's get this show on the road."

Excerpt copyright © 2008 by Sarah Mlynowski.
Published by Delacorte Press, an imprint of Random House
Children's Books, a division of Random House, Inc.

WITHDRAWN

Hastings Memorial Library
505 Central Avenue
Grant, NE 69140